Olav's Story

by Bill Flowers

One Printers Way
Altona, MB R0G 0B0
Canada

www.friesenpress.com

Front Cover by Morgan Flowers Winters
Edited by Valerie Compton

This is a work of fiction. Any character that resembles someone alive or dead is purely coincidental.

ISBN
978-1-03-913417-1 (Hardcover)
978-1-03-913416-4 (Paperback)
978-1-03-913418-8 (eBook)

1. FICTION, CRIME

Distributed to the trade by The Ingram Book Company

Dedication

To the memory of William Robert Mesher, my brother-in-law
whose tragic death came while I was writing "Olav's Story."

PART I

———

"Scars have the strange power to
remind us that our past is real."

Cormac McCarthy
All the Pretty Horses

Prologue

My name is Olav Williams. I was about a year and a half old when my mother, Abigail Williams, was strangled to death in front of me at our home in Twin Rivers, Labrador. That was in the winter of 1996.

I grew up not knowing what it was like to have a mother. The closest I had to a mother I think was my aunt Grace, my father's sister. She was always good to me and seemed to understand the stuff that motherless children tend to go through.

Looking back, it seems that most of the time I felt like someone who was pushed out to sea in a rowboat and told to navigate without oars or a compass. Whether that is a fair characterization or not, I don't know—but it is how I felt.

For most of my life, I did my best to avoid stories of my mother's killing or reading reports about it. I worked hard to keep all that out of my thoughts. It only brought on nightmares. Besides, I didn't trust any of the writers who put their stories out in print because they often took liberties in their editorializing, in order to colour the story.

I was an only child, so growing up in Twin Rivers became a lonely existence. I don't know if one is born an introvert or if a person is conditioned into becoming one, but it seemed to me that my early life experiences were a breeding ground for introversion. I had and still have to fight it all the time. It doesn't give me any pleasure to tell you that many folks considered me a misfit at school and in the community.

But when I left Twin to go to university, certain things happened that put me on a journey that would bring about some profound, life-changing events. During that time, opportunities came that encouraged me to be a bit more open and to talk about the deep, darkness that seemed to flood my brain.

No one could have prepared me though for where this would lead. My encounters set off a chain of events that compelled me to tell the story of what really happened to my mom and the many people who were connected to her. I felt it was the very least I could do to honour her memory.

In the last couple of years, I realized that I knew enough about my mother's life and her death from personal knowledge, police and newspaper reports, and court transcripts, that I could put pen to paper and start to tell her story.

Now in my last year at law school, I discovered I can crank out papers and assignments at record speed and that affords me some free time. I also find that my thoughts keep returning to the events that were set in motion seven years before.

But as you will find out, this is not only my mom's story but also the story of several people who impacted her short life and mine.

Olav Williams
Halifax
Nova Scotia
April 2019

CHAPTER 1:

Me - Olav

DALHOUSIE UNIVERSITY, HALIFAX, MARCH, 2019

I was born in Twin Rivers, an Indigenous Inuit community in Labrador on August 16, 1994, not long after the first Gulf War—Desert Storm. I have some Inuit blood in me from generations back. I haven't yet pinpointed that, but I will in time.

With a name like "Olav" I thought I must have been named after one of the Andersens farther up the Labrador coast where there are many families of Norwegian ancestry. On caribou hunting trips to the barren lands, my father often met up with hunters from these families around a place called Sweet Home, near Cape Strawberry, and they would end up travelling together.

But in fact I was named for one of my father's war buddies—a second-generation Canadian named Olav Jensen. His father came to the country from Denmark and was some how connected to the offshore fishery. I'm told that the elder Jensen, a fellow named Knut, came over to train fish plant workers. He met a pretty girl from one of the fish merchant families and became a Canadian citizen as soon as he could. Olav was their son.

Sadly, Olav Jensen was killed in the war when his vehicle came into contact with an improvised explosive device a week before Desert Storm ended. I guess my old man thought he would honour his friend by naming me after him.

I have a photographic memory. I am not bragging about this—just stating fact. This didn't become clear until I was given some kind of memory test by the school board when I was in grade five. They said it was an ARCA test. The test, an Assessment of Recall and Cognitive Ability, was developed by some shrinks at Johns Hopkins University in the 1970s. The results of the test and a later report by the psychologists administering it concluded that I had exceptional recall ability. The report mentioned photographic memory.

I know one thing, whatever label it is, shit gets burned in my memory and stays there. I can call up stuff like sights, scripts, or sounds at any given moment.

There are not many of us in the world really. Every few years there is an international meeting of persons with photographic memories and high recall performance. It is like the gathering that celebrates redheads I read about one time, but definitely not in the same numbers.

I have followed their meetings on the Internet. They seem to do fun things—competitions and shit—and I plan to attend one some day when I can find the money. They are always held in New York City, which isn't cheap.

I have read the *King James Version* of the Bible from cover to cover and if you want to quiz me, pick any book, Old or New Testament, doesn't matter, any chapter, any verse, and I can tell you what it says.

You can pick any page number from *The Old Man and the Sea* or *The Grapes of Wrath* and I can recite every paragraph written on that page. I've also read all the works of Shakespeare, and can rhyme off passages at length for anyone who wants to experience death by boredom. Christopher Plummer would have loved to have been able to rent my brain.

For a social studies class in high school, I read every volume of the Royal Commission on Labrador and the one on Aboriginal

Peoples. I have even read the Warren report on the assassination of John F. Kennedy. I didn't agree with its conclusion that the assassin Lee Harvey Oswald acted alone in November of 1963, but hey, we can all have our theories!

Most my age would not have heard tell of the Watergate scandal in the United States. But I've read all that stuff—everything that Woodward and Bernstein wrote. I can tell you about the informant Deep Throat, as well as Haldeman and Erlichman and all the other players. John Mitchell. John Dean. Do you know who Sam Ervin was? I can tell you exactly how he led the Senate investigation into Watergate and Richard Nixon's role in wiretapping the headquarters of the Democratic Party.

My point is everything I see and hear, I retain.

One of my favourite pastimes in school every now and then was "fact-checking" the stuff that teachers were telling us. Some of them really hated being challenged. Once when I was in the tenth grade my history teacher was trying to explain our freedoms as Canadians and said that "Canada has always been a free country and our soldiers have and will always fight and die, to make sure it remains free."

I looked around the class and noted that most eyes were glazing over as was usual in history classes. Suppressed yawns. I thought it might be a good time to challenge the teacher—perhaps it would wake up some of the students. I put up my hand.

"Yes Olav."

"Your saying that Canada has always been free is factually incorrect and misleading," I said.

The teacher's eyes came open wide. He wasn't smiling.

"We like to *think* we have always been free," I continued, "but in reality, we haven't."

"Okay," the teacher said. "Class, perhaps we should let Olav have a chance to give us some lessons in history. Do you care to share your knowledge of a time when Canada has not been free Olav?"

He was being sarcastic and that threw me for a small loop because it was clear to me that the teacher was going on the defensive.

"Not that long ago actually," I said. "October, 1970—during what was termed the October Crisis. Who knows what the FLQ was?"

I looked around the class. Blank eyes. I looked at the teacher, who was starring back at me with a red face. I read his mind. He was struggling to remember what FLQ meant, if in fact he ever knew what it meant.

"The FLQ was a militant organization in Quebec whose goal was Quebec independence. Its name was le Front de libération du Québec and in 1970 they kidnapped a Quebec provincial government minister and a British diplomat. They murdered the cabinet minister but the diplomat was released after being held for a month and a half.

"In response, Prime Minister Pierre Trudeau implemented the War Measures Act and, by doing so, every Canadian lost their right to security. Police and military in that period of time were allowed to enter, search and make arrests in any home in the country, without a search warrant. Canadians lost their freedoms during that period."

Perhaps trying to test the extent of my knowledge, the teacher asked me how long this situation was in effect.

"It was in effect until April of 1971," I said.

"And how many people were arrested?"

"497," I said.

"Thank you for that piece of history, Olav."

"You're welcome," I said .

Most in the class now had their eyes on me, and I could see that the teacher had become more agitated. He was shifting on his feet and still red in the face.

Before the class ended the teacher instructed me to stay behind for a few minutes. When there was just the two of us, he told me never to say that he was misleading a class again. He told me to be careful with the kind of words I chose in the future. He was quite angry. I nodded my okay though I could not help but feel that there was a deeper reason he called me in front of him. He resented being upstaged in the classroom and he spoke to me to show me who was boss.

* * *

I had no trouble getting through school and aced every exam I wrote. I even won an award from the Governor General.

I tried tutoring some students in high school, but I lacked patience and quit. Most had their brains scrambled from alcohol and drugs. I remember during one history class about the Second World War, one of the students put up her hand and asked the teacher if Mussolini was a type of pasta.

That level of knowledge and awareness of the world concerned me a bit, because teachers would never fail to remind us at our monthly assemblies that we were "Labrador's future leaders." To drive home the point, the principal would say in her squeaky, irritating voice that "perhaps one of you could even become Prime Minister of Canada someday!"

I'd look around the room then at my boots each time I'd hear that and think, "Holy shit—are you kidding me?"

I was never interested in drinking or drugs. Guys would pressure me sometimes to have a beer with them. Peer pressure I guess. I did try rum and coke a couple of times when I was eighteen but I didn't like its taste. I hated the two Ds that came with use of alcohol: the dehydration and the depression. I naturally have low levels of serotonin, so I am prone to depression anyway. I did not want to aggravate that even further with the use of alcohol. I sized it all up as an incentive to stay away from the stuff and protect brain cells.

In my last year in high school, one of our classmates died from alcohol poisoning during the Christmas break. I heard that he and several friends were playing chicken and daring each other to drink straight London Dock rum—that black one hundred and eighty proof shit that guys often smuggled in from the French island of St. Pierre off the south coast of Newfoundland. The contraband often made its way back to Twin Rivers.

They would bring cases of it into the community, water it down to make two bottles out of one and then bootleg it for a hundred bucks a bottle. It returned a lot of money and would always be worth the penalty of having your boat and engine confiscated. Bootleggers would just find more second hand equipment from somewhere and go at it again.

In any case, one of the kids who was playing chicken went to hell with the joke and downed glass after glass of that rum. His eyes sunk back in his head, and his lungs began to shut down. Then he went into convulsions, threw up and choked to death on his own vomit.

The school brought in grief counsellors to help students "process" the tragedy and bring them some "closure." Personally I thought the parents should have a good deal of counselling to help them try and do something about keeping their kids in line.

The weekend after they put the kid in the ground, sure enough, the same bunch was at it again. It was a never-ending cycle in Twin Rivers.

Apart from my "gift" of a good memory, I am also an introvert. That is my own diagnosis, but my loner-type behavior meant that I was labeled a lot of different things in Twin Rivers. I am sure many introverts have had similar experiences and had to endure the same kind of shaming. I was called things like nerd, stuck-up, loser, social misfit and lots of other stuff. Grown-up folks even said that it would do me "a world of good" to get out and socialize more. Whenever people would say that to me, I'd have to bite my tongue and hold back from screaming, "Thank you for being so judgmental, now get the hell out of my face!"

I do need to do better though, and curb my attitude some. And I'm working on that. I am going at my own pace though, and not at the whims of someone else who thinks I should be a certain way.

* * *

In 2009, our school received an invitation to participate in the Labrador Drama Festival. It was held every two years in one of the communities along the coast. That year it happened to be Dark Harbour's turn to host. I wasn't part of any cast (I'm an introvert, remember!) but I was part of the group that was helping organize the stage props and do some prompting from behind the side curtains and stuff like that. Mostly, I just looked forward to the weekend trip away from Twin Rivers.

The competition was stiff and our production of "*Thoughts From The Last Codfish in the Sea*" went tits up—a complete failure. It was a play we wrote ourselves, partly comedy but with some serious messages. A couple of our actors didn't show up because they were off partying somewhere and were late arriving. The director, our drama teacher, was foaming at the mouth. Some students tried to fill in for the two no-shows, but it didn't work. Our production was yanked after the first act.

Later there was a reception of sorts in the gym. A person named Jackie Strickland came up to me and introduced herself. She said she did some volunteer work at the school and helped organize the festival. She wanted to say that she felt badly about what happened to our production, but she'd read the script and thought it was brilliant. I thanked her on behalf of the students but didn't tell her that I wrote most of it.

She asked me if I was part of the Williams family from Twin Rivers, who had a murder in their family some years back. I think I have a pretty good read on people and couldn't help but think that this question was the real reason she came over to talk to me. I told her I was an only child and that yes, I was part of that family. She said she knew Abigail from the eighties when she was in high school in Dark Harbour and she thought that Abby was a lovely young person.

She expressed her condolences for my loss. The expression on my face must have told Jackie that I was getting more interested in our conversation and she invited me to her place for lunch the next day. I said I would be happy to visit though unease began to set in. I really didn't know whether I should get involved in those conversations. I knew that her son, Mose Strickland, had been convicted of my mother's murder and was now serving a life sentence. I began to wonder and speculate why she would want to meet with me.

She gave me her address and phone number and said she would pick me up about eleven-thirty.

* * *

At noon on Saturday, I sat down with Jackie to spaghetti and garlic bread. She was not long retired from the provincial government and her husband died two years earlier of a heart attack. In addition to Mose, she had a son Alan with her husband in Dark Harbour. Alan struggled with mental illness. She said although his illness was controlled by medication, he was very much a stay-at-home guy.

Jackie married into a family that owned the main grocery store in Dark Harbour. The business also sold dry goods, operated gas pumps and a liquor store, and provided supplies to fishermen. She took over the enterprise when her husband died. It was a thriving business, but at her age she said she didn't need the money and over the past six months had been in negotiations with someone who was interested in buying her out. She said she had no plans to give it to Alan to run because of his mental condition. He was there at the table next to her, crunching like hell on garlic bread as she spoke about him.

She finally got around to telling me the real reason I was invited there. She wanted to tell me about her older son Mose.

* * *

Jackie finished clearing away the dinner dishes and came into the living room with two glasses of water and sat beside me. Alan was gone to his room, where he spent most of his days playing video games.

"I knew your mother quite well, Olav," Jackie said.

"Oh?"

"Yes, she and my son Mose were a young couple, in late 1987. I also knew her parents, Reverend Absalom Peters and his wife Rhoda from the church here in Dark Harbour."

I was beginning to sense where this conversation might be headed.

Jackie talked about how Mose was so well liked in school and how good an athlete he was. She also wanted me to know how much she liked my mother.

"Why are you telling me all this?" I asked.

"When Rev. Peters and his family moved away in February 1998, a lot of people around town thought that Abby was pregnant and that they were moving away so she could have an abortion. Mose was pretty certain that she was going to abort the baby."

"Do you know what happened for sure?" I asked.

"We are not certain. Mose told me he had a letter from Abby just after she got to Toronto and that she expected to have an abortion."

"With the reverend's Catholic upbringing, do you think he allowed an abortion?"

"That's why I thought we would have this chat. I believe there might have been a baby born that was put up for adoption. I guess the child would be about twenty-one years old now."

"That would be about right."

"It is possible that you have a sibling somewhere and I have a grandchild, who neither of us have ever met."

"That's incredible. The possibility never occurred to me. Can we track the person down?"

"It's possible," Jackie explained. "Provinces are making it easier for adopted kids to get in touch with their birth parents these days. It has to do with a person's right to know, especially considering genetics and health related stuff. Ontario is one of those provinces that is bringing in a law to open adoption records."

I nodded and took a sip of water.

"Again I am speculating, but the possibility is there," Jackie continued.

I thanked her for her hospitality and for telling me this information. I remember being shaken and a bit bewildered by the conversation for the remainder of that day. But the thought of having a brother or a sister somewhere was rather exhilarating.

CHAPTER 2:

Old School, Old Souls

St. John's, Fall 2012

It was quite an experience coming out of Twin Rivers (pop. fifteen hundred) and plunking myself down on the campus of Memorial University. I don't know if culture shock is the right expression, but it certainly awakened me to a new reality.

I knew I had to learn to be a bit more outgoing in this environment. It didn't seem to leave me a lot of choice. I had to fight the uneasiness I felt about letting new people into my life, and didn't really know what to expect when it came to learning in university level settings. Some teachers in grade twelve tried to prepare us for the change. They gave us pamphlets and showed us a couple of videos about life on campus and orientation. That helped—a little. It tended to paint a rosy picture of university and, I thought, it was more about marketing than what a cash-strapped student like me might expect to experience.

I stayed in res in my first year. Hell just finding my way across the parkway to the dining hall was a challenge.

As I got ready for my transition to university, I made a plan to do a graduate degree in law. I did some preparatory reading for law school and noted one senior prof at Dalhousie University who said that students with backgrounds in math and the sciences made some of the best law students. I concluded there and then that my undergrad would be a major in math. I also knew the international reputation that Memorial University had for its earth sciences programs—that being one of the best in the world—I thought a minor in that area in environmental studies would be an interesting place to focus some of my interests.

Memorial is a very large university with an enrollment of about twenty thousand students. At its centre, or at least what I consider its centre, is the library. The Queen Elizabeth II Library is a beautiful piece of architecture on campus with a couple of million volumes of books, journals, CDs and the like. For me it was love at first sight when I entered the building. I expected that this would be my home over the next eight semesters for my free time between classes.

I was studying a science text and making notes for an assignment, at the library one day in the fall, shortly after I arrived for my first year. I was feeling that I had enough information for the assignment, and found I was looking out the huge glass windows toward the hills every few minutes—thinking about the debt I would owe at the end of my seven years!

It was a grey kind of day with the hills partly fogged in. Some would say typical Avalon Peninsula weather. On my way out for a bathroom break, I saw this young lady engrossed in some books two carrels down from where I was sitting. She looked up at me and smiled. I smiled back and continued on my way to the bathroom. We didn't speak that day but we did make eye contact again as I was on my way back to my study space. I continued to sit and gaze out the windows for a while but this time I began to daydream as to what that smile might mean!

Later that week, back in my usual carrel, I took another jaunt to the bathroom, and I'll be damned if she wasn't there again just a few carrels away. She saw me and waved this time. Coming back from the bathroom, I had to track down a science journal, so a little time went by before I got back to my carrel. This time her carrel was empty. When I got back to my desk I found a piece of paper folded up and placed in the clip of my pen. I opened it to find a happy face looking at me, with just the word "Sophie." That made me smile.

I was pretty intrigued and have to admit that it occupied a lot of space in my mind that night and for the next few days. I had no contact information and actually I didn't really know who might have put it there. Could have been anyone, but I was ninety-nine percent certain who did it and let me tell you, it was pretty damn sexy!

Another week later, we were back in the library again. This time it was her who left her carrel to go somewhere and as she did she passed by where I was sitting. She had a mischievous look in her eyes as she breezed pass me. In expectation of my seeing her again, I sketched a little picture of "*The Thinker*" a couple of evenings before, and put the word "Olav" by it. I placed it in the pen clip on her desk then went back to my studying.

We kept our smoke signals going for another few days, but one of us was going to have to make a move soon. That was me! I decided to push back my introversion and be bold. I walked up to her carrel and introduced myself.

"Hi, I'm Olav," I said.

She held out her hand, smiled and said, "Sophie."

"I have to tell you that this has been fun and very intriguing," I said. "I love the mystery."

"It's old school communications," she said. "But then I've been told I am an old soul!"

"That's interesting," I said, smiling. "Most folks back where I grew up think I have no soul at all."

Sitting back in her chair, she asked, "Why would they think that?" She had a genuine inquisitive expression on her face.

"Well that might be an exaggeration—it is an exaggeration actually," I said. "But I've always been a little shy and less outgoing than most I grew up with."

"Really? It takes some outgoingness to come over and introduce yourself, so I can hardly believe that."

"Well thank you. I guess it takes all kinds," I said, and paused a moment as we continued our eye contact. God she was beautiful! "It is a very nice day—interested in walking up to the Starbucks for coffee?"

She stood and put her books, water bottle and laptop in her shoulder bag. Sophie was picture perfect in her jeans shorts, a light, yellow coat and sneakers. She was just slightly shorter than me.

"Let's go!" she said.

We walked down the stairs together and out the front entrance. Of course, I had no way of knowing at the time that I was meeting the one person who was about to change my life forever.

* * *

Sophie O'Brien came from along the Irish shore in Newfoundland, down Renews-Cappahayden way. Her parents and their ancestry had a long history in the fishing industry so she was coming from a bit of money. Old money.

She was very bright—but a bit shy, a lot like me in many ways. She had Celtic in her blood and I loved all things Celtic. Sophie was planning to study medicine.

I loved her Irish accent and hoped it would rub off on me. I have to tell you though, that I needed her beside me most of the time as a translator on my first trip down that way to meet her family. It was quite funny at times, but oh so cool.

I was intrigued by the history of the area and all the connections back to the old country and having Sophie in my life with her wavy, dirty blonde, shoulder length hair and hazel eyes, I was experiencing a little piece of heaven for once. When she was around, Twin Rivers would become the last thing I'd want to be thinking about.

The family's kitchen parties were steeped in Irish-Newfoundland music and culture. Her father and her siblings played fiddle, mandolin, tin whistle, guitar, concertina and the bodhrán. Sophie was good with the fiddle as was her sister. I couldn't sing worth shit but I did enjoy the musical talent and the feasts they would host. Fish and Brewis, Irish Stew, Jiggs Dinners, lobster boils on the beach. You name it. They even had this great Newfoundland dog, whose name was Papa Bear. He was just over three years old.

He loved to catch balls and Frisbees and was as much at home in the water as he was on dry land, webbed feet and all. When Papa would emerge from the water he would give everyone within a twelve-foot radius a shower whether they wanted one or not.

The dog drooled—and drooled—and drooled some more. But no one cared. Everyone loved Papa Bear. He was central to the family.

I entertained a vision of my future at a law firm, with a home in St. John's and perhaps a cottage down that shore. It was a charming thought, provided I could get through some of the shit on my end.

It was three years since Jackie Strickland told me about the likelihood of my having a blood relative somewhere. I was pumped about it at the time, though I did not give it a lot of attention for various reasons. Not really good reasons. Mostly I was uneasy about how the person might react if we did make contact. This kind of thing can come as quite a shock to the adoptee. Then I had the adoptive parents to consider and they might not want anything to do with me, so I held off making efforts to track this person down. I estimated this brother or sister of mine to be about twenty-four years old.

When I told Sophie about my 2009 meeting with Jackie, she became intrigued about the idea of my having a relative somewhere whom I'd never met. She told me I owed it to myself and to my mom's memory to find this person.

"This is your family," she said. "It's your opportunity to complete the circle. Besides you need to know this person and have a relationship with him or her because you never know when one of you might need an organ transplant."

She was already thinking like a doctor. "Let me help you," she said.

The thought of working with her in some detective-like stuff was exciting, and the results had the potential to be life changing. We set about making a plan of action.

CHAPTER 3:

Travis – War Vet

Travis Williams was born into a large poverty-stricken family on October 31, 1967 in Twin Rivers. He and his siblings often went to bed hungry at night. Their alcoholic father had little education and could not get steady employment. He often took out his frustrations on his children, his wife and their dog.

Travis became immune to the treatment and began to concentrate as much as he could on his own physical development, working out at the school gym. As soon as he was of age he enlisted in the military, mostly to get away from the hellhole he grew up in. He fit right in. He became a very focused young man, committed to the service. When he was twenty-three, he decided he wanted to be one of those heading for the desert as tensions in the Persian Gulf were boiling over.

Travis had a keen eye with apparent nerves of steel and he seemed to sport an eternal skinhead. He did have some facial hair, though, in the form of a goatee that gave him kind of an evil, Vladimir Lenin-type look. He cherished that. He loved to pose in uniform with an assault rife. Travis was ready for war and, he itched, fidgeted and champed at every bit before he got his transfer orders to fly across the world. He could not wait to get his boots on the ground in Kuwait and to get into some action.

Photos and videos of his time in the desert showed a jovial Travis popular with his comrades, always carrying on for the cameras.

Most members of the coalition cared little about the threat from Iraqi scud missiles. Those often missed their targets, landing harmlessly in desert sands like empty metal containers. It didn't take long for coalition members to discover that Saddam's army was not what it was cracked up to be. His army was mostly untrained with weaponry that in the opinion of some was not much advanced from pitchforks.

What was risky, though, was the logistical effort involving convoys of armoured vehicles during Operation Desert Storm. Saddam's army was good at placing Improvised Explosive Devices.

A week into Desert Storm, as Travis was part of a ten-vehicle coalition convoy advancing closer on a strategic target, his vehicle came into contact with an IED. The explosion ripped the vehicle apart, killing three of its occupants. Only Travis survived that attack, but not without several injuries including taking shrapnel to his left leg.

Travis returned from the war in late 1991 with the nickname "Trance," something he acquired from his comrades for his ability to spot deadly installations that the enemy had camouflaged among the desert sands and rolling hills. He would stop, fix his gaze on a target as though he was in a trance, and warn troops who were then able to blow up the land mine from a distance.

This skill likely came from his earlier experience hunting caribou on the barren lands in northern Labrador and Quebec. He made his first trip in to the hunting grounds with his older brothers at the age of twelve. The skill required both twenty-twenty vision and an ability to size up a situation on the spot. It came in handy in the Gulf, where he received a commendation for his success from top military brass leading the Canadian effort in Desert Shield and Desert Storm.

Following the war he returned to small town Labrador as a celebrity. Many of the fifteen hundred locals of Twin Rivers on the coast of Labrador, would walk up to him in the only coffee shop in town and shake his hand. Mayor Eleanor Rowe (Ellie) even organized her own version of a ticker tape parade held the day Travis arrived home.

I have a news clipping of his arrival back home that day describing how he flew in on a chartered Islander aircraft paid for by the local council. Before landing, in a salute to the town and its native son, the pilot circled three times, each time a little lower than the one before, so Travis could have a look at the large, cheering crowd that had gathered at the small airport to welcome him home.

The people of Twin Rivers had not seen anything like it. As the parade made its way through town, horns honked, banners flew and through a megaphone, the mayor signed an order and, declared the day "Travis Williams Day." The parade was followed by an event at the town hall with food and drink, and a slide show of Travis at various locations in the war theatre with his comrades. There was yet another speech from the mayor about how proud she was of Travis, and lots of lively music.

News headlines included: "Patriotism at its Finest," "Exemplary Service to the Cause of Freedom" and "Local War Hero - Role Model." The role model part I am sure was meant to encourage more Labrador youth to join the military and go to whichever war needed them.

After the euphoria, Travis settled back into the community and later decided to go to college in Corner Brook in the fall of 1992 to study heavy equipment operation. After a couple of months at the college he met Abigail Peters. They discovered that they were from the same part of the Labrador coast. Travis spent a lot of time by himself and was no stranger to using drugs—something that he thought helped him cope with his bad memories from the war. In time, he began to get restless, yearning for female company. He and Abby hit it off and started a relationship.

Their relationship received only lukewarm support from Abby's parents. Her father was tuned in pretty well to the grapevine in the area and there was word around town that Travis was into drugs and maybe even dealing.

Still in defiance of her father's disapproval, the two continued their relationship. They were after all, adults.

Once back home after graduation, Travis was given a job with the Twin Rivers town council maintaining roads. He liked the work, and the equipment reminded him of the armored tanks and vehicles that he'd become familiar with during the war. He liked the feeling of being at the controls of a big machine that wielded so much power. It also meant he could be alone much of the time and to some extent be his own boss.

He really did not like taking orders from civilians most of whom he thought were idiots or nobodies. They could not match the experience he had in defending the freedoms these people enjoyed.

He came back from the war with an attitude that seemed to say, "I'm a veteran and you're not." That kind of attitude. He had to be better than everyone else. If someone said they could piss fifteen clapboards, Travis would say, "Well I can take a piss standing on my head and still write my name in the snow." He had to one up you every time.

Travis knew everyone in town and got in the habit of visiting Andy's Place for a few ales and a game of pool, after clocking out from work. These were days when he had his roadwork under control and he could kick back and relax. On days following a winter snowstorm he could not do that as much, but he was glad to be out there plowing snow all hours of the night. Overtime was good.

Funny thing though, even after hanging around the bar as much as he did and knowing most everyone in town, there was no one person that he could truly point to and consider a close friend.

He was friendly enough to the townspeople, but often he could not wait to be alone and escape into his own world to relive his wartime antics. The whiskey and soda and sometimes a bit of crack cocaine coloured his moments of glory, but it also brought back things he would rather forget.

During his first summer on the job, a contracting company from outside the community won a bid to upgrade the road to the airport and to extend and resurface the airstrip with new aggregate. The company brought in their own men and equipment despite having made a promise that they would hire local workers.

None of this sat well the townspeople and it angered Travis especially as he saw some potential, perhaps a supervisory role for himself, somehow being mixed up in the project.

There was talk in the town of organizing a protest when the ship carrying the equipment was due to arrive at the dock, but this was cancelled on short notice. The mayor said it was too late for it to serve any purpose and she didn't want to risk any negative attention that would come with possible arrests.

In fact the protest was cancelled mostly because the media didn't show any interest and the mayor would therefore not get her face on the television screens that evening. She had ambitions that far outweighed that of being mayor of little Twin Rivers.

Even though the protest was cancelled, this did not stop folks from talking and expressing their disgust, especially at the local bar in the evenings.

One evening shortly after the project got under way, Travis was sitting in Andy's with some town employees slamming back a few cold beers, when three men from the construction project walked in to the watering hole. Travis felt the time was right for him to saunter on over and introduce himself.

The encounter ended in a ruckus that saw roughed up testicles and facial lacerations with Travis being on the delivering end. He didn't hesitate to deploy some martial arts that he had learned while in the service. It resulted in an assault charge being laid against Travis, but after some skillful argument by the legal aid lawyer that it was a first offence and that Travis was likely suffering from PTSD, the Crown agreed to drop the charge.

Even though Travis was beginning to carve out a life for himself at Twin Rivers, he was also starting to show his teeth. He was there to let folks know what it meant to "fight for your rights" when you feel you've been hard done by.

CHAPTER 4:

Mose – From the summer of 69

Mose was conceived in upstate New York in August, 1969 during the Woodstock folk festival. His mother, Jackie Strickland, had just finished her final year studying social work at Memorial University and she and two other companions managed to somehow thumb their way down to Bethel, New York to take in the great music event at Yasgur's Farm.

This was a graduation celebration they could not pass up. It was the summer of love, the make love-not-war era, and there was plenty of long hair, headbands and grass (not the kind you mow.) Many artists at Woodstock riled their audiences as they performed songs that swore on the "establishment" and protested the war in Viet Nam.

Somewhere between the music, the pot-filled air and the rain, Jackie met a guy named Joe Longshadow, a Native American and a member of a tribe from Montana. They took to each other right away (the acid helped), and it was not long before they managed to borrow a tent, crawl inside out of the rain, and consummate their relationship.

Over the next few days they were inseparable. Jackie managed to convince Joe to come home with her following the festival. He did, and in short order found work with the newly organized

Native Association of Newfoundland. He was a good fit for the role. He had long braided hair resembling that of Archie Belaney, the Englishman who in the early twentieth century appropriated First Nations culture, passed himself off as a Canadian Indian, and took the name Grey Owl.

Joe was always itching for a fight so he decided to stay for a while.

David Moses Strickland was born on May 27, 1970. He was the quintessential love child, what with his immaculate conception at Woodstock. He was almost a year old when he was baptized the following April, but already trouble was brewing in paradise between Jackie and Joe. The novelty of a new country was wearing off for Joe and he began feeling hemmed in by the limitations of the island landmass so damn far out in the North Atlantic. From what I could gather, his restlessness came about more because he had a girlfriend back home on the reservation. When their partnership deteriorated and became irreparable in Joe's eyes, he decided to move back to the United States, not giving a second thought to leaving Jackie a single mom.

After returning home, Joe fell deeply into alcohol, drugs and gambling. He was broke all the time and resorted to stealing money to support his addictions. He was your textbook deadbeat dad and made no effort to work so he could send money to Jackie for the support of their child.

Within a year of his return to the states, Joe's sister Martha, who Jackie had also befriended at the festival, called Jackie and told her that Joe was dead. She said it could have been an accidental overdose, but most likely it was suicide because he seemed to be headed down a very dark path from the depression he suffered.

Jackie promised Martha that she would never speak ill of him to Mose and that she wanted his family to know of her condolences. They said some prayers over the phone while smoke from smouldering sweetgrass circled each of their heads. They gave thanks to the Creator for Joe's life.

Jackie cried herself to sleep for several nights. She had held out some hope that she and Joe might reunite. As deadbeat a dad as Joe had been, at least he was Mose's flesh and blood. Now there was no one. She became overwhelmed by gloom with a heavy sense of responsibility as she began to consider her future.

With her social work degree in hand, Jackie now had to look for a permanent job. The short-term work she had been getting since graduation was drying up. She had to look for something better. There would be no more free time for her. She had another mouth to feed.

She began scanning advertisements in the *Evening Telegram*, Newfoundland's daily newspaper, and made as many phone calls as she could to people who she thought might know of opportunities and even to some who she thought perhaps might have some political influence.

She became distraught when her efforts turned up nothing—until one day she spotted an interesting ad in the *Telegram*. The government was looking for a manager of social services on the coast of Labrador in the small, isolated community called Dark Harbour. The job was attractive. She would be supervising several staff, and it came with subsidized housing and a northern allowance.

Despite her serious reservations about going so far up north, she decided she had to apply for it. She felt her chances were good. She knew that it was difficult to recruit people for jobs in northern communities. Hence the incentives like northern allowance.

She was right. Within a fortnight someone from the social services department called her for an interview and a few days later she was offered the job.

Jackie set about packing up suitcases and cartons for her and Mose, and took the next coastal boat from Lewisporte in Newfoundland and headed to the coast of Labrador as a civil servant.

Sailing into the harbour, Jackie looked in at the community and its surrounding bleakness and seriously second-guessed her decision to accept the job. She said several silent prayers and had to dismiss the thought of boarding the vessel again on its voyage south and getting the hell flames out of there.

* * *

It wasn't long though before Dark Harbour became home for young Mose. He was outgoing and made lots of friends. In no time at all, it seemed, he was off to kindergarten. Mose loved outdoor activities especially during winter, and he would often be seen sledding with friends over on Rose'ill. The hill, named for the generations of Rowe families who had lived at its foot for one hundred and fifty years, was a popular location with kids once the snow arrived.

Mose became very well liked at school among both teachers and students alike. He grew into a handsome teenager with a dark complexion and shoulder length, jet-black hair that gave him movie-star looks. He was also a good hockey player, and local folk even speculated that Mose might even be good enough to be drafted to the National Hockey League. He was the captain of the team and with the combination of his swagger and hockey skills he was sought after by the town's young girls.

While his academic performance was average, he was getting through high school although at a slower rate than his classmates. He had trouble with math and that meant having to repeat a couple of grades.

Through high school, Mose had a string of girlfriends ranging from one-night stands to three-month relationships. He detested his time alone with his mother because she would be forever lecturing him about sex and the use of condoms. He had no time for that and often made up excuses like having to go to study group just to get away from her nagging.

Mose was so popular with girls that his teammates would often razz him about it. In hockey practice someone would say things like, "Mose when are you going to learn to share with your teammates?" or someone else would shout, "Hey Mose, have you started on your second cock yet?"

Most of the time he shrugged it off but would often fire back as good as he got. Truth be told, most were pretty jealous of the young Casanova.

Mose continued his practice of bouncing from girlfriend to girlfriend until the day that he took a serious look at Abby.

Abby and Mose got together in the fall of 1987. She had turned sixteen in March of that year. He was nearly two years older but still at her grade level owing to his trouble with math. Most people didn't know that even as young as he was, he was struggling with a drug addiction and he occasionally dabbled in the sale of illegal drugs.

Despite all of this, the guy was personable and likable with a good heart and somehow he passed the criteria that Abby's father, Rev. Absolom, laid down. Moses's mother Jackie had married a local well-to-do merchant in Dark Harbour and they became the biggest donors to church coffers. That probably helped getting Mose into Absolom's good books. The reverend could not afford to alienate those folks. The other reason that may have played a role in meeting the reverend's approval criteria is that his name was Moses. Being named after the guy who parted the Red Sea to lead his people to freedom, couldn't be all bad.

Mose and Abby became very close. They went to movies together, to the local fast food restaurant, they sat together in class, went for rides on snowmobile, and she would attend all his hockey games.

Even though Mose was welcome at the reverend's house, it was only for dinners, or spending time in the living room watching television. There was no alone time at the manse. But when they did manage to get some time alone, hormones being what they are in teenagers, they had to fight like hell to avoid sex and both knew that they could not ward off that temptation for much longer.

CHAPTER 5:
Rhoda

St. John's, 1950s

Rhoda Kavanagh was born in St. John's, Newfoundland on July 25th, 1941. By her own description, she was a townie. The term, invented by Newfoundlanders, was used to draw distinction between those from the city and those who came from the smaller, fishing outports around the island.

Her mother, as was common in those days, stayed at home to raise the children. Rhoda was the middle child in a family of three siblings. The eldest, a boy, died at the age of eleven from complications brought on by diphtheria. That left only the two girls, Rhoda and Francine, the youngest.

Her father was part of a Water Street fish merchant family and a big businessman. He was also a World War II veteran who went overseas shortly after Rhoda was born. He landed on the beaches of Normandy on June 6, 1944 as part of the allied invasion on D-Day. He survived the invasion but suffered injuries to his legs and lived with shell shock and partial deafness for the rest of his life.

Shortly after I began writing this story, thanks to Francine, I came into possession of a diary that Rhoda started when she was in her last year of high school. She kept it going for about seven years and abruptly stopped contributing right about the time she married.

I was able to conclude from her writing that she was an active and smart student with lots of opinions and evaluations of her teachers as well as many of her friends and family.

In social studies, she tended to challenge the thinking of the day. It was the early post confederation-with-Canada era, and many anti-confederates still had some very strong feelings about Newfoundland having relinquished its status as an independent country and becoming annexed as the tenth province of the Dominion of Canada.

Rhoda's early views of confederation with Canada were likely influenced by the company her folks kept in the Water Street business community, especially among the many merchants involved in the fish trade. They were an independent lot and fought hard against confederation, fearing they would lose control of their business empires.

In an entry dated October 10,1955, Rhoda noted the very liberal views of some teachers in the social sciences. "Mr. Best in social studies today, kept talking about how confederation was such a good thing for all of Newfoundland. He said the old days of fishermen beholden to merchants will soon be gone and that will be a blessing for Newfoundland. I raised my hand and said there were many who would not agree with that statement and that a lot of people still feel that confederation with Canada was a bad thing. The teacher made me stay after class to explain what I meant. It was like detention, but I got the feeling he did not want to hear any opposing views like I was putting forth."

A little later on in her journal I came across this entry. "I remember my father being very shaken by the results of the second referendum in July, 1948—the one that decided we would join Canada. Then on the official date of confederation, March 31, 1949, I saw him crying. I was only seven years old but I saw the tears. 'Newfoundland is no longer a country' he said, 'Mark my words. You will not recognize Newfoundland in a few years.' I don't think I will ever forget his words that 'Newfoundlanders will become nothing more than another bunch of beggars heading to the mainland to find work!'"

I found it sad to read those notes. Even though it was true that Newfoundland would not be immune to the changes that came with the times, it must have been a painful experience to those who viewed association with Canada as a loss of independence. But then it is easy for someone like me to look back and judge history when I have not walked in the shoes of either those who were for or those who were against confederation.

But Rhoda, it seemed to me, was passionate about her roots and her culture. She was also a brave young person who was not afraid to express her opinion even though she was a young female in a world dominated by men.

Later, as I learned in her journal, she accepted the reality of being a Canadian. "We have to look to the future and make the most of this thing with Canada I guess. As strange as it is to refer to ourselves as Canadians, I will always be a Newfoundlander first." I noted that she had this last sentence underlined.

Rhoda continued her studies through high school with the intention of becoming a nurse and going north to work in remote locations. In this entry she expressed a deep concern for the health of the people in outports especially in Labrador, which lacked health care facilities and practitioners. "This is my high school graduation year. I have been accepted into the RN program at St. Claire's Hospital. It will take me three years to get my RN. I have read about the International Grenfell Association in Labrador and northern Newfoundland and how it is a constant struggle for the mission to find nurses. I would love to go north and help wherever I can to bring health care to the people who need it so badly."

But shortly after beginning her training at St. Claire's, she began developing health troubles of her own. Through her diary, it became evident that Rhoda had something of a concern about her physical well-being, noting along the way how "very thin my body is compared to others my age, and I am often exhausted."

After fainting one day in a class at the hospital, the doctors diagnosed her with anemia and put her on iron pills. They advised her to eat more foods that were rich in iron but it looked like she would need to be on medication for the rest of her life. Some of her diary was laced with colourful language about her disgust for liver and she resented having to eat the stuff! "That is the most repulsive food item I can think of. I would rather have to eat codfish tongues every day!"

When she asked if her condition could interfere with her fertility, she was told that it could, but it would be important to keep a good balance of iron in her diet and to take the medication, if she wanted to start a family.

Her diary indicated that following the fainting episode and starting her course in iron supplements, she began to feel better and more energetic. She vowed to improve her diet she said "because I have ambitions that will require good physical and mental health."

Rhoda grew up in an environment that was all things Catholic. A huge framed picture of Pope Pius XII hung on the living room wall of her parents' home as well as in the classrooms of her school. The local bishop was a family friend and often a dinner guest at their home and her parents were significant donors to the church. One parish hall in the city had a large room named after the Kavanagh family in recognition of their contribution toward its construction. It seemed that on balance the Kavanagh name was synonymous with the Catholic Church.

Rhoda practiced her faith all through her high school years and while she was doing her nurses training. One night a week she would attend a bible study class at the parish hall. She enjoyed those evenings out, perhaps mostly for the social opportunity that came with it. At one of those classes, she met a young church deacon, who introduced himself as Absolom Peters. They were close in age and though there was an attraction there, at first they both tried to deny it. In the following weeks and months, the two became close friends often meeting for tea or lunch. Rhoda's diary noted that they were becoming attracted to each other "in a way that would not be allowed by the church. I am feeling as though I have sinned for even thinking this could be possible."

Absolom had plans to become an ordained Catholic priest within the year, and the conflict that he was beginning to feel about that kept him awake night after night.

Rhoda, trying to fight back the attraction, wrote about the crisis in her diary. "Absolom says he loves me and will renounce the Catholic Church and join the Anglican Church. He does want to follow his calling he says but also wants me in his life. I am not sure about this big step. It makes me nervous and I wonder how my family would take this. Absolom is a very strong-minded person and wants me to promise to marry him. I don't know what to do."

Absolom did prove to be strong-willed and kept pressuring Rhoda. Her diary suggested that she felt she had to follow him because he was "a man of God." Numerous entries toward the end of her seven-year journal, described her conflict with herself, with Absolom and with her faith.

She was at that crossroad described by Robert Frost where "two roads diverged in a yellow wood."

CHAPTER 7:

Abigail – A Rainbow in the Storm

A bigail was born as an only child to the Peters family on March 7, 1971. Her father was the Anglican priest at the local church and her mother, a nurse, was then a stay-at-home mom, but very much involved with voluntary work at the church.

Although Absolom was originally Roman Catholic, he opted to leave the Catholics and join the Anglican Church after meeting and falling in love with the woman who became his wife. It was clear that the reverend's views coincided with that of the far right wing of the church and he was well known along the Labrador coast for taking to the pulpit and raising hellfire about the sins of homosexuality, abortion, alcohol and drugs.

On a beautiful Sunday morning though in June, 1971, Reverend Absalom Peters and Rhoda beamed with pride as they presented three-month old Abigail Mae to be accepted into the church congregation at St. Timothy's in Corner Brook. There was good reason to beam—I saw the photos and Abby was indeed a beautiful baby.

Shortly after Abby came along, the family moved north to take charge of a local parish on the coast of Labrador in Twin Rivers.

Abby's father ministered to the Anglican congregation there for four years. In the summer of 1975, they relocated in order to another parish, two hundred miles to the south.

The congregation at Dark Harbour was a richer one owing to the success of the local fishing industry. Absolom was delighted to get a change of scenery, to see a new set of faces in the congregation, and to dream of bigger potential for the church bank accounts. Abby, though, at five years old, was upset at having to leave her friends and she occasionally threw temper tantrums that drove her parents crazy. Her mom and dad tried to convince her to look at it as a new and big adventure. They told her she would make lots of new friends because she would be entering kindergarten in the fall. Besides, the family had to follow whatever God had in store for them.

School records show that Abigail was a top student from kindergarten on up. By the time she was sixteen Abby had developed model-like sex appeal. She often tied her long black hair in a bun on top of her head with strands falling to either side, or sometimes she wore it pulled back in a ponytail. She had big innocent, dark eyes and a strong resemblance to a young 1970s Linda Ronstadt. Those dark eyes overlooked her hourglass figure that made her stand out in a crowd.

By this time she was taking an interest in the opposite sex, and hooked up with the occasional boyfriend, each of whom was carefully screened by the reverend. Most did not meet the reverend's standards and were screened out of Abby's life altogether.

Since she had turned thirteen, Absolom lectured Abby on her physical development, her menstrual cycles, the sacredness of the family, and the need for abstinence in the face of temptation. He told her she could have a boyfriend but sex out of wedlock was a sin and was therefore forbidden. His view was that sex was for procreation and nothing else. Abby's mind became full of metaphors like coming home to the mouth-watering smell of pizza in the oven only to be forced to fast, or being at the beach on a hot summer day and not allowed to take a dip in the ocean.

Her father was forever on his high horse and at night she would wonder whether her parents had sex before marriage and whether they were actually preaching what they had practiced.

Abby resented not having an older sister with whom she could talk to about those things. She could not talk to her grandparents. They were over on the island of Newfoundland and too far away. In any case they probably had an even stricter view of the world than that of her father. She could not talk about private things with her teacher. Miss Thompson, who she referred to privately as Miss Manners, was a close friend of her parents and a regular churchgoer. Then there was the guidance counsellor who seemed to deliberately avoid any topics even remotely relating to sex. Feeling alone and lost, she was left to somehow educate herself on the forbidden topic.

During Christmas holidays in 1987, Abby managed to convince her parents to let her go to a party one night between Boxing Day and New Years. Abby assured them that there would be no alcohol served at the party—just some snacks and non-alcoholic punch.

She was past her curfew when she returned home that night only to meet her parents who were sitting in the kitchen waiting for her. This lack of respect angered her father. He got up close to her face to lecture her and when he did he thought he detected the smell of alcohol. When Abby admitted that she had had a couple of drinks, the law came down like a sledgehammer. No dating for the rest of that school year. She was grounded, then ordered to bed, but not before the reverend put his hands on her head and said a prayer for her forgiveness. The prayer lasted fifteen minutes.

By early February, Abby came to realize that her period hadn't happened when it should have. Now she felt absolutely alone. She was not allowed to date and talk with her boyfriend Mose, and school personnel were useless, so the only avenue open to her was to talk to her mother. Her mother was most often loving and understanding toward her, but Rhoda did not interfere when the reverend began his preaching and lawmaking.

While her mother was disappointed at the possibility of family disgrace that an illegitimate child would bring, she shed some tears, whispered some prayers and crossed herself a few times. In the end she agreed to take Abby to the health clinic for a pregnancy test.

The test came back positive. She was pregnant and about to join the damned.

The following Sunday, the congregation was shocked when the preacher announced that his family would be moving almost immediately to Toronto so he could further his studies. No one suspected that it might have anything to do with their pregnant young daughter. No one that is, except Mose. He knew that his encounter with Abby at Christmas could have some unplanned results but at times he felt emboldened by that. It was a blissful thought—the idea of him and Abby having a child together. But the sudden departure to the anonymity of Toronto could only mean one thing. An abortion.

CHAPTER 8:

That Day

FEBRUARY, 1996

People in Twin Rivers remember that cold February 26 in 1996 and shudder.

School was closed as the wind chill dragged the temperature below the minus fifty-five degree mark that morning. At quarter to eight the bus driver, Mose Strickland, went outside to start the bus and let it warm up. Even though the engine started, the wheels on the bus would simply not go round. They seemed frozen in place. If you think it cannot get this cold just ask anyone who has driven school buses in these environments. Mose turned off the engine and went back indoors.

He poured himself a cup of coffee and called the school office to say the bus was completely frozen up. Ten minutes later, the radio station in Goose Bay announced that the school in Twin would be closed for the day.

All day long, gusting winds created that cutting, low drift of snow in open areas that is such a bitch to face in wintertime.

Mose was a rock star with the children whom he drove to school each day. He had the bus configured with loudspeakers at the front, mid-section and back, so that he could speak to the kids, joke with them and play some of the latest music. His most popular performance was farting into the microphone and sending the kids into the stratosphere howling with laughter. Mose liked his job.

He came to Twin Rivers the previous year from Dark Harbour, having taken a labour job with a construction company building social housing contracted by the town council. A little while after he arrived, the job of bus driver came open at the school. The previous driver got convicted of a DUI while driving the bus, putting fifty-four children at risk. He was summarily fired at the time he was arrested. Mose applied for the job and was a shoe-in given his experience operating the school bus in his home community.

A short time after his arrival in Twin Rivers he started a relationship with a young lady, a blonde bombshell named Jennifer Morris. She was beautiful and sexy, though not altogether smart. Many thought Mose just wanted her for sex.

But now that he had a more stable job, Mose set about building a two-bedroom house and settling in to the community. It took him eight months to build the place and when it was ready for occupation he and Jennifer moved in and began sharing their lives together.

* * *

The weather began to get a little milder by late afternoon, so Mose decided that he should warm up the bus and drive it around the community to rebuild power to the battery. He also needed to visit the Riverside Co-Op on Main. Mose didn't have a car, though he did have an older, second hand Ski-doo that worked only half the time and a small aluminum speedboat with a fifteen horsepower Yamaha outboard motor that he brought with him from Dark Harbour.

Just before five o'clock, Mose went into the grocery store where he stopped and talked with Abigail Williams. They'd met and chatted several times around the community after Mose arrived in

Twin Rivers. They hugged now, and even though she was wearing a down-filled parka, the feel of her in his arms and the smell of her hair close to his face made him weak at the knees. They had been more than friends during their school days in Dark Harbour.

Each time they met, she talked about her husband Travis Williams and their son. Mention of her husband always raised jealous emotions somewhere deep down in his heart that he had to conceal. But he could do that.

Mose told her he was happy for her and he also spoke about his new house and that he now had a live-in partner, Jennifer. Abby could barely refrain from rolling her eyes skyward, but she was polite about it and told him how happy she was that he had a house here in Twin Rivers.

Since Abby had walked to the store and because it was so cold outside, Mose offered her a ride home on the bus that he was driving. Although this was not allowed by the school, he thought he would risk it given the cold weather and, besides, Abby had her small son with her.

When they finished checking out their groceries, they boarded the bus, with Mose carrying both his and Abby's bags. He closed the bus door and they drove away from the store parking lot heading up the hill toward Abby's home on Groswater Street.

Parking by her house, Mose offered to bring her bags in, an offer she graciously accepted. She said Travis was still at work but would be home soon.

They went into the house. He placed her bags on the island counter and turned to leave.

* * *

Abby froze as her attacker entered her living room. She had just turned on the CD player and was listening to Bruce Springsteen as she began to fold baby clothes. She felt a sharp, nervous pain run trough her abdomen as she stared at the wild-eyed person there to do some damage. The attacker kicked an end table out of the way, that just barely missed coming into contact with the baby's head, and a lamp crashed to the floor. The baby wailed for a moment, then stopped.

The child, a toddler, was standing by the entertainment centre chewing on a squeaky rubber toy.

Abby let out a scream as the attacker grabbed her by the arms and threw her against the wall, breaking the glass that covered a framed picture of her parents.

"Fuck!" It was hard to tell whether the voice was male or female.

Abby's screams became muffled as she felt powerful hands pressing in on her throat.

Gagging, she tried to speak to plead for her life but could not get any words out. She motioned toward the baby as her eyes locked with the devil's and she seemed to be saying *whatever you do, do not touch the baby*. These were most likely the last lucid thoughts that ever went through her beautiful brain.

The attacker turned her so that she faced the wall and wrapped something around her neck. Abby felt the thrust of pain. In a mafia-style execution, the killer tightened and tightened and held it until Abby went unconscious. She was no longer breathing. The attacker loosened the strap and let her petite, lifeless body fall to the floor.

It was all over.

For a few moments the killer sat there with adrenalin pumping and heart pounding not knowing whether to laugh or cry, alternating between sobs, a hysterical laugh and muttering something unintelligible. The killer looked around the room, then down at the motionless body, and sat for a couple of minutes with his head in his hands.

* * *

The lone police detachment in Twin Rivers, housing just two officers, received a phone all from Travis Williams at six twenty that evening. Travis was frantic on the phone and within five minutes, the officers pulled up to the Williams residence. Senior Officer John Stanton and his partner, Constable Jake Lewis knocked on the door. Travis, with the baby in his arms opened the door. He appeared to be in shock.

He held the small baby close to him as the police did their best to calm him down. When they went to the living room to view the scene, Constable Lewis, always a little queasy around corpses, threw up the supper that he had finished eating a half hour earlier. This was a very out of the ordinary scene for a small community on the Labrador coast, where such things just did not happen.

Travis would not let go of the baby. While holding his dead wife, Travis got some of the blood on his hand that had trickled from Abby's nose. It got transferred to the pale blue pullover that the baby was wearing. Travis kept repeating "I should have come home sooner. I should have come home sooner."

The police read Travis his rights and advised him to consult a lawyer, as he was an immediate suspect. Travis waved that off, feeling he had no need for that but the police strongly suggested that he contact a lawyer. They gave him the legal aid number in Goose Bay and persuaded Travis to get on the phone to duty counsel. Travis called. A Mr. Black answered. Black simply advised Travis not to speak to anyone and that he would fly out to the community at first opportunity.

Senior Officer Stanton called in a local fellow, a special constable from the community who was deputized and could do police work in emergency situations. Caleb Moores met the police officers at the Williams residence at seven o'clock. He immediately set about to place yellow crime scene tape around the perimeter of the house.

Stanton ordered Constable Lewis to watch the scene. He told Lewis to call social services to come and get the baby right away and to take photos of the body from all angles. He wanted close-ups, especially the marks around the neck where the murder weapon, whatever it was, had been applied. He reminded Lewis not to move anything as he got on the telephone to his bosses in Goose Bay.

Stanton and Moores took Travis to the station at about seven fifteen that evening.

CHAPTER 9:

Twin Rivers - A Winter Funeral

FEBRUARY, 1996

On February 26 at seven thirty in the evening Newfoundland time, Abby's father, now a bishop in St. John's, received a call that no parent should ever have to take.

Rhoda stared at Absolom for several long seconds. One hand covered her abdomen and the other covered her mouth as she backed up toward the chesterfield. Her body shook, but at that moment she seemed beyond the ability to cry. The shock was too deep. Her husband did his best to console her, but was having trouble himself trying to stay focused. They could not believe what they were hearing. How could God take their daughter this early in her life? Even after all his theological study and his every day closeness to the Holy Spirit, Absolom failed to see how something like that could be inflicted on his family.

The bishop opened a bottle of communion wine and poured a full glass, blessed it and drank it all down—then another, until he had to start on a second bottle.

"God will be good to her," he said over and over. "He will look after us. Your Will be done O Lord. In the name of the Father, the Son and the Holy Ghost."

Rhoda sat there, her whole body now engulfed by dreadful, heaving sobs. They seemed to be a mixture of love, loss, pain and childhood memories of Abby. Memories that would pierce her heart forever like the blade of a knife.

At that moment she had no use for her husband or his God. Her mind went back to Absolom's treatment of Abby, uprooting the family every so often to go and do something to further his own ambition. She thought about those stupid two years spent in Toronto and all that entailed. It made her sick to her stomach. It was just a matter of time and the bishop was going to get one hell of a piece of her mind.

At eight o'clock the family doctor arrived with some sedatives for Rhoda. The bishop's assistant and his wife also came over and offered to stay the night with the couple.

Rhoda and her husband went to bed at about ten-thirty after responding to multiple phone calls of condolences. By this time Absolom was well down into his second bottle of sherry.

During the night, church staff got on the telephone and arranged for a chartered plane for Absolom and Rhoda so they could fly directly to Twin Rivers.

* * *

The bishop woke early, dehydrated and with a pounding headache. In his stupor he thought at first the news about Abby was all a bad dream, but looking at Rhoda next to him, he became wide awake, got up, went to his study to pray, and then set about packing for the trip to Labrador.

The assistant and his wife prepared a hot breakfast, although Rhoda, fearing she could not keep down solid food, just sipped tea. By ten o'clock they were headed for the airport.

They were told that weather was closing in along the coast of Labrador and they needed to leave without delay to try and get ahead of the storm. The crew said they expected a tail wind and advised that the flight would be about four hours with a short re-fueling stop in St. Anthony.

* * *

The twin otter tossed and bumped as it began its descent through the clouds and flying snow. Absolom jumped wide-eyed when he heard a sudden, loud crash that sounded much worse than its actual cause. The de-icers had kicked in breaking away the buildup of frost on the propellers. Pieces of ice hurtled past the plane, some coming into contact with the leading edge of the wing, causing the loud bang. With his lips moving, and eyes shut tight, Absolom said silent prayers and crossed himself several times. Rhoda sat there like a statue. She didn't give a shit about the flight nor the turbulence. If she had her way she'd open the damn doors of the plane and jump to her death so that she could be with Abby.

The weather was clearer as the plane got closer to ground level. It was a smooth landing on the gravel airstrip a couple of kilometers in back of Twin Rivers. Absolom lifted his eyes to heaven and mouthed, "Thank you, Lord."

Rhoda appeared to be still in shock as she deplaned while Absolom just seemed to be relieved to get down the steps of the aircraft and on to solid ground. People joked that he kissed the ground like Pope John Paul used to do. But I doubt he did that. His lips would have frozen to the ground.

They were greeted by Rev. Theophus Brooks and his wife. Rev. Theo, as folks called him, was the pastor in charge of The Holy Church of His People in Twin Rivers.

Rhoda was dressed in some sort of a black cape that fluttered in the wind. Her husband held her arm as they walked to the waiting vehicle. They went immediately to the church where Rev. Theo, trying to give them some comfort, said some prayers before he took them to the manse.

The bishop's grumpy demeanor was nothing new to Rev. Theo. He had to deal almost daily with his crankiness. He railed on about the size of the church, its maximum capacity, and drafty old windows. Whatever he could find to complain about, he did. Rev. Theo felt like telling him hey, you're the guy with the budget and you're the boss of this church. Give me some money to do some upgrades. But he didn't go there. There is a time and place for everything of course. Instead he assured the bishop that he had spoken to the school principal and the funeral would be held in the gym. They expected the entire community to attend.

They sipped tea and ate biscuits with bakeapple jam while Rhoda sat in a rocking chair in the living room, staring straight ahead at nothing. She was in very bad shape.

They were informed that the police had custody of the body and said they had sent it to Goose Bay for an autopsy. Absolom protested. He got on the phone and in a booming voice gave orders to the senior officer. No autopsy.

He was told it is too late for that.

"The autopsy is being carried out as we speak," he was told. "We are required by law to ensure an autopsy is done in the case of a suspicious death. We will report to you when we get feedback from the pathologist."

Being that there was no funeral home in Twin Rivers, Rev. Theo gathered together a group of people from the congregation to help, as he always did when there was a death in the community.

* * *

Once the body was released, Rev. Theo's helpers got to work preparing it for viewing and burial.

A local carpenter and his son built a beautiful casket that included hand-carved messages from Scripture on its cover. The homemade nature of the work pleased Absolom and Rhoda.

Jesus was a carpenter, the bishop reminded everyone.

The day before the funeral, Absolom began insisting that the burial part of the ceremony take place in St. John's. He was prepared to take the body back on the plane with him. By this time, community folks had already finished digging the grave, never an easy task in Labrador's mid-winter. Absolom's reasoning was that at least she would be resting in a cemetery close to where her mother could visit, bring flowers, pay respects, and sit with her daughter and pray whenever she felt the need to.

Word about the bishop's plan got back to Travis who was being held at the police station. Once she had heard about it, his sister Grace Williams-Johnson knocked on the door at the station and asked if she could see Travis.

They took her to the holding cell where Travis was. He was very unkempt and looked like he hadn't slept in days. He asked about the baby.

"Baby is fine," Grace said. "He is with us, and I don't want you to worry about him."

She told him that the bishop was running roughshod over everyone and taking control of the situation. She told Travis that he was going to take Abby's body to St. John's with him on the plane once the church ceremony was over.

Travis put his foot down. "Fuck the bishop!" he yelled at Grace. "That's not happening!!"

Travis became angry as hell at the thought of Absolom taking Abby's body to St. John's while showing so little concern for his side of the family, especially Abby's son.

"She will be buried here in Twin Rivers," he said. "I don't give a goddamn what the bishop thinks."

Absolom quickly backed off after he got the message from Travis. Rhoda spoke up in support of Travis's wishes and that brought Absolom back down to earth. After some minor debate he agreed with Rhoda that internment would be in Labrador.

The family held a wake on February 28, the day before the funeral. It was an open casket at the parish hall. Many from the community came out to the wake, bringing cards, flowers and condolences. Grace gently carried me in her arms to view the body for a few moments.

The next morning, pretty much the entire community came out to attend the funeral. Even the huge space in the school gym could not hold all the people. The service started at ten o'clock. Just before it got underway, two of the pallbearers nailed the casket shut. Many in the congregation jumped at the first bang from the hammer that echoed up through the rafters.

Travis was allowed to attend the ceremony. He sat with a police officer on either side of him. As he was led into the gym, Travis noticed Mose Strickland in the last row back. He appeared to be stricken with grief.

Grace sat with me in her arms in the seat directly behind Travis and the police officers. He hung his head throughout the service, avoiding looks from the congregation and trying not to imagine the hate brewing toward him.

The choir sang several hymns and anthems, and two different friends of Abby's did Scripture readings. The first being from I Corinthians, the gold standard on love in the New Testament.

After the second reading the bishop went to the front of the gym. It was very tough for him to speak about his own daughter and he was uneasy about having Travis at the service. He had been told the evening before that although Travis was in custody, the police were not convinced at this point that he was the killer.

The bishop avoided his usual hellfire, and decided instead to tell the congregation of some of his memories of Abby. The congregation listened and uttered polite laughs from time to time when Absolom managed some light-hearted thoughts. Many wept. He thanked the congregation for all they did to help Rev. Theo and ended with the Lord's Prayer, emphasizing, "Thy Will be done."

At ten forty-five a.m. the casket was carried back down the aisle to be put aboard a vehicle for the trip to the cemetery. The bishop and Rhoda stood at the door hugging and shaking hands with people as they filed out of the gym and into the bleak, cold of the Labrador winter day. They did not so much as glance toward Travis. Rhoda did manage to hold me for a few moments before Grace took me to the car.

Following the burial many attended the reception at the parish hall organized by Rev. Theo's helpers. There was a slide show running that the family prepared. It was projected on the wall with instrumental violin music. A violin version of "The Rose" brought yet more tears. Over near another wall, a large cork easel stood out showing a collage that included pictures of a beautiful smiling Abby with Travis. But most were of her holding and jostling with the baby. She seemed to be a very happy and proud mom.

There were two or three shots of Abby with her parents.

People helped themselves to the light food and beverages that folks in the community had prepared. Some walked over to speak to Grace, to offer condolences, and to make playful eyes with me.

Of course Mayor Ellie was on hand acting as consoler-in-chief. She went around shaking every hand she could and even made a speech. She talked about how the murder resulted in such a loss to the family and the community. All true, except that she went on for way too long.

"The community must pull together and learn from what has happened," she said. "Life must go on. We lean on each other in this town and now we come together to help the family heal. Tomorrow will be a better day."

That last part was code for "my name will be on the ballot for election to the House of Assembly at some point in the future."

CHAPTER 10:

The Investigation

An hour after the incident was reported to Major Crimes in Goose Bay, the regional headquarters for police in Labrador, a staff sergeant, James Albright, an inspector, Maxine Smith, and constables, Alan Hardy and Richard Greene boarded the detachment's plane for the forty-five minute flight to Twin Rivers. They landed at the airstrip at quarter to nine that evening. Caleb met them in a paddy wagon, a suburban, and took them immediately to the crime scene.

The inspector who had some training and experience in forensics began looking over the scene and the body. There was very little blood but some marks on Abby's neck indicated that she had been strangled by some kind of cord.

Working with gloved hands and with the inspector making notes, the police gathered each piece of evidence, including clothing from the body, the broken picture frame, and the shards of glass, and photographed each piece. Then they placed the evidence in separate bags and labeled each bag.

There was no sign of the murder weapon.

Once the staff sergeant and the inspector were finished examining the scene and securing the evidence, Caleb and one of the constables set about placing Abby's body in a body bag. Before zipping the bag, Caleb had one more close-up look at the marks on Abby's neck. The lines were red or orange and didn't appear to be blood. Then they carried the body out of the house and loaded it aboard the suburban to take it back to the plane to be transported to Goose Bay for the autopsy. It just so happened that the forensic pathologist was in Goose Bay doing an autopsy on another body, so the work could be performed in relatively short order.

After the body was situated aboard the plane, all hands climbed back aboard the suburban and drove to the police station.

* * *

The police had to wait until Travis's lawyer arrived before they could begin questioning him. Wilson Black, legal aid counsel, was scheduled to arrive on a flight the next morning. In the meantime, everyone sat down and had coffee with Stanton, Lewis and Caleb. They just sort of chatted. Stanton had been stationed in Twin Rivers for several years, while Lewis was relatively new. Caleb being from the community knew everyone. They asked Stanton if they had any information or clues about why something like this would happen.

"I knew the couple probably more as acquaintances," Stanton said. "Very well respected in town. He worked on some heavy equipment for the town council."

Stanton poured Carnation milk in his coffee and gave it a stir.

"Travis is a vet. First Gulf War—Desert Storm," he said, munching on a Purity brand Jam Jam cookie.

"Did they have many friends?" Staff Sergeant Albright asked.

"She certainly did. A very outgoing person. Not sure about Travis. Bit of a loner."

"Is he known to drink much?"

"I was told he likes to drink some and is often seen coming out of the liquor store," Stanton offered.

"Any history of PTSD?"

"None that I know about," Stanton said.

"Did he say anything when you met him at the door?" Albright asked.

"He just kept repeating, 'I should have come home sooner'. It seemed clear to me that he was in shock."

Stanton was getting a bit uneasy because he didn't want his comments to contribute to colouring anyone's judgment before questioning the suspect.

The staff sergeant decided to probe a bit further. "Any third party who might be in the picture?"

"No, I don't believe so. But can't be sure."

Caleb, knowing the town folk better than anyone, thought he would offer two cents. "There is a fellow here, Mose Strickland. He moved to the community about two years ago. Drives the school bus. I have heard people say that he and Abby had had a relationship in high school down in Dark Harbour. Seems well liked by most everyone but I have heard that he may be selling drugs. Maybe we should keep an ear out for any rumblings on that front."

"Yes, please do," Staff Sergeant Albright said.

"If we can piece together some motive as to why someone would do this that will help focus our investigation," Albright suggested. "Inspector, can you check if there have been any recent changes to life insurance policies and the like."

"The Mayor called a couple of times wondering what we could tell her so far," Stanton said. "She will be very much on top of this and likes to advertise her leadership and the community as being safe and tough on crime. She will want a charge laid as soon as possible. I know we don't answer to the mayor, but she does have a lot of influence in the community and at higher levels in the government, especially the department of justice. You should be aware of that."

"Thanks, that is helpful."

* * *

Lawyer Wilson Black arrived on the early scheduled flight the following morning.

Black was tall with long hair and a goatee. About forty-five years old. He liked to dress down most of the time at work and wore jeans as much as he could. He spent his career in legal aid and considered himself a champion of the downtrodden.

He went straight to the police station for a private meeting with Travis. He was given a copy of Travis's police record. It was clean. The lawyer spent most of the morning asking him questions and getting his side of the story.

Travis was nervous. "What if I get convicted?"

"Let's not get ahead of ourselves. Depending on the evidence, you could be charged and tried for first-degree murder," Black explained. "If you are found guilty of first degree it would be twenty-five years without parole. If they find you guilty of second degree the sentence would be ten years, with possibility of parole after that. 'Course there is the possibility of the lesser charge of manslaughter as well. But one step at a time okay? We are early in the information gathering stage. Everything we have so far points to circumstantial evidence."

"If I have to go to trial, where will that be?"

"It would not be held here in Twin Rivers," Black said. "It would be pretty much impossible to get an impartial jury. It will likely be in Goose Bay or Corner Brook. If we have to apply to the court for a change of venue we will, but I am pretty sure the Crown will agree that it would not be in Twin."

"I didn't do it," Travis said sadly. "I got home late from work. Overtime. How could anyone think that I would I kill the person I loved?"

Black tidied up his notes and his briefcase and notified the staff sergeant that Travis was ready to make a statement.

CHAPTER 11:

Eye to Eye

The morning after the murder and after his initial consult with Travis, legal aid lawyer Wilson Black and Special Constable Caleb Moores escorted Travis to a small room that served as an interview space. It had a table that could seat four people. The table and chairs were very heavy so as to prevent a person from a sudden movement like picking up a chair and throwing it at someone. There was also a bracket on the table to which a suspect could be handcuffed at times, although the police didn't use it.

Staff Sergeant Albright and Inspector Smith came in and sat down across from Travis and Black. They placed a small hand-held tape recorder in the middle of the table. Albright introduced himself and the inspector and began questioning.

After getting routine questions out of the way, they started into the substance of the interview.

"Travis, where were you between five and six p.m. on February 26, 1996?"

"I was working."

"What are your work hours?"

"Eight-thirty to four-thirty. I had to do some overtime yesterday. I had a meeting at five with the town manager and the works supervisor."

"What are their names?"

"Wendell Cooke is the town manager and Mike Rowe is the supervisor of works."

The inspector made a note of the time and the names to cross reference with the town manager.

"What was the meeting about?"

"It had to do with some road clearing on the outskirts of town and whether we had the budget to continue snowplowing services to those areas."

"When was the meeting over?"

"About five thirty—maybe twenty to six."

"What did you do then?"

"I left to go home but I stopped in the store to pick up some milk and eggs, then I went on home."

"What store?"

"The Riverside Co-Op."

"Who tended on you at the store?"

"I checked out my things with Marcia Penney."

"What time was that?"

"It was close to six I think."

The inspector made a note to follow up with the store to get a copy of the receipt.

"You speak to anyone else in the store?"

"No."

"What did you do next?"

"I drove on home."

"What happened when you got to the house?"

"I went inside and put my things on the island in the kitchen. I called out to Abby. There was no answer. The baby was crying quite hard."

"Keep going."

"So I went to the living room and that's where I found her. She was on the floor."

"That's where you found Abby, your wife?"

"Yes."

"How did she seem to you?"

Black whispered something to Travis.

"She appeared to be dead," Travis said.

"Travis, do you have any idea why someone would want to do this to Abby?" Staff Sergeant Albright asked.

"No, I don't," Travis said. He put one hand up to his eyes as though he was beginning to cry.

"Where did you and Abby meet?"

"We met in Corner Brook in January, 1992. We were both going to community college."

"How long were you married?"

"We got married in 1993."

"Travis, you were in the Gulf War, yes?"

"That's correct."

"Have you had any episodes of what we call PTSD—post traumatic stress disorder?"

"No."

"Is there anyone in the community who you think might have some reason to kill Abby?"

Again, Black whispered something to Travis.

"I don't know. But she did have a friend in high school in Dark Harbour who is now living here."

"Who's that?"

"Mose Strickland."

"Do you know him?"

"A little. Not much."

"Would you say he is a friend of yours?"

"No, not at all."

"Travis, you had a charge laid against you a couple of years ago for a brawl you started at Andy's Place."

Black whispered to Travis and then interjected, "Mr. Williams's record is clean. He doesn't have to answer that."

The interview ended about two hours after it began. Travis, although a bit shifty-eyed during the interview, managed to keep his composure, except nearly breaking into tears a couple of times. The police told him that they had more work to do and they had to continue to hold him at the station, though they would release him under escort to attend Abby's funeral.

After the interview, Inspector Smith went to speak with the town manager who confirmed that Travis was at the town office for a meeting between five p.m. and six p.m. She also went to the store and spoke with Marcia, the checkout clerk. She recalled seeing Travis at the store about five to six and she rang him in at the check out for some groceries that he picked up. The inspector asked her to retrieve a copy of the receipt, which she had no trouble finding. The inspector satisfied that she had witnesses confirming Travis's whereabouts between five p.m. and six p.m., returned to the police station and reported to the staff sergeant.

Just before supper on the twenty-seventh, the police received an anonymous call on their tip line. The male voice on the other end said he lived two doors away from the Williams residence. He wanted to report that he had seen the school bus parked by Travis's house the evening before at about five-twenty p.m. The caller said he didn't think anything of it at the time, but looked down the road again about ten minutes later and the bus was still there running. A minute or so after looking at the bus a second time, he saw someone leaving the Williams residence and get aboard the bus and drive away. He couldn't identify the person from that distance. It was coming toward dusk. But it was the school bus and Mose was the only driver of that bus.

Special Constable Caleb began deducing as to who the caller might be, and he determined that the few people he knew living two doors from the Williams residence were all solid, respectable people and that this was not likely a crank call.

The police decided this tip information was enough to bring Mose in for questioning.

CHAPTER 12:

The Family Peters

TORONTO, 1988

Abby came back to Newfoundland and Labrador from Toronto after her father received his doctorate in theology. Absolom returned as the clergyman for a local parish in Corner Brook but he had his eye on big advancements in the church. Bishop for sure, but maybe even becoming Primate, the head honcho for all of Canada.

Abby was happy to be back. Even though she enjoyed Toronto most of the time, she couldn't see herself staying there for long. She finished up high school in the city and made a few friends but was always a little restless about wanting to get back home and possibly find a good job on the coast of Labrador.

Her family kept her pregnancy very much to themselves. This was the real reason for their sudden departure from Dark Harbour.

I remember Rhoda explaining to me that a few days after getting to Toronto, the three of them had a sit-down family meeting, about how they would deal with Abby's pregnancy. Absolom with his staunch Catholic upbringing told Rhoda and Abby that he had prayed to the Lord for guidance in the matter. He said the message he had been receiving from on high was that under no circumstances should Abby have an abortion. She'd need to take her pregnancy to term and when the birth happens, she would be forbidden to see the baby, neither could she learn of its sex, and once delivered she would give the newborn to the authorities to be placed in the system for adoption.

Abby could go to school in Toronto but would stop once her pregnancy began showing. She would have to resume in a different school after the baby was born.

Absolom was as cold as a Greenland iceberg as he gave his instructions. It was almost as though they were simply considering the future of an animal. Not a young teenager and a child. Abby's wellbeing and that of his own flesh and blood grandchild seemed irrelevant to him.

As for who the father was, Absolom had no interest whatsoever in learning who sired this thing, although he had to have a good idea. Rhoda knew because Abby told her. The evening with Mose between Christmas and New Years had to be the time at which time the child was conceived. Abby had not been with anyone else.

Rhoda was disgusted with Absolom's attitude. It was the 1980s after all, and there was nothing she would have enjoyed more than to have a little grandchild in her life to divert her attention from Mr. Fire and Brimstone. But again she refused, or was afraid, to challenge her husband, so his word became law.

By the end of her second trimester, Abby was feeling a natural attachment to the active little being inside her. She marveled at how her body could support a tiny fetus, nurture it and grow it into a real, living human. She had natural mothering instincts. This little one, who was growing and starting to kick, depended on Abby in every possible way, to keep it alive.

She felt an indescribable love for her child. She was constantly touching her belly and cradling her arms around it as if to protect it from harm or to rock it to sleep. More and more, Abby's mind was occupied with imaginings of her, Mose, and the baby as a family. She had a deep longing to see Mose and to be with him.

Before they left Dark Harbour, Abby and Mose managed to get together for the briefest of meetings. She told him she was pregnant and asked him to keep it secret, even from his mother. She loved Mose's reaction. His eyes lit up and he couldn't get a coherent sentence out he was so excited. He became very distraught when she told him they had to leave in the coming days, to go to Toronto for two years so her father could continue his studies. When he asked what about the baby, Abby said she didn't know what would happen.

She dreaded the end of the pregnancy and having to part with the baby. She could barely stand to think about it. With the forced adoption, it would be like a double dose of post partum depression. She even contemplated seeking help from a shelter where there were programs for pregnant teenagers. She hoped that they could help her and maybe even move her back home to Labrador where she could be among friends.

Abby spoke with her mother about the idea. Although Rhoda was sympathetic she was very much afraid of how Abby's father would react. Abby tried to convince her mother that she could go back to Labrador and have the baby and someone locally would take the baby and raise it. That way Abby could still have a relationship with the child. It would be like a native custom adoption. But Rhoda told her that her father would not want that. The baby had to be born here in Toronto. It had to be done in secret so that it did not bring any shame to the church.

"How can a little baby bring shame to anything?" Abby asked, not understanding such reasoning. "What kind of warped thinking is that?"

"It is what your father believes," Rhoda explained. "Sex outside of marriage is wrong. He feels he would not be able to preach the truth to his followers, if we have an illegitimate child in the household. It would be hypocritical."

"So he will be preaching a lie. Because regardless of what father says, the baby will still exist. His God surely knows that. And why would he want to preach anyway to such people if they are so shallow as to condemn me, and my baby? If God is what you say he is, then He will not condemn me. Don't you preach the idea of 'letting the little children come onto me'?" Abby pleaded.

"It's the way he thinks."

"Well, it is archaic thinking. Mediaeval even. And it makes me sick. My father better realize that he is responsible for destroying lives here. Including yours, mother, by denying you the right to see your grandchild. And that has to go against any vows he ever made to his fucking church and his God!"

"Abby dear, please don't use that language!"

Abby went to her room. Her heart aching, she cried herself to sleep.

CHAPTER 13:
The Cloud Gathers

FEBRUARY 27 AND 28, 1996

Mose was just about to sit down to watch the evening news to see what he could find out about Abby's murder when a knock came on the door. Jennifer answered.

"Sorry to be bothering you at this hour, but we need to speak with Mose Strickland," Stanton told her.

Mose came to the door.

"What's going on?" Mose asked.

"We would like you to come down to the station with us. We need to ask you some questions in connection with the murder victim."

"Do I need a lawyer?"

"No, not necessary."

Mose went and put on his outer winter clothing and got aboard the suburban.

Within a few minutes they pulled up to the station.

Special Constable Caleb led him to the interview room where he was met by Staff Sergeant Albright and Inspector Smith.

They all sat around the table. One of the officers placed the tape recorder on the table between them and Mose and Albright moved into the substance of the interview.

"Mr. Strickland, apart from your job, what has been occupying your time lately?" the staff sergeant asked.

"I've been building a house."

"Been building it yourself?"

"Yes. Doing all the work."

"Mr. Strickland, did you know Abigail Williams, formerly Peters?"

"Yes, I did. This is a tragedy."

"How well did you know her?"

"We went to school together in Dark Harbor. Same class."

"How close a relationship would you say you had with her? Just friends, girlfriend perhaps?"

Mose glanced around making eye contact with the people in the room.

"We went together for a while."

"What does that mean?"

"As boyfriend and girlfriend."

"When was that?"

"In the fall of 1987."

"How long did you go together?"

"We broke up after Christmas that year."

"What was the reason for the break up?"

"I think her parents had a lot to do with it. He was the minister at the church there."

"Anything else happen that you know about?

"No. Not long after we broke up, they moved away. In February, I believe."

"When did you see Abby next?"

"When I moved here to Twin. In 1994."

"Did you see Abby socially after you came here?"

"No. She was married. I saw her a few times around town, and said hello. Things like that."

"Now let's go to Monday, February 26, 1996. Did you see Abby that day?" Albright asked.

Mose shifted in his seat. He began to feel a sweat coming on.

"Yes, I did. In the store. She was there with her baby."

"Did you talk with her?"

"Yes, we spoke and chatted a while."

"What did you talk about?"

"I told her about my new house and my job and my new partner."

"Did she seem upset or anything? How was her demeanor?"

"She seemed fine. Happy."

"What did you do after you spoke with her?"

"We checked out our groceries."

"Who checked them out for you at the store?"

"Marcia I think her name is. I remember it from the badge she was wearing."

"What then?"

"I offered Abby a ride to her house. It was very cold, and she had the small baby with her."

"So you gave her a ride to her house on the bus?"

"Yes."

"What time was that?"

"It was after five I'd say. Maybe five twenty or so. Thereabouts"

"Did you go in the house with her?"

"Yes. I carried in her groceries."

"How long were you there?"

"Just a few minutes. "

"How many minutes, five, ten?"

"Between five and ten, just chatting."

They concluded the interview about an hour after Mose was brought to the station. He was then released and allowed to go home.

* * *

At about eight-thirty p.m., a call came in at the station from someone asking to speak to Staff Sergeant Albright. It was

Mayor Rowe. She asked the sergeant how the investigation was coming along.

"We still have a lot of work to do. Everything points to circumstantial evidence. No eyewitnesses," Albright explained to the mayor.

"Does that mean you have not charged anyone?"

"Yes, so far we have not laid a charge."

"Then why is Travis in custody?"

"We are holding him for his own protection at the moment."

"I wanted to pass on a piece of information that might be helpful, and maybe it is best if I come to the station to speak to you in person." Although the mayor was a bit forceful, she sounded a little nervous.

"Yes, you are welcome to do that Mayor. Can you come by in the morning?"

"Yes, I will be there about nine."

* * *

The next morning Special Constable Caleb met the mayor at the main entrance and escorted her to the interview room.

Without shaking hands, Staff Sergeant Albright introduced himself to the mayor.

"Please tell us your name and occupation," he said.

"My name is Eleanor Rowe. I am mayor of Twin Rivers. In my second term."

"Okay mayor, what did you want to pass on to us?"

"I have heard that Mose Strickland was likely to be interviewed in connection with the murder."

"We have already spoken with him."

"Obviously I don't know what he told you, but a friend of mine who was also a friend of Abby's told me that Abby and Mose were a couple in high school. Abby told my friend that they conceived a child during Christmas of 1987. The following February, Abby's family moved to Toronto so her father, a priest, could do a graduate degree."

Except for the part about a child being conceived, this corroborated some of the information that Mose gave them.

"Who is your friend?" Albright asked.

"Trish Paul. She is a teacher here."

"And she was also a friend of Abby's?"

"Yes."

Albright made a note of the name.

"Go on."

"Abby told Trish that they had to move away so no one would know about the child."

"What happened to the child?"

"Abby didn't say. My friend would only speculate that the fetus was either aborted or that the pregnancy was taken to term and the baby was offered out for adoption."

"How do you think this information can help the investigation?"

"I just put it out there for you to consider that the murder could have been a crime of passion. Jealousy."

* * *

With the interview over, the police officers sat in the room going over what they just heard.

"Even if we can corroborate this information, we are still in circumstantial territory," Staff Sergeant Albright said.

"I think we should speak with Trish Paul to cross reference this and perhaps she may also offer a few other clues besides," Inspector Smith suggested.

"If it is evidence that the Crown will want to use, it will need to be corroborated. Otherwise it is hearsay. We can check hospital records in Toronto. No birth date, only approximate. Baby would likely have been born in September. But we should do that," Albright said.

"I will get on to that," Smith offered.

Looking at Caleb, Staff Sergeant Albright said, "Let's bring Miss Paul in this afternoon. Go to her place at noon so you don't have to go to the school."

* * *

About twelve forty-five p.m. on February 28, Special Constable Caleb and Constable Hardy went to Trish Paul's residence to ask her to come to the police station.

"You are not a suspect," Hardy explained. "We just want to ask you some questions about your relationship with Abigail."

"Sure, no problem."

When Albright and Smith came into the interview room, Caleb and Hardy had already seated Miss Paul.

Recording the interview, Staff Sergeant Albright began.

"Miss Paul we understand you were a friend of Abigail Williams. Is that correct?"

"Yes, that's correct."

"How would you describe your friendship?"

"We were close friends. I am shocked at what has happened."

"How long did you know her?"

"Ever since she moved here in 1993, I think it was."

"How did you get to know her?"

"I met her at a school event. I think it was a Christmas concert. She invited me to her home for New Year's Eve that year. She said she was new to the town and wanted to get to know people. We had a few things in common. Her father was—is a priest, as is mine. So we had things to talk about. We also liked similar music, children and dogs. They didn't have a pet, but she said she was planning to get one if she could convince her husband. Travis wasn't sure about a dog, she said. Something about bad memories from his growing up."

"Did she say anything about an earlier relationship?"

"After we got to know each other quite well, she told me about a relationship she'd had in high school."

"Where was this?"

"In Dark Harbour."

"Who was the relationship with?"

"Mose Strickland."

"Would that be the same Mose Strickland who lives here in Twin Rivers? The fellow that drives the school bus?"

"Yes, same person."

"What did she tell you about the relationship?"

"That they went together a few months and that she got pregnant in late 1987."

"For this person Mose?"

"Yes."

"Did she say what the outcome of the pregnancy was?"

"No," Trish said, "but she did say they moved away to Toronto because her father wanted her pregnancy to be kept under wraps."

"So you don't know if the baby was born or whether it was aborted?"

"She didn't tell me. And she wanted me to keep it all secret. Just between us, she said."

"Did she give you any hint at all why she wouldn't say?"

"I think it might have been because she was afraid of her father. I didn't want to probe."

"How well do you know Mose? The bus driver at your school."

"I know him, but not well. We are not friends."

"Ever witness any anxiety or outbursts on his part anywhere around town since you have known him?"

"Being our bus driver he attended a school staff Christmas party last year. I remember seeing him talking with one of the male teachers outside the main door in the entrance. They both seemed agitated, though it didn't come to blows."

"Who was the teacher?"

"Stanley Rose."

"Okay. Well, thank you Miss Paul. We appreciate your time and we apologize for interrupting your day."

"You're welcome."

Special Constable Caleb offered her a ride in the suburban, but she refused, preferring to walk instead.

"Okay," Staff Sergeant Albright said. "I don't think we are any further ahead. The work that you have done inspector, checks out with Travis's story as to his whereabouts at the time. We will wait for reports from the lab on blood samples, and fingerprints to see where that gets us. When can we expect that back?"

"At least two weeks," Maxine advised. "Certainly doesn't help that we have no murder weapon."

"The marks around her neck do not seem like bruising to me," Caleb offered. "I looked at them close up and they look like some kind of paint or dye maybe."

"What kind of cable do you think might have been used?" Albright asked.

"Not sure. Not likely an ordinary piece of marine rope. A narrow leather belt maybe that could have had dye colors in it. Electrical wire perhaps, though I am not sure if the colored synthetic covering on a wire would rub off on human skin. We can have that examined."

"Maxine, talk to your people at forensics on that," Stanton told the inspector. "They may already know something."

The inspector nodded in agreement.

"This may well be a crime of passion as the mayor suggested," the staff sergeant continued. "We have evidence that he was the last person to see her and to be seen with her, and he was at the scene where she died between five and six p.m. It looks like we could be narrowing in on him. In the meantime I am also going to call the regional superintendent in Goose Bay first thing in the morning."

CHAPTER 14:

A Hotel Liaison

ST. JOHN'S, NEWFOUNDLAND, OCTOBER 1994

Eleanor Rowe was an enigma. Young for a mayor at thirty-one, she was still single. She worked out regularly and was in good shape. She liked to ride around town on her trail bike. She even did her grocery shopping on bike when she could, and would strap her stuff down behind her seat in a milk carton. She felt this had benefits from a physical exercise viewpoint, but mostly it helped keeping her in closer contact with her constituents.

Like most politicians, she loved being photographed with folks, especially doing ordinary things like riding her bike and grocery shopping. Ellie would organize a bike marathon every spring to raise money for cancer research. She had exceptional political instincts.

Many around town liked to refer to her behind her back as "Miss Twin," because of her dogged political drive and ambition. She ran the town as if it was her own fiefdom. She was known to have something of a temper and to be short with staff at times. Many blamed that on her flaming red hair and her willingness, it seemed, to throw even her grandmother under the bus if that meant achieving her ambitions.

Mayor Ellie was also a micromanager. She liked to poke her nose into work at all levels of her organization and that irritated her managers to no end. She made it her mission to personally oversee every aspect of the organization and give orders, making the town manager's job almost redundant. She came by her covert nickname honestly.

Often her team at the town office would make subtle suggestions about management training courses but she would not hear of it. She didn't feel that anyone could teach her anything. She preferred to gallivant off to municipal and provincial meetings around the province and a couple of times a year, around the country. She called those events "networking" and "professional development."

Ellie liked to market Twin Rivers and she took every chance she could get to put it on the map. She loved the media and the media loved her. She really stepped that up a notch after Travis came to work for the council. She relished the notion of having a Gulf War veteran among her employees and she felt that the world should know about it. It was good for her political image. To the consternation of many other employees, she zeroed in on his work and his well-being.

In 1994, she surprised Travis when she told him that she wanted him to go with her to the annual municipalities convention in St. John's in October. She said there would be many who would like to meet him because of his military service and his experience in the Gulf. It would make sense that he come she said, because municipal works was high up on the agenda that year.

Travis wasn't sure about the idea. He thought that his supervisor should go, if anyone. Besides he thought, he was not long married and wondered how that might look to people in the community, taxpayers' dollars and all. He and the mayor were roughly the same age, she a little older, and despite being a micromanager, she was easy on the eyes.

She told him to talk it over with the works supervisor, as if that would make any difference. If Ellie said he was going to St. John's, then Travis was going to St. John's no matter what the super might say. End of story.

The convention was held in the Hotel Newfoundland. A swanky place in the downtown area that overlooked the St. John's Harbour. It had a gym, pool, hot tub, a rock garden with tables, and great dining. A real upscale attraction. Big entertainment personalities had been known to stay there. Kenny Rogers, Bob Dylan, Dolly Parton. Many from the Royal family darkened the doors of that hotel. As did Bill and Hilary Clinton.

Travis loved the beautiful venue, but he was not used to these kinds of gatherings, meeting strangers, and "working rooms" as politicians like to say. He did meet some fellows from around different bays in Newfoundland that he felt comfortable with and many mayors came by to shake his hand. During the break on the first morning, the premier who was there to open the convention came over to congratulate Travis, to welcome him home and thank him for his service.

Earlier in the morning when it came time for Mayor Ellie to introduce herself, she made sure to point out "a decorated veteran and hero of the Gulf War, now at home serving his community in Twin Rivers, Travis Williams!" There was standing applause. Travis stood and took a bow.

Travis did a few interviews later that day for television stations, the regional newspaper, and some radio stations. It was all done in a scrum format. They were interested in his service in the Persian Gulf and wanted to talk about his homecoming as well as his injury. He didn't like being in the spotlight and felt hot sweats coming on. The bright lights, the camera equipment and loud bustling of people around him reminded him of his awakening in the war theatre in a hospital bed after his leg injury, where he'd lost a lot of blood. He managed to maintain his presence of mind and stay in the moment, but he made his answers short and to the point.

Mayor Ellie was watching from the side as Travis spoke to the media. She had a pleased look on her face as if taking full credit for his contribution to Desert Storm.

On the evening of the second night, the organizers held a dinner and dance. There was no shortage of beer and spirits.

Prior to the evening reception, Mayor Ellie asked Travis to come to her suite for drinks. Travis was a little uneasy about it, but accepted her invitation. He made sure to belt down a couple of stiff rum and cokes before he went and knocked on her door. A bottle of rum, mix and some ice had been sent to his room, compliments of the hotel, with a note that thanked him for his service.

The rum made his lips numb, and he began to feel more relaxed as he strode down the corridor to Ellie's suite.

Ellie met him at the door in a very low cut top and short skirt. She had a well stocked bar and some light snacks that were arranged on a tray nearby. Her bar was more than just a mini bar. It was stocked with full size bottles and a good variety—all paid for by the taxpayers of Twin Rivers. She justified it as an entertainment expense while doing business with people like the Minister of Municipalities.

She poured drinks for herself and Travis. They stood close to each other near the narrow mahogany table that held the liquor and the food.

"How are you enjoying yourself?" she asked him.

"It's going fine. Met a few people."

"How does it feel to be a rock star? Media attention and all."

"I'm not cut out for that. Not a politician."

"Politics can grow on you," Ellie commented.

"I don't think it will for me," Travis replied. "I don't have any ambitions that way."

"Keep options open," she said. "You would get elected easily in Twin. Up and down the coast for that matter. Maybe provincial politics. Look at the States. Military service, especially seeing action, almost seems like a requirement for becoming a senator or a president."

"Not interested."

"As I say keep your options open. Never say never." Her eyes locked with his, and she moved closer to him.

Travis was feeling a little overwhelmed and not sure what to do or how to react.

On the one hand she was his boss, but yet she was trying to encourage him to have a life in politics, so she may have been regarding him more as an equal. And he felt an undeniable attraction to her.

The thought of a sexual relationship with a boss somehow excited him. It reminded him of something Jack Nicholson said in *A Few Good Men* about there being no greater turn-on for a man than every morning having to salute a female officer who outranks you. Jack seemed to express the notion better than Travis could rationalize it in his head, nevertheless the thrill was there and in full force. Her body language was provocative to say the least. It all left him confused.

"I want you to know that you can come to me in my office at anytime if you have any problems at work." She took his hand. "Don't be shy to do that," she said in a near whisper.

Feeling his heartbeat increase and a rush of blood through his loins, Travis succumbed to the temptation and pulled her into his embrace.

* * *

Over the next year, the encounters between the mayor and Travis became frequent. They often met in her office, sometimes at her residence, and even travelled together a couple of more times for work.

Travis began working lots of late nights and this was starting to raise flags in Abby's mind. By the middle of 1995, Abby was out and out suspicious and confronted Travis on more than one occasion.

Abby had hoped to get a job at the town office but with the small baby she put that off to some point in the future. Travis thanked his lucky stars that Abby was *not* working at the office.

By Christmas 1995, it was clear to some town staff at least, that they were witnessing a love triangle in full bloom.

CHAPTER 15:

The Arrest

TWIN RIVERS, FEBRUARY 29, 1996

Staff Sergeant Albright talked with his boss, Regional Superintendent David Barton, in Goose Bay about seven-thirty on the morning of the twenty-ninth, the day of the funeral. It was early, but Staff Sergeant Albright had Barton's cell phone number. The staff sergeant began the conversation by informing Barton of the lack of eyewitnesses which meant, at this point at least, that an arrest could only be made based on circumstantial evidence. "Well, except for a small baby that may have been at the scene, but the baby is only about two, or less than two years old."

Albright could hear Barton sipping coffee.

"The pathologist has given us his report determining the cause of death to be asphyxia by strangulation and places the time of death as between five and six p.m. on February 26," Albright said.

"Okay. Go on."

"We have evidence that shows that Travis, the deceased's husband, was not at the scene when she died. He was in a meeting at the town office until about twenty to six. Then he left to go home, but he stopped at the co-op for milk and eggs. We have a witness who tended on him and a copy of a cash register receipt showing a sale for the items he said he bought. The time stamp on the receipt is five fifty-six p.m. We are still holding him here for his own protection. I am pretty certain we can rule him out as a suspect."

"Yes, sounds like it. What else do you have? Was there any kind of weapon discovered at the scene?"

"No, there was no weapon that we could find. We have been looking at the marks on her neck and they could have come from quite a narrow red-colored belt. The dye from the belt may be what has left the color. The bruising is more purple in color and it is not dried blood."

"Any tracks around the house?" Barton asked.

"No, the snow around the place was pretty well beat down and some frost had formed, which covered the ground even more overnight."

"So you have nothing."

"Well, we do have a person of interest."

"Oh? Who's that?"

"Mose Strickland. The school bus driver here."

"How is he of interest?"

"We can place him at the scene between five and six p.m. at the approximate time of the murder. He also knew the victim and had a relationship with her in Dark Harbour back in the eighties. Got her pregnant and she may have had an abortion. We could be talking about a crime of passion here."

"Yes, that sounds possible, if not likely," Barton said.

"Other than a crime of passion, there is not a lot of motive that we can suggest."

"If you want my advice, Jim, I think this fellow Strickland is arrestable based on the information you have. You should go ahead and lay the charge."

"Thank you sir, that is the direction we thought we would be heading," Albright said and hung up the phone.

The staff sergeant called his team together.

"Okay. Here is what we do," he said. "Stanton, you, me and Caleb will go out and bring Mose in. We will arrest him and bring him into Goose Bay for a bail hearing. I will talk to the Crown as soon as we have him in custody and we can do the information once we are back in Goose Bay."

"Should we wait until after the funeral?" Stanton asked.

"Yes, we should do that."

"In the meantime," Stanton continued, "we can release Williams. He is wanting to go to the funeral, of course, and we should still have two officers attend with him, for his protection. Stanton, please go and tell Williams he is free to go. He is no longer a suspect. You should coordinate that with the officers who will go to the church with him. The service is scheduled to begin in a couple of hours."

* * *

Stanton, Albright, and Special Constable Caleb Moores knocked on Mose's door at one-thirty p.m. Jennifer his common-law partner opened the door with Mose right beside her. It was a cold afternoon. Even colder, where the words that came from Albright. "Moses Strickland, you are under the arrest for the murder of Abigail Williams."

Mose was stuck for words. His eyes were wide open. "No, no," he said. He was near tears. "Jennifer can you—I'm—what's going to happen to me? This is a mistake."

Albright read him his rights, including that he had the right to retain and instruct counsel without delay, that he had a right to remain silent, and anything he said could and would be used against him in a court of law.

They asked him if he understood what was just read to him. Mose answered that he did.

Special Constable Caleb Moores took Mose by each wrist and brought them behind his back, while Stanton placed the handcuffs on him.

"This is wrong," Mose said. "Wrong, wrong, wrong. I did no such thing. I could never harm Abby."

They drove back to the police station and took Mose to the holding cell. They explained to him that they would be taking him back to Goose Bay for a first appearance and to enter a plea. They advised him to contact a lawyer as soon as possible.

"I don't know any lawyers,'" Mose said. "But I will get mother to contact a friend in St. John's who could recommend one to me. Can I get to a phone to call her?"

"Yes, we can do that."

* * *

Wayne Osmond III of the firm Osmond, Goodridge, contacted Mose after he was taken to the Goose Bay police station and processed.

Osmond told Mose that his firm specialized in criminal defence. He said he also had a person in Goose Bay who works with him, a private lawyer, Susan McDonald, who acts as an agent for Osmond, Goodridge. He asked Mose if he had made a statement to the police yet. Mose said he hadn't.

"I can't afford to pay you," Mose told Osmond.

Osmond told him that he did contract work for legal aid so he didn't need to worry about money.

"Okay," Osmond said, "don't say anything to the police or to anyone. I will have Susan be in touch with you tomorrow. Sit tight."

CHAPTER 16:

Normalizing the Abnormal

Travis stayed with his sister for some months after he got released from detention.

He was not really keen on going back to the house right away. He needed some time to get past the murder. He didn't like the thought of reliving the scene day in and day out with all the reminders around the house.

He tried going back to work two weeks later but that had its problems. Some co-workers tended to look at him in a suspicious kind of way. At the office, staff would often be whispering to each other when he was around. That kind of behaviour played on his nerves.

It took him some time to adjust to the reality of Abby's death and he went into periods of heavy depression for weeks on end. He was also drinking a lot and got caught drinking on the job at one point. Even though his supervisor was sympathetic, he wrote Travis up and put the letter on his personnel file. That added to his stress.

He took Ellie up on her offer to come and see her if he had any issues at work. She was sympathetic and offered him some time off with pay to help him move past the whole affair. She suggested that he see the school guidance counsellor who was a trained psychologist. Travis didn't want to do that. He had trust issues, and

Twin Rivers was a small community. But Ellie said people in the community would understand given what he had been through.

"Yeah, but my guess is that a lot of people in this town are blaming me for Abby's death."

"You don't really know that. You shouldn't be so hard on yourself," Ellie tried to reassure him.

"I think I need to take some time off. I have some work to do at the house. So thank you for allowing me to do that."

Ellie hugged him before he left. "Call me anytime," she said.

In the following weeks, with the help of his brother-in-law, Travis made alterations to the house in the part where the murder took place. I guess he wanted to make those changes in particular so that it would lessen his memories of the murder scene and Abby's body. He painted the walls of the living room and put up a half a wall between his living room and the kitchen. He also changed the carpet and the furniture.

By the middle of April he felt good enough to move back into the house and to get back to his job at the town. Grace agreed to babysit.

* * *

After Abby's death, his clandestine affair with Mayor Ellie began weighing on Travis. Their encounters after the evening at Hotel Newfoundland became more intense as time went by.

His cheating on Abby, one so innocent and perhaps a little naïve, was hitting him like an avalanche. He began to feel resentment toward Ellie for her boldness and her seductive ways. He cursed himself for not being stronger and resisting the temptation. He cursed the alcohol that took away his inhibitions and made it easier to fall under her spell. He was now facing the unforgiving, cutting edge of guilt.

He also began to think what his future would look like if he started giving Ellie the cold shoulder. How would she treat him at work? These situations were not normal. It was usually the male in the senior position taking advantage of his position to engage in sexual misconduct with a female. He was fully aware of the power imbalance between them and began to worry about his job. He decided he better not piss Ellie off and it would be best to let things ride at least for now.

As a war veteran though, he felt he had some marketable skills, perhaps in the security business, though that would likely involve a move away from Twin, which would be away from the support of family like his sister Grace.

He was not ready for a move to another town.

Travis decided to get some counselling, but not locally. The employee assistance program at work paid for workers to consult counsellors in circumstances like his. He felt it would be worth his while to give that a shot, but didn't hold out a lot of hope that it would pay off. He just wasn't the kind of guy who could open up his troubles to a stranger.

CHAPTER 17:

News of the Affair

Mose's bail hearing came and went. He was denied bail, despite Susan's strong argument to release Mose back to Twin Rivers if he assured the court that he would remain in Twin Rivers until trial. But the judge didn't buy it, saying he was a flight risk, and remanded him back to Her Majesty's Penitentiary on Quidi Vidi Lake in St. John's while he awaited the preliminary hearing.

"How the hell could I be a flight risk," Mose said to Susan. "I have no money to get anywhere. I have a Ski-doo that works only half the time and a small boat that I wouldn't go across the river in. Neither do I expect that I have any friends anymore who would help me get out of Labrador. So hardly a flight risk for fuck sake! Can't we appeal?"

"If we were to appeal, given they consider you a flight risk," Susan said, "the judge would post bail so high that we would never raise the money in any case. So you are effectively denied bail regardless. We just have to be patient and be ready for trial."

"That is easy for you to say."

Mose was overwhelmed by the thought of having to sit out time in a jail, notorious for the traffic of illicit drugs, and inmates with a reputation of playing tough games with those who were guilty or awaiting trial for the murder of young and beautiful women.

He felt he would probably be lucky even to be alive by the time the preliminary hearing came around. Susan told him that the department had counselling services available and that she and her legal team would always be available to do what they could to ensure his protection.

Her assurances did not work to comfort Mose at all.

Back in prison, Mose had to suffer the hard stares and threats of other inmates as well as the coldness of the guards. He didn't like what he saw. It took him a long time to get used to using the toilet in his cell while in full view of the guards and he hated the showers. Often the water was cold or only lukewarm and he was uneasy being naked in front of other men. He cursed his life and wondered how in God's name it had come to this.

His mother, Jackie, came to visit him while he was awaiting the preliminary hearing. He was surprised and overjoyed to see her. Her heart sank when the guards brought him out with handcuffs on. They sat in a visitors' area at a table across from each other. Jackie wept at first.

"My God, Mose," she was trembling as tears trickled down her face. "What is going on?"

"Someone got this all wrong," he said. "My lawyer in Goose Bay, Susan, says all the evidence is circumstantial. She said that means there were no eyewitnesses to the crime and that they will have a hard time proving that I did this."

"I am hearing stuff around Dark Harbour that you have been selling drugs in Twin Rivers. Is that true?"

"What does that have to do with whether I killed Abby?"

"People will want to make you look bad," his mother told him. "You should speak to Susan about it. Maybe she can get letters of reference as to your character."

"I will speak with her."

"And what about your relationship with Abby and her pregnancy? Will that come into it?"

"I don't know. Something else I will have to cover with the lawyer at some point. If there were no eyewitnesses, I guess the lawyers are going to use everything they can to build a case against me. Like a crime of passion or something. But you must believe me when I say I could never do a thing like that to Abby. Never."

"I believe you, and I love you."

"I love you too, Mom," Mose said.

Jackie didn't offer any money to help Jennifer come to St. John's to visit Mose, although she could have. She had the means to do it, but she did not know Jennifer very well, and the couple of times that she did meet her, Jackie considered her a bit dumb—something of a scatterbrain. Jackie held out no hope that Jennifer and Mose were in a relationship for the long haul.

* * *

Two weeks later, Mose received a telephone call from Susan. She told him she was checking in on him.

"How are you doing?"

"They call this the Lakeside Hotel. I guess I should consider myself lucky to be staying in such an upscale place."

"You sleeping okay?"

"Naw, too many nightmares and shit. People screaming down the hall all hours during the nights."

"You eating?"

"Food is the shits. No good to complain, no one listens."

"Can you tell me who Stanley Rose is?" Susan asked.

"He is a teacher in Twin Rivers."

"So you know him?"

"Not well."

"Someone in Twin is saying that you know him quite well. We are getting messages coming back from Twin that you may have supplied drugs to Mr. Rose. Is that true?"

"If I did, what would it have to do with Abby's murder?"

"To your knowledge, have the police in Twin Rivers been keeping an eye on you so to speak?"

"Not that I know about."

"It's a pretty small place and most people know everyone else's business," Susan said.

"Well, if I were in the drug business I wouldn't be advertising it in the papers or putting it on posters around town or anything."

"No, but the local police have a good idea what happens in Twin, and I would not be surprised if they have heard you've been trafficking."

"What would that have to do with the murder, though?"

"Since the case is being built on circumstantial evidence, proof beyond reasonable doubt is going to be difficult for the Crown. They will piece together a profile of you, which they will do anyway, but it will be especially important to them in this case. If you have been dealing drugs in the past that will have a huge effect on a jury."

"Can they do that?"

"We will argue to disallow it because you have no charges or any convictions on your record."

"But once something like that goes into people's ears they won't forget it," Mose said.

"If the Crown does try to bring in that issue, we will challenge its admissibility."

"I see. Seems pretty weak to me."

"Well, the Crown has to give us full disclosure of their evidence and judges do not look kindly on the idea of surprise evidence or witnesses. We have nothing to prove and you are innocent until proven guilty, Mose. The Crown has the onus to prove beyond a reasonable doubt that you killed Abby. So we need to prepare for the chance that the Crown might try to profile you as someone who has engaged in covert activity."

"Okay, well thank you for these lessons in law. I am sure they will make me sleep easier tonight."

"Is there anything else you want to tell me, Mose? We don't need any surprises coming at us at trial, so if there is anything that you think might weaken our defence you have to tell me. I have already explained the rules around lawyer-client privilege, so you need to feel free to give me information."

"No."

Susan waited in silence for a few moments.

"Okay, I will check in again with you in two to three weeks or sooner if for any reason something comes up and I need to speak to you."

* * *

Susan put down the phone feeling as though Mose did have something else to tell her but she decided not to probe anymore for the time being.

About ten days later, Susan received an anonymous call from someone in Twin Rivers. The female voice was saying that she wanted to make sure that Mose's lawyer had all the information.

"You need to tell me who you are, otherwise I am not willing to take the information," Susan told the caller.

"Why is that?" the caller asked.

"Because if it is something that may need to be entered into the court record, we have to have the source, and you may need to testify."

"Okay, my name is Trish Paul. I am a teacher in Twin Rivers. I was a friend of Abigail Williams."

"Okay. Is your given name Patricia?"

"Yes."

"I've seen your name in police documents. Okay Ms. Paul, just so you know, I am going to record this conversation."

"That's fine."

"Okay, thank you. Now what is it that you have to tell me?" Susan asked.

"There are two pieces to what I am about to tell you. Abby was a good friend of mine, and she was also a friend of someone I know well. Eleanor Rowe."

"The mayor."

"Yes. Mayor Ellie."

"Go on."

Trish reiterated the story about the relationship between Abby and Mose in high school, Abby's pregnancy, and her family's move to Toronto.

Susan was making notes.

"Do we know the result of the pregnancy?" Susan asked.

"Not certain. Abby didn't tell me. There are some who say the baby was aborted, but others say that she had the baby and put it up for adoption because of her father's beliefs"

"What is the role of the mayor in this?"

"I understand that she made a statement to the police, telling them about Abby's pregnancy and suggesting that the crime could well have been a crime of passion. Mose acting out in a jealous rage. Maybe you have seen this in the records."

"Why would the mayor take such information to the police?"

"She says she felt they might be overlooking that piece and that she thought it might help them in their investigation. She says she will be talking to the Crown prosecutor. I expect she will be a witness at trial. I thought you should know that."

"Is there anything else you'd like to tell me?"

"There's one more thing that you might want to be aware of. Since October, 1994, the mayor and Travis have been carrying on an affair. Travis was cheating on Abby for over a year and they are still seeing each other. I have no idea if that has any relevance, but I leave that information with you to do with it what you will."

"Has this been well known around town?"

"Not as well known as you might think. Some town staff knew what was and is going on. But generally around town, not much out there."

"Thank you Trish."

"Thanks for taking my call." Trish hung the phone.

The conversation with Trish got Susan thinking that there must be a lot more to this than meets the eye. There was clearly a love triangle at play here, if not a rectangular affair.

CHAPTER 18:
Going to Trial

The judge heard various pieces of evidence presented by the Crown prosecutor at the preliminary hearing in Goose Bay in January of 1997. He accepted that the Crown had enough evidence to proceed to trial. Mose did not attend the preliminary hearing.

"The court will be in touch with both counsel to work out a date for trial," he said and banged his gavel on his desk. "Court is adjourned."

* * *

"How you doin'?" Wayne Osmond III asked Mose. Osmond acting as part of Mose's legal team, was visiting him at the pen in St. John's.

"Had better days. Some asshole who already found me guilty of killing Abby kicked me in the nuts a couple of weeks ago. Been pissin' razor blades ever since. I wouldn't wish it on my worst enemy—well except maybe the guy who kicked me. Jesus I need to get the fuck out of here!"

"I'm sorry to hear that. Did they take you to the Health Sciences?"

"Yes. They put me on some opioids for pain, and something to ward off infection. For what good all that did. The prison controls handing out meds and they can be slack. Sometimes even missing my doses for a day or more, because they don't give a shit."

"We now have a trial date Mose."

"How exciting. Will there be a jury?"

"Yes, there is always a jury in a first degree murder case."

"What is the date for trial?"

"It will begin on Monday morning October 13. The first thing will be to select a jury. Mose what can you tell me about your relationship with Abby?"

"I told the police about my relationship with her."

"Did she get pregnant with your child?"

Mose stared back at Osmond. "Yes, she did."

"How did you feel about the pregnancy?"

"I loved Abby and I was happy that she was pregnant."

"I understand she went away with her family while she was pregnant. Do you know what happened to the baby?"

"I had a letter from her saying she thought she would have to abort the pregnancy. But I think that her parents were responsible for forcing her into that. I know she wanted to have the baby."

"What did you do about it?"

"I tried to get in touch with her, but her parents wouldn't let me speak to her."

"So you don't know for certain whether there was an abortion or perhaps the baby was born and put up for adoption."

"No, I don't know for sure."

"Mose, what the Crown is going to try to do is demonstrate that you killed Abby in a jealous rage over how she denied you your baby, and how she went off and married another man."

"That's not what happened."

"You were at the scene at the relevant time of her death. How are we going to convince a jury that you didn't commit that murder?"

"Well, we are going to have to. It's your job to raise doubt in the minds of the jurors, isn't it? That's how Susan explained it to me."

"Yes, it is."

CHAPTER 19:

Shamans

Meeting Sophie lifted my spirits in ways I cannot even begin to describe.

Back in high school I'd had a couple of girlfriends who couldn't put up with my awkwardness and ditched me in a matter of days. I didn't go to school dances because I was too shy to dance and thought no one would want to dance with me anyway. I was in a gutter so long that it felt as though the gutter was a normal place to be and it was where I was supposed to be.

Sophie made me see that I was as good as the next person, and that increased my confidence in myself. Boosted my self-esteem I guess.

She was interested in learning all she could about my background, and when I told her about the loss of my mother at a very young age, she cried on my shoulder. I was starting to fall in love with her.

I told her many stories about my growing up in Twin Rivers.

Although Travis always made sure I had a roof over my head and food to eat, he had a drinking problem that often turned into a form of terror that he inflicted on me. I would hear him screaming at night in his room when I thought he would be asleep. I am certain that the PTSD and the death of my mother combined to haunt him. These events shook me to the core.

I was a gifted child who stood out on school records, though Travis paid zero attention to that and he did nothing to show that he appreciated my gift of memory. He seemed to be wrapped up in his own world of which I just happened to be an unfortunate by-product. He would often make fun of me for being different and anti social. I think he might have thought I was gay, but he never did say it.

When I would try to tell him about a bad dream I'd had or that someone had made fun of me in school, he would brush it off and tell me to get over it. Sometimes he would read my report cards, most often he wouldn't. He would never attend parent-teacher meetings. He thought that was nonsense and a waste of time.

I was afraid of him, and being that there was just him and me living at the house, I became the one who had to absorb all his shit.

I have some old photograph albums that I don't look at too often. Too many reminders of my mother, and they tend to get me down. I thought happy memories were supposed to be good, but they work the other way for me. There are some pictures of me with Travis after my mother's death. Riding on a snow machine, building a snow fort and a snowman. All are smiling, happy images. But pictures do not tell the whole story. In fact they can be downright misleading. I don't have to tell you that.

When I was about five I remember my aunt Grace one day bringing some sweet bread down for us. It had come right out of the oven and was still warm. She was always happy to see me and I would show her some of my schoolwork or talk about a new game I'd learned. But this time, she gave me the loaf of bread to put on the table, and as I was going to the table with it, I dropped it. Aunt Grace had her dog with her and of course he bolted at the bread and gouged a big piece out of it.

Travis went completely berserk. He had just come home from work and was hungry.

"You stupid, fucking, useless little prick!" he screamed at me. "Get the fuck out of here and go to your room and stay there! I don't want to see you anymore tonight."

Grace tried to defend me but Travis told her to mind her own business. She went home in tears and I went to my room hungry and in a state of terror.

Of all the stuff I faced in my screwed up life, the worst were the repetitive nightmares that would take hold of me. Similar dreams that would come and go each time leaving me frightened and drenched in night sweats.

The night terrors most always involved the same person—a male relative who is now dead. Although that person is dead in my dream, he continues to move around like he is refusing to be buried. He is even moving his body while in the coffin awaiting burial. Eyes open. In some dreams he steps out of the coffin and comes toward me. I am afraid he will touch me because I am thinking his skin will rub away from his bones if he touched me. I can smell the stench of death on him, as he gets closer. Each time, his hands move toward my throat. His eyes, unblinking, are staring right through me from his expressionless face. At this point I am trying to say something but words won't come. There is no one around to hear me. I try to holler and only strange sounds come out. Then I wake up gasping for air and sweating.

I have to tell you that there were times I thought about ending it all. I thought about how it might feel to be free of what I saw as some kind of entrapment. Demons came from out of nowhere and crowded in around me like angry, dancing shamans. I thought my life was of no use to anyone and that people would not miss me even if I did decide to go and jump over the wharf.

Sophie and I were seeing each other for a period of months before I related any of this to her. She was curious and wanted to learn more.

"Have you had any nightmares lately?" she asked.

"Yes, just last week."

"Same scenario?"

"Pretty much. Same person haunting me. Am I possessed or something?"

"Mother of God, Olav, your head doesn't spin around on its axis does it?" she laughed.

"Ha ha—like Linda Blair!"

"Why do you think you have these? Have you ever spoken to a psychiatrist about it?"

"No, I haven't."

"Is that something you think might help you? Talking to someone like that might help you understand why these things happen."

"Maybe," I said. "I will give it some thought."

"There is a doctor over at student health services here on campus. She is a psychiatrist and she provides counselling services to students. Her name is Dr. Lynda Lau."

"Let's talk about it some more before I make that leap."

CHAPTER 20:

Becoming Sleuths

Sophie and I started our detective work to track down my sibling by searching the Ontario government website and finding out what the governing rules were. Something was telling me that although there was a recent law enacted that allowed for the opening of adoption records, it would not be as simple as going to a library and locating a book.

The first thing we did was to enter my name on their adoption disclosure register as a person interested in searching for an adopted relative.

The more we looked into it, the more it seemed to become a lesson that would help me prepare for law school: exceptions to the law.

The first hurdle we discovered was that adoptive parents had the right to veto any disclosure. They could elect to do that, but whether they did in this case was another matter.

The other complicating factor was that we had little to no information as to the date of birth, nor in which of Toronto's forty or more hospitals the baby might have been born. Or if indeed the baby was born in a hospital at all.

We decided to contact the Bureau of Vital Statistics in Ontario to see if we could open a conversation with someone there who could help guide us.

After several frustrating minutes of answering multiple robotic prompts, our introductory call led us to an agent named Deanna Sewell. Her voice was friendly and welcoming.

We told her the story of my mother's pregnancy, her family background, the year and approximate date of the birth. She asked if I had registered on the disclosure register. I told her I had.

She said she would email us a package of information that we should study. The application was online and she offered to send us the link for that as well.

"I am here to work with you through the process and please understand that I can only do what the law allows me to do. That should go without saying, but breaches, for example of orders like no disclosure or no contact, can be subject to fines of up to fifty thousand dollars," Deanna told us.

"We understand that," I said.

She gave us her email and her direct line and we hung up. We felt we were making real progress now that we had a direct contact, and set about planning our next steps.

* * *

Six months after our initial contact with Deanna Sewell at Vital Stats in Toronto, we received an email from her saying that they had located a birth certificate in the archives registering a baby girl born to Abigail Peters on September 14, 1988. The baby was registered as baby Tamara Peters.

It was the only Abigail Peters in the records for the time period that we specified. It was pretty certain that I had a sister. Somewhere.

There was no abortion after all, and our instincts about the reverend's views of abortion probably proved correct.

Deanna offered to speak to the people at adoptions records on our behalf. She told us that if she could match the names of the adoptive parents to a document signed by Abigail, she would pass that along to us. She would also check whether the parents had signed any non-disclosure documents. We would be on our own on the search after that.

I told Sophie that the first thing I should do is contact Jackie to let her know what we have so far discovered.

I called Jackie in Dark Harbour later that evening. We were on the speaker so I could introduce her to Sophie. Jackie was very pleased to meet her and asked her where she was from and about her family. Jackie said she was familiar with that area in Newfoundland.

"I will tell you that the purpose of our call is to let you know that we are tracking down the child that Abby had in 1988. And she did have a child. Our contacts in Toronto tell us that Abby had a baby girl on September 14, 1988."

"Oh my God," Jackie whispered. "I had this feeling all these years, that I had a grandchild out there somewhere."

"We are very excited about this and can't wait to hear from Toronto again. Our contact there is searching adoption records to find out who the adoptive parents are. After she gets that information we will do our best to track them down. But right now we are pretty much intoxicated on the news that there is a sibling out there."

I didn't want to dampen Jackie's spirits after this news but I did have to tell her the possible negative part to this.

"The other thing you should know," I said, "is that the adoptive parents may have signed non-disclosure statements and if they have done that it will make the search much more difficult."

"Yes, I understand," Jackie said. "But I should tell you, in case this becomes relevant, that your grandmother Rhoda was stricken with kidney failure after Abby was born. I learned this through my contacts at the church here. It was before they came to Dark Harbour and for a long time she had to be treated by dialysis.

Eventually they determined that one of the family could donate a kidney and she had a successful transplant. But the important thing here Olav is this: the kidney disease was of the type that is genetic and it is often known to skip a generation. I didn't want to tell you this when we met in 2009, because I was afraid of what trauma it might cause. But it is important that you know."

"Yes, it is, and important for my sibling," I said. "Thank you for the information."

"Good luck with the rest of the search," Jackie said. "If there is anything I can do, just get in touch with me."

We exchanged email addresses and hung up the phones.

"Should we tell the bishop and Rhoda?" Sophie asked.

"I am not sure," I said. "Right off the top, I am thinking no, since Absolom was mainly responsible for the child going up for adoption in the first place. So why would he care?"

"Well, his views may have changed over the years."

"That's true, and I guess the premise of the open adoption records about health matters might be a motivating factor. Why don't we wait until we actually locate Tamara and then decide whether to let them know? Although she is not likely to be going by Tamara now."

"Okay," Sophie said. "That makes sense to me."

CHAPTER 21:

Opening Day

GOOSE BAY, LABRADOR, OCTOBER 13, 1997

The date for the Strickland murder trial had finally arrived. Mose was flown to Goose Bay from St. John's on the Friday before and held at the Correctional Centre. Susan met with him on the weekend to prepare him for what to expect in the coming days. They discussed how he should behave in court: not to stare at the jurors, how he should dress, and whether or not he would take the stand to testify in his own defence.

"I want to testify," Mose said.

"It would not be until near the end of the trial so we have some time to think about that. No need to decide now," Susan said. She told Mose that they would hear a lot of suggestions put forward about him by the prosecutor and this will upset him. "It's important that you not respond in anyway to the things they are saying even though you will feel like screaming out and rebutting what they are saying. Don't do that. Keep your cool. Very important," Susan said.

* * *

On Monday morning the courtroom benches were filled with the hundred or so people whose names had been called as potential jurors. The trial would be held before Judge Martin Estridge.

After a morning of challenges by counsel on both sides, the court was finally able to seat eight men and four women to act as jurors.

It was all pretty foreign to Mose. The courtroom seemed very formal and cold. As he was led in he looked around at the sea of faces and shuddered. The judge cloaked in black with some sort of red sash, was seated up on a pedestal so everyone could see him. He seemed to be looking down at a flock of obedient little lambs. Mose looked at the unsmiling faces of the twelve characters in the jury box and shuddered even more. These were the people who would hold his fate in their hands.

He'd read somewhere that an accused person is entitled to a trial by a jury of his peers. He looked at the twelve people in the box and thought, yeah, right. God help me. Most looked like they came from some sort of privilege—stuffed shirts. They were all old enough to be his parents or grandparents, and they were pretty white.

Mose expected the Crown to specifically point out the fact that his father was a Native American so as to plant a certain notion in the heads of the jurors. Many on the jury he speculated would still have the comic book versions of hostile Indians imprinted on their brains. The cowboys and Indians version.

This was not going to end well, Mose predicted.

* * *

The Crown Prosecutor was a fellow named Isaac P. Morgan, Esquire. He had stacks and boxes of files, which probably impressed spectators in the visitors' gallery. Morgan strutted and flitted around the courtroom as though he was walking on air, leaning over to whisper to this one and that one, his robes and grey hair flying and grabbing everybody's attention. The man sure had a flair for the dramatic. Like the shit you see in movies and on television.

Mose met Morgan a few months earlier when the Crown came to him and his lawyer to offer a plea deal. Morgan had proposed that they would recommend voluntary manslaughter to the judge if Mose would plead guilty to that. Although the maximum penalty for manslaughter is life in prison, the Crown was offering a six-year prison term, and he'd be eligible for parole after serving a third of the time. It would not be subject though to credit for time served.

"But I would have a criminal record," Mose said.

"Yes, that's correct," Wayne Osmond advised him.

"Then Mr. Morgan can take his offer and stick it up his ass," Mose said. "I'm not pleading guilty to anything."

Osmond tried to convince Mose to take the deal. "You'll be out in twenty-four months," he said.

"I will take my chances. I am not a murderer."

"Okay, I will take that back to the Crown and tell them we are going to trial."

* * *

The trial began with both counsel making opening statements to the jury. Morgan made some convincing points to the jury. He stood in front of the twelve men and women on the jury benches, occasionally pointing at Mose and his defence counsel.

"The Crown will show that the accused, Mr. Strickland, was at the scene within the time period in which Abigail Williams was murdered," Morgan thundered. "He admitted that to the police. "

Morgan paced in front of the jury.

"Ladies and gentlemen," he continued, "you will also hear evidence that Mr. Strickland and the victim, Abby, had a deep and complicated relationship that went back over ten years.

"Now the defence will put forward its argument that the case is based on circumstantial evidence. That is, that there were no eyewitness who came forward to say they actually saw someone do the killing. The strangulation." Morgan paused for effect, while looking several jurors straight in the eye.

Morgan looked at each person in the jury box as he concluded his opening statement.

"But ladies and gentlemen, when you the jurors piece together the facts along with Mr. Strickland's own admission of being at the scene, you will conclude that Mr. Strickland acted in a jealous rage that resulted in the murder of a young and beautiful mom, a wife, and someone who was a friend to many in the community. You will have no choice but to find Mr. Strickland guilty of the murder of Abigail Williams. Thank you."

Morgan nodded at the judge and waltzed gracefully back to his chair like an eagle coming in for a landing. His opening remarks seemed to echo through the courtroom like bells tolling at a funeral.

Mose could only hang his head, body language that was not winning any points with the jury.

This was going to be a battle and Mose could only hope that the team working on his defence was up to the task.

CHAPTER 22:

Road Blocks

I received an email from Deanna Sewell about two months after we spoke to her about the birth registration. She asked us to call her to discuss her latest news.

She told us that adoptions had processed an application involving a baby Tamara Peters in late September, 1988. She said that baby Tamara had been adopted into a family somewhere in Ontario. However, she could not give us the name of the couple nor their address because by default under the old legislation the file was closed and allowed to remain closed even after the new law came into effect.

That was what we were afraid of. We were stymied at this point.

"I have learned that both myself and this sibling of mine could be exposed to a genetic disease," I told Deanna. "What do you suggest we do?"

"What you will have to do in that situation is make a case to the court asking for an order to open the file. That could take some time unfortunately and cost a lot of money. The other thing is there is nothing stopping you from taking out an ad in one of the papers in Ontario for a few days and hope the person will come forward voluntarily. But there is no guarantee that would be successful. Whichever route you choose will end up costing some money."

"I will think about that ad idea. Do you know of any lawyers who practice in that area of law?" I asked her.

"I will email some names to you."

Sophie and I looked at each other. "Well now it looks like we could have a legal battle on our hands," I said. "Just what we need!"

I had no idea what to do next. I had zero money to pay a lawyer or to pay for an ad in the paper, which I was certain would be very expensive, and there was no one in my family that I could turn to for help. Jackie of course had an interest, and offered to help in anyway. Maybe a source there, but what was the court going to need to prove our genetic exposure if we went that route? The complications were beginning to mount.

"What do you think of my asking Jackie to help out with the money part?" I asked Sophie.

"I have a feeling she would be happy to do that. Why don't you contact a couple of lawyers from that list that Deanna is sending and get an idea of costs," Sophie suggested. "You could also do both the ad and the legal route. Doesn't have to be one or the other. Research those costs and after that we can talk with Jackie."

"Good thinking," I said but the thought of being beholden to someone, weighed a bit on me.

* * *

I received a quote from a firm in Toronto which was offering to represent me on a ten thousand dollar retainer with an estimate of another eight thousand to see the process through to the end. They also estimated that it would likely be ten months down the road before the case could be heard, there being such a backlog on the court docket.

The time estimate was disappointing and when I asked the lawyer if it could be moved to the top of the docket where health is the basis of the claim, he told me only if there was a pressing need—for example I would have to be in need of a kidney right now in order for that to happen. Since that was not the case we were stuck with the ten-month time period, maybe longer.

But money was the big hurdle right now. Eighteen thousand was one hell of a lot of cash. I stressed about this for days. I knew Sophie wanted to help, but there was no way I was going to take that kind of money from her. There was only one option. Jackie.

She proved to be as good as her word. When I briefed her on what needed to happen and the kind of legal costs involved, she offered to help without any questions asked. She would front the money for the legal bill as well as for an ad in the paper. That was one hurdle out of the way. I told her I was a little fearful of having that debt hovering over me and that I had been really reluctant to approach her. "This is family," she said, "and we are going to do what ever is required to unite us. I don't want you to worry about repayment Olav."

"That is so considerate of you Jackie," I said. "I cannot tell you how much I appreciate it."

"At some point, after you have made your first million we can talk, but until then, don't worry," she said with a laugh.

Following the call with Jackie, I emailed instructions to the lawyer in Toronto to begin drafting the application and get it filed as soon as possible. I told him I would have the ten thousand dollars to him in a few days. He replied the next day and said to be patient. "We will be well down on the docket," he reminded me. "It is not going to happen overnight."

CHAPTER 23:

Jury of One's Peers?

Mose felt like the walls were closing in around him. This courtroom was colourless and unfriendly. The judge was sitting between two flags—the Canadian and the Newfoundland flag on either side of him—and up above him on the wall was a 1960s portrait of the Queen. This was her courtroom. The crime was committed against her, the Sovereign.

The place was icy cold. No one gets to feel comfortable. Not in these rooms. Even the lawyers who were supposed to be representing him seemed stiff and unreachable. The only friendly face that Mose could find in the room each day was that of his mother.

Jackie was there every day to listen to the "factual" testimony that was all designed to paint a picture of her son as a murderer. To her they were fabricating a case based on lie after lie.

The bishop and Rhoda were also in the courtroom, though Mose placed them among the unfriendly crowd, or at least the bishop was for sure. Mose went out of his way to avoid eye contact with them.

Mose tried to turn his mind to some less threatening things outside the courtroom—something involving more pleasant times. But these became fleeting thoughts because no sooner would he think of something pleasant then just as quickly he would come back to that big, black thundercloud hanging above his head. It covered the whole sky and went on forever. Pains darted in his stomach and his bowels would start to feel loose each time he thought about the possibility of life in prison.

He tried to get a read on each of the jurors but that was next to impossible. They were stiff and most just sat and stared straight ahead. There was one juror who made eye contact with him and as soon as that happened she dropped her eyes to the floor and then quickly glanced around to see if anyone in authority had been watching her. She seemed to be terrified that she had committed a crime or something.

So this was a jury of his peers?

In a jury trial, someone else gets to decide who one's peers are. And that can be offensive. So if someone said this jury was a group of Mose's peers, I'm pretty sure he concluded he was screwed. Royally.

* * *

One by one on the first afternoon and into the next morning, the Crown paraded witnesses into the courtroom to swear their oaths and sit in the witness box to give evidence. There were few objections and little cross-examination from Mose's team to the first few witnesses. The Crown witnesses included Staff Sergeant Albright, Senior Officer Stanton, Inspector Maxine Smith, pathologist Dr. Sheldon Nolstrom, and Dr. Shannon Bennett, psychiatrist, who had examined Mose and pronounced him fit to stand trial.

One of the first witnesses was the forensic pathologist, Dr. Sheldon Nolstrom. He outlined his vast experience in carrying out autopsies and writing reports on causes of death. He told the court the details of when the body came to his attention and how he pinpointed the date and time of her death.

He described the victim as having suffered trauma to her throat and airway caused by an object that was wrapped around her neck and tightened until she could no longer breathe.

He also noted that Abby's physique was rather on the petite side and he speculated that she would have been easily overpowered by a person of average size.

During his testimony, the Crown put the autopsy photos into evidence, at which point they were handed to the jury for viewing.

Each juror looked at a photo and then handed it on for observation by the next juror. They could have been looking at a fresh-out-of-the-oven item in a chef's competition. Not one showed any sign of emotion. It took Mose all he had to keep from screaming obscenities at them.

Mose heard some sniffles coming from behind him during Nolstrom's testimony. They were coming from Rhoda. He felt sorry for her having to live through all that pain again.

"Dr. Nolstrom, how would you describe the marks on Abby's neck?" Morgan asked.

"There were abrasions where it appears the skin had been chafed by some type of string or cable or perhaps something like a length of electrical wire."

Susan stood to object.

"The witness is speculating about the murder weapon, my Lord, without any factual evidence on which to base his suggestions."

"I am not going to accept that objection counsellor. The court would just as soon hear expert testimony as to what all reasonable possibilities there may be as to the murder weapon," the judge said. "Please continue with your examination Mr. Morgan."

"Thank you, my Lord. Go on, Dr. Nolstrom," Morgan instructed his witness.

"From the photos taken at the scene, the marks appeared to be orange or a shade of red at that time. By the time the body got to me, some discoloration had taken place and the marks had darkened in color. They were on the sides of her neck and in the front and a small lesion on the back of the neck, likely being the point where the attacker applied the most pressure."

"Dr. Nolstrom, in your professional opinion, please tell the court how Abby was killed."

"She was choked to death," Dr. Nolstrom stated. "Strangled. Technically speaking her death was asphyxia by strangulation."

"Thank you Dr. Nolstrom. I have no further questions for this witness."

"Any cross Ms. McDonald?" Judge Estridge asked, looking down over his reading glasses.

"Yes, thank you my Lord." Susan got to her feet.

She was in her late thirties and a very attractive brunette with longer than shoulder-length hair. Her deep brown eyes scanned the courtroom through a pair of Calvin Klein wire-rimmed glasses. Her eyes could be steely when necessary. There were rumours that Susan would likely be on the list for the next round of Queen's Counsel appointments and perhaps on the provincial court bench within five years.

She scanned back through her notes, dragging it out for some seconds so that the doctor would squirm in the witness box a little longer.

"Dr. Nolstrom, you are aware that the Crown has been able to produce neither an eyewitness, nor a confession, nor anything resembling the murder weapon. Correct?"

"Yes."

"Now, you speculated in your testimony that the attacker used a string or a cable or perhaps a length of electrical wire. These are your words."

"That's correct."

"How wide were the marks on Abby's neck, say the widest mark? When I say wide I mean the width of the mark going in a north-south direction?"

Susan placed her thumb and forefinger to her own neck and moved them apart to be sure the doctor understood what she was asking.

"The widest mark was just slightly less than a centimetre."

"That would be a little narrow for a piece of electrical wire would it not, Dr. Nolstrom?"

"I don't know ma'am."

"You don't know."

"No ma'am."

"Dr. Nolstrom, would you consider yourself an expert in matters related to the sizes of electrical wiring typically used in home construction?"

"No, I don't."

"Are you familiar with the characteristics such as colors or the widths of electrical wires?"

"No, ma'am I am not."

"If you know nothing about those kinds of wires, then why would you suggest that the murder weapon could have been a piece of electrical wire?"

"It is speculation."

"Speculation?" Susan asked looking at the jury.

"Yes, ma'am."

"Did the Crown or the police ever inform you that Mose Strickland had a house under construction?"

"Yes, I was advised of that."

"Why do you think they advised you of that?"

"That is a question for the police," Dr. Nolstrom said.

"But I am asking you Dr. Nolstrom. You surely would have had some interpretation as to why they would tell you that. So what was your interpretation?"

"It was one piece of information that came to me as part of a larger unsolved issue."

"Then what did you conclude from that information?"

"I didn't conclude anything ma'am."

"Yet you held out the possibility of electrical wire being the murder weapon in your testimony. Why did you do that?"

"I am speculating as to possibilities."

"Your speculations are not based on any fact and can mislead the jury and this court, would you not agree Dr. Nolstrom?"

"I do not wish to mislead anyone, ma'am."

"Well whether you wish to or not, your words have meaning and consequences."

Susan, frustrated with the smug, pat answers from the doctor, began to raise her voice slightly.

"So let me put this to you Dr. Nolstrom," she continued, "you admitted under oath that the police told you that Mose Strickland was building a house in Twin Rivers. In the same breath you mentioned the possibility of electrical wire as the murder weapon. What would any reasonable person piece together from that? I suggest the purpose of your testimony was to plant in the heads of the jurors that Mose had easy access to the weapon that was likely used in the murder. That I suggest Dr. Nolstrom is misleading the jury because it is pure speculation."

"That is not my intent," Dr. Nolstrom was grasping at straws.

"No matter what your intent, the effect of your speculative words is out there. It's on the record. Words matter Dr. Nolstrom," Susan argued.

"Given that there were no eyewitnesses to the death, that in and of itself leaves everything open to a lot of speculation," Dr. Nolstrom stated.

"Well, you know my client is innocent until proven guilty and proven guilty beyond a reasonable doubt. That leaves no room, NO ROOM for speculation Dr. Nolstrom," Susan said.

Her steely eyes were now penetrating those of the doctor making Nolstrom very uncomfortable. He looked as though he needed to get the hell out of the witness box as quickly as possible.

"Now you said it could have been a string or a cable or a piece of electrical wire, but you are not certain what caused the death. Correct?"

"No, I am certain that the cause of death was strangulation. But the particular weapon could have been any number of possibilities."

Susan felt she had made some progress in discrediting Dr. Nolstrom as a witness, so she took her time to look back through her notes and move to another issue.

"Dr. Nolstrom, did you take and preserve any tissue or fluid samples from the body?"

"Yes. This is done as a standard practice and preserved in case of future DNA relevance."

"How long, Dr. Nolstrom, are such samples preserved?" Susan asked.

"As long as the Crown wants it preserved. It is their call."

"Did you recommend to the Crown that in this case where the murder weapon was not in evidence that as a matter of due diligence, the Crown should order that the samples be preserved indefinitely?"

"No, I did not recommend that. As I said, that matter is within the purview of the Crown."

"In retrospect do you think you may have been negligent in not recommending that?" Susan asked.

"No, I do not. The matter was out of my hands."

"I have no further questions, my Lord."

* * *

On the afternoon of the second day of trial, the Crown prosecutor I. P. Morgan introduced witness, Mayor Eleanor Rowe.

A couple of newspaper articles I read noted the grandness of her appearance as she entered the courtroom.

It could have been Queen Elizabeth herself stepping down from the portrait above the judge's head. Eleanor was even a little late, fashionably as they say—not quite enough to irritate the judge but just enough to suggest to the crowded public benches that she was a busy and important person. I am sure it was all she could do to keep from giving a little royal wave to the spectators.

She sat in the witness box, head held high, and waited to get started. When the clerk went over to administer the oath she snapped to her feet, put her left hand on the bible and held the other in the air. She made sure to face the judge. She could have been a president being sworn into office on inauguration day.

She wanted the people and the media to hear her every word. This could give her some front-page coverage tomorrow.

Eleanor described herself as a friend of the deceased.

"How did your friendship with Abigail start?" Morgan asked.

"Abby applied for a job at the town office. She was well quali-fied with a diploma from a business course she'd taken at the com-munity college. I spoke to her a few times about it and we kind of hit it off from there. She didn't take the job at the time because she discovered she was pregnant and decided to hold off on working until a later date after the baby was born."

"What was the nature of your friendship with Abby?"

"We were not really close friends but we did meet for coffee, though not often. I would also see her at community events. A few times I visited at her home at her invitation for dinner and drinks, cookouts, that sort of thing. Usually with a few other friends."

"Now Ms. Rowe, on February 28, 1996 you met with the police in Twin Rivers to make a statement concerning Abby's death."

"Yes, I did."

"Please tell the jury why you felt it was necessary for you to have a conversation with the police."

"Twin Rivers is a small town and as its mayor I pretty well know everyone and I tend to get a lot of information coming at me. I think it is safe to say that the town was in shock after Abby's death. This type of thing is very unusual for this or any community along this coast. Everyone was talking about it of course.

"I was hearing that no one had actually seen the attack on Abby so there was a lot of speculation going on as to how her death might have come about. I knew the police would be searching for clues and possible motives to try and piece together what may have happened and who was responsible. So I went and spoke to them to tell them of something that had come me to my attention which might help them in their investigation."

"What was that information?" Morgan asked.

"It had to do with a relationship between Abby and a person in town. It was not really well known and I thought it might be something relevant that the police could easily miss."

"Who was the person that you were referring to who had the relationship with Abby?"

"It was Mose Strickland."

"The accused," Morgan said, pointing his hand toward Mose.

"Yes."

"What did you tell the police about that relationship?"

"I told them that a friend of mine who was also a friend of Abby's, a mutual friend so to speak, had told me about the relationship that went back to the mid eighties."

Wayne Osmond objected to this statement, saying that the witness was entering an area of hearsay.

"I agree," the judge said, "Mr. Morgan, unless you can bring evidence to the court to corroborate the witness's testimony I will not allow her statement."

"There is another Crown witness who will corroborate what Ms. Rowe is saying," Morgan replied.

"Then I will allow it," Judge Estridge stated.

"Thank you, my Lord."

"Please continue, Ms. Rowe," Judge Estridge instructed her.

"My friend told me that a while back Abby related to her that she had been in a relationship with Mose Strickland that began in Dark Harbour in 1987. She said that it had become much more than a casual relationship. That, in fact, Mose had gotten Abby pregnant in late 1987."

"What happened to the child?"

"Not certain. But the family left Dark Harbour, in early 1988. Abby's father was a priest and he decided to take the family to Toronto during a period in which he was doing a graduate degree. People speculated that it was either for Abby to have an abortion or to put the baby out for adoption. No one seems to know exactly."

"So why would you relate this story to the police?" Morgan asked.

"The fact of the pregnancy not being well known around town, I thought that it might be a clue that would help them in solving the matter as to who did the killing. They seemed to appreciate receiving the information."

Morgan let that sink into the jury's minds for a few seconds and looked at his notes.

"No further questions, my Lord."

"Any cross, Ms. McDonald?" the judge asked.

"Yes, my Lord," Susan got to her feet and turned to the witness box.

"Ms. Rowe, do you know Travis Williams?"

Morgan objected and asked the relevance of this question.

"My Lord," Susan said, "the relevance will become clear a little later and I ask the court for some latitude to pursue this."

The judge pondered the issue for a few seconds.

"Okay, let's see where this takes us. I will allow you to go down that path, but keep it narrow counsellor," Estridge said. "Please proceed."

"Ms. Rowe, shall I repeat the question?"

"No—yes I do know Travis Williams," Eleanor said.

"Would you say you know Travis Williams very well?"

"No, not too well," Eleanor said with a smirk.

"How close a relationship do you have with Travis Williams?"

Eleanor began to fidget. Sweat beads started breaking out on her forehead.

"He works for the town and I am the mayor."

"Please answer the question, Ms. Rowe," Susan said. "I repeat, how close a relationship do you have with Travis Williams?" Susan asked again, "and let me remind the witness that she is under oath."

"Not close," Eleanor stated.

"Not close," Susan said, repeating Eleanor's words.

Susan stared at Eleanor for a few seconds.

Silence in the courtroom.

"I have nothing further for this witness, my Lord," Susan told the court, all the while continuing that steely stare into Eleanor's eyes.

Susan returned to her seat, put down her notes, and looked again one last time at the now unsmiling figure in the witness box.

"Any re-direct, Mr. Morgan?"

"No, my Lord."

"Please call your next witness, Mr. Morgan."

"Thank you, my Lord. The Crown calls Ms. Patricia Paul."

Trish swore her oath and gave her vitals. Responding to Morgan's questions, she stated she had been friends with the mayor and with Abby as well. Her testimony confirmed that which Eleanor related to the court about Abby and Mose having conceived a child. It was the corroboration that the judge expected in order to dispel the issue of hearsay raised by the defence.

Morgan was satisfied that he had gone far enough with Trish and that the jury had absorbed her testimony.

"Thank you Ms. Paul, I have nothing further, my Lord,"

"Cross Ms. McDonald?"

Susan got to her feet.

"Yes, thank you my Lord."

She paused, looking back through her file. Susan was effective at making good use of silence.

"Ms. Paul, you called my office on April 18, 1996, yes?

"Yes, that's correct."

I.P. Morgan looked up puzzled and fully engaged, ready to pounce.

"Please tell the jury why you called me."

"I called to tell you that Ms. Rowe would probably be testifying for the prosecution, though I learned later that you would already have known that."

"What did you expect her to testify about?"

"That she would testify regarding the relationship between Mose and the deceased Abby Williams, and about how Abby had gotten pregnant with his child."

"Thank you Ms. Paul. What else did you tell me?"

"I told you that Ms. Rowe and Abby's husband, Travis Williams, had been carrying on a romantic relationship."

Someone among the court audience made a slight gasp.

I.P. Morgan decided to step in.

"My Lord, we object to these questions. We had no notice that this Crown witness would be a witness for the defence," Morgan pleaded.

"Mr. Morgan, you know the rules about disclosure as well as I do and that counsel for the accused has no obligation to reveal their defence strategy to you."

"Yes, I understand that my Lord, but it seems that the defence wants to go down a particular path such that we have no alternative but to treat this witness as hostile."

The judge decided to recess the court to give him time to consider Morgan's request to cross-examine his own witness.

The court resumed a half hour later.

"I have considered your request to apply Milgaard in the case of this witness Mr. Morgan, and I am granting that request."

"Thank you, my Lord."

"Please continue, Ms. McDonald."

"Ms. Paul when you say that Eleanor Rowe and Travis Williams were carrying on a romantic relationship, how do you know that was the case?"

"There was a lot of discussion in certain circles that it was going on."

"What circles?"

"Among staff at the school and other employment places."

"Objection, this is hearsay my Lord," Morgan interjected.

"Agreed," the judge said.

"Counsellor, please limit your questioning to facts."

"Ms. Paul, to your knowledge how long was the relationship going on?"

"Since 1994. And it is still going on."

"And how do you know that?"

"Abby told me."

"So this relationship was happening while Abby was still alive and married to Travis?"

"Yes," Trish replied.

"In her statement, Ms. Rowe said she was a friend of Abby's. With friends like that who needs enemies, wouldn't you agree Ms. Paul?"

"Counsellor," the judge was glaring down over his glasses.

Morgan started to object but decided to take his chances on cross.

"I withdraw that last statement. Nothing further, my Lord."

"Mr. Morgan, you may now proceed."

"Thank you, my Lord. Ms. Paul, you seem to be playing some kind of game here in a case in which the stakes are very high. Do you agree that the stakes for everyone here are quite high Ms. Paul?"

"Yes, I do."

"So let me remind you that you are under oath and the court expects to hear the truth," Morgan lectured.

"You do not need to remind me that I am under oath, sir, and my only goal is to help people get to the truth," Trish lectured back.

"Now Ms. Paul, you know the accused, Mr. Strickland, yes?" Morgan continued.

"Yes, he works for our school as the bus driver."

"Have you ever witnessed any circumstance where Mr. Strickland showed any outbursts of anger or violence?"

Trish told the court about the altercation with Stanley Rose at the school.

"Do you know what this altercation was over?" Morgan asked.

"I later found out that Stanley owed money to Mose for drugs."

"How did you find that out?"

"Talk around the school."

Morgan decided to let that sink into the minds of the jurors but Susan's objection interrupted the flow.

"This is hearsay and speculation," she stated, "and further, it should interest the court in knowing that Mr. Strickland has a completely clean police record."

"I agree with your objection, Ms. McDonald," Judge Estridge said turning to the jury box, "and I instruct the jury to disregard that last statement from Ms. Paul. Please continue Mr. Morgan."

"Now, Ms. Paul, turning to your testimony regarding the relationship between Eleanor Rowe and Travis Williams. Have you ever seen Travis and Eleanor together in what you would interpret to represent two people in a romantic relationship?"

"No, I have not."

"Has Eleanor Rowe, your friend no less, ever told you that she was involved in a relationship with Travis Williams?"

"No, she has not."

"Has Travis Williams ever told you that he was involved in a relationship with Eleanor Rowe?"

"No, he has not."

"The Crown submits then my Lord that the entire testimony from Ms. Paul today except that confirming evidence given by Eleanor Rowe on direct, is based purely on conjecture, and should be stricken from the record."

"I accept that submission Mr. Morgan and I hereby instruct the jury not to consider Ms. Paul's testimony concerning a relationship between Eleanor Rowe and the husband of the deceased."

Susan shook her head and looked at her co-counsel.

"Thank you my Lord," Morgan said and sat down with a satisfied look on his face.

* * *

Susan McDonald and Wayne Osmond felt they were at a point where they needed to decide whether to put Mose on the stand. Although Mose was anxiously waiting his turn to speak to the court, the lawyers had to weigh the benefits of giving direct testimony versus the risk of being torn to shreds by the prosecution.

They believed that they had raised enough issues during the trial to plant seeds of doubt into the minds of at least some of the jurors, and given the circumstantial nature of the evidence, they saw their job as simply to raise doubt.

The onus was on the prosecution to prove beyond reasonable doubt that Mose not only did the killing but also that he did it with full intent. That he planned Abby's execution.

The lawyers were also uneasy about putting Mose on the stand due to his demeanour. He was a bit shifty-eyed under questioning, which could make him look like he was hiding something. Even during their own questioning of Mose, Susan noticed that he tended to avoid eye contact. They felt that under attack from Morgan, his whole testimony could go to pieces and he'd end up hanging himself in front of the jury.

Susan and Wayne decided to advise Mose against taking the witness stand.

CHAPTER 24:

Who?

Amanda Reynolds was at the end of a year-long clerkship at the Superior Court of Ontario in June, 2014. She already had a job lined up as an associate with a major firm in Toronto as soon as her articles were complete at the court. She was looking forward to the day when she would be called as a lawyer by the Law Society of Upper Canada.

Mandy, as everyone called her, was very smart and had no trouble breezing through Osgoode Law School in Toronto. She was an active student, a good debater, and won several moot competitions, one of them a national competition that was held in Vancouver. Many on the faculty, including the dean, took note of her achievements and it became clear that she had a brilliant career ahead of her in law.

Mandy grew up as an only child in a family in Thunder Bay, Ontario. The family was not endowed with a lot of money. Her father, being an administrator at city hall, and her mother a nurse, meant they were ensconced squarely in the middle class. After Mandy's arrival as a baby, her parents opened an education savings account and over the years managed to salt away enough money to see her through grad school. Mandy was very close with her parents and she frequently reminded them how much she appreciated the sacrifices they made in order to finance her education.

"Some day I will be in a position to pay that back to you," she would tell them.

Mandy found her clerkship boring at times. She was anxious to get into the rough and tumble world of trial law and litigation. Even though she was bored, the clerkship did allow her an opportunity to scan the kind of cases coming before the court and she often enjoyed reading about them in the newspapers after filings took place.

A couple of weeks before the scheduled end of her clerkship, she began the filing process for the Olav Williams application asking the court to open an adoption file. These kind of applications caught her attention and, as with several other similar applications that had come in during her clerkship, she decided to read a bit deeper into the document.

As she read she came across the words "baby Tamara" born in Toronto to Abigail Peters in late September, 1988. Mandy knew she was adopted because her parents practiced full disclosure with her and told her what her birth name was. They felt Mandy was entitled to know about her biological origins.

Just as she read the words "baby Tamara," someone came to her office door wanting her attention. Mandy had to cover her mouth to suppress an audible gasp.

"Jesus," Mandy thought, "this is me they are talking about!"

Reading further into the document, she noted a sense of urgency since the applicant was claiming possible "exposure to a genetic kidney disease" and that it was of utmost importance that the child that Abigail gave up for adoption in 1988 be made aware of this very significant health matter.

Mandy felt weak and a hot flash went through her body. With her head spinning, she got up and left her desk to go to the washroom. She had to get ahold of herself so she went out onto the street to walk and get some fresh air. She stopped by a coffee shop and sat staring out the window, wondering what to do next. After twenty minutes, she concluded she had to go home to Thunder Bay to talk with her parents.

Back at the office she met with her boss, one of the judges, to explain why she needed a few days off to go home. She understood and told Mandy it was important that she talk with her parents to discuss what to do, and to take what time she needed.

She went back to her office and made arrangements to fly home on the first available flight. She felt as though she was in a bubble for the remainder of the day. She was excited about a sibling in her life but afraid of what that might mean. Would there be chemistry? Would they like each other? So many emotions and fears engulfed her. She locked herself in her office and began to cry. Mandy picked up the phone and called her mother to say she was coming home for a few days. She said she needed to talk but would get into it more when she got home.

"Is everything okay?" her mother asked.

"Yes, I am fine," Mandy said. "Just that something has come to my attention that we need to talk about."

"Quite often that means one of two things, you're getting married or you're pregnant," her mother said trying to prod.

"No, nothing like that," Mandy replied. "No need for you to worry. I will see you tomorrow."

* * *

Following the winter semester at Memorial, I went home to Twin Rivers for the summer break. I was working my summer job at the Co-Op store for minimum wage. It was a dull job but I hoped to save a few dollars to help out in the next semester.

Sophie too was back at her home on the Irish shore so I didn't have her to lean on. I missed that support. I couldn't wait to get back to university for the next semester to be with her again.

One afternoon while I was having coffee with some of the staff in the store lunch room, my phone rang with an 807 area code—one that I didn't recognize.

I answered. "Hello, this is Olav."

"Hi Olav, this is Mandy Reynolds calling from Thunder Bay."

"Who?" I said.

"Mandy Reynolds," she said. "I believe we may have something in common. Our mother Abigail Peters."

I was not shocked because I did have a few nutcases calling me after my ad came out in the paper.

"Just a sec," I said. I left the lunchroom and found a more private place to continue the conversation.

"Whoa," I said. "I hate to have to ask this, but how do I know this is not a prank call?"

"I've read your application to the court to open an adoption file. I work in the registry for the Ontario Superior Court. I know that seems hyper-coincidental and it is—but here I am!"

"Okay, but you could also be someone who has read my ad in the paper," I said.

"What ad?"

"The one in the *Globe*. I've already had several prank calls."

"How did you know they were pranks?" Mandy asked.

"When I queried them on certain facts, they either gave me wrong answers or just didn't answer," I said.

"Okay. I didn't see the ad," Mandy said. "But your question is a fair one. I guess we could submit to DNA tests. I'd be up for that."

"How did you get my cell phone number, if I may ask?"

"When I found out your name, I used Canada 411 to track it down," she said.

"Do you know anything about Abigail's family?" I asked.

"My parents told me they spoke to my biological grandparents for the exact reason that you talk about in the application. The possibility of a genetic disease. They wanted information in case we needed it in the future. Their names were Rev. Absolom and Rhoda Peters, of St. John's, but Abby was raised on the coast of Labrador. She was quite young when I was born." Mandy was able to name the communities in Labrador where the family lived.

This was sounding legitimate and less likely to be a prank.

"Do you know why you were born in Toronto?" I asked.

"Not exactly, but I do know Abby's father was studying there at the time."

I was pretty certain that this was my sibling. "I take it that you are obviously interested in our getting to know each other. Otherwise you would not have called."

"Yes, and I am totally looking forward to meeting you in person." Mandy sounded pleasant and genuinely interested. That sure was a relief.

We chatted about school and how each of us was doing academically. She asked me a few things about Twin Rivers and the coast of Labrador—cultural stuff about life on the coast, the Indigenous peoples and their lifestyles.

From my court application, Mandy would have known that Abby was dead, and when I mentioned it she became a little distressed on the phone. I didn't tell her the nature of her death or the situation with Mose, not at this time. But she did tell me she'd done some research finding newspaper articles, after she read my application.

"I will fill you in a lot more about the family when we meet."

I gave her my email and asked if she would send me a photo of herself. She said she would do that and provide other documentation, which would show that she was born to Abigail Peters.

We made a plan to get together later in the summer. She was willing to come into Twin Rivers, but truth be told I diverted her from that idea. I was not altogether keen on her meeting my father. We made an alternate plan to meet up in St. John's. Sophie could also meet her then. I thought it best to explain the family dynamic when we met face to face.

"I should mention to you," Mandy told me, "that I moved your application well up on the docket so that in case we didn't get to connect this way, at least the application would be heard quite soon. But if you are satisfied that I am the person you are looking for, then the application can be dropped and you will save a lot of money."

"Yes, and I do appreciate that very much," I said. "I look forward to us meeting soon."

"I am glad we spoke," she said, "and I am really excited about the prospects of having a brother. And I would want you to meet my parents at some point. They are looking forward to meeting you."

"Same here."

"Olav," she said, in an expression that I will always remember, "we have to honour our mother's memory."

"I am with you on that." I found that I was quite moved when she made that last statement. A feeling of peace engulfed me.

We hung up the phone and I called Sophie with the news.

CHAPTER 25:
Untruths

GOOSE BAY, OCTOBER 16, 1997

The Crown called one final witness on the last day of trial. It was Stanley Rose, the teacher that Trish Paul had referred to in her testimony who had had an altercation with Mose at the school. Trish had testified that Stanley and Mose had been involved in a drug deal, though Susan was successful in convincing the judge to disallow that evidence.

Morgan's strategy was to paint Mose as something of an unseemly character who was, at times, prone to violence.

Stanley admitted that he had gotten into a brawl that Mose had started. He described Mose as being explosive and said he could go into a tantrum at any given moment.

When invited, Susan chose not to follow up with any cross-examination.

"The Crown rests its case my Lord," Morgan advised the court.

"Will you be calling any witnesses, Ms. McDonald?" Judge Estridge asked Susan.

"No, my Lord," Susan replied.

"Counsel, are you both ready to proceed with closing arguments?"

Both Morgan and Susan answered in the affirmative.

"We will adjourn for twenty minutes and when we return the Crown will lead off with its closing argument."

* * *

Crown prosecutor Isaac P. Morgan got up and moved from behind the table where he was sitting facing the twelve members of the jury. He adjusted his tie and made sure his lawyer's tabs were sitting perfectly. All eyes in the packed courtroom were on him and he soaked up every second of it. He spoke without notes and in a voice that rose and receded—a voice designed to evoke different emotions as he placed emphasis on carefully planned words and phrases.

"Ladies and gentlemen of the jury," Morgan began. "You have an important responsibility here today. It is perhaps the highest civic duty that anyone can ask of you."

Morgan never failed to remind the members of the jury of their important role in the administration of justice.

"All week long you have been hearing details of the terrible crime that has undoubtedly shaken the town of Twin Rivers and other communities. The family, friends, and neighbours of Abigail Williams have been emotionally drained over these past number of months because of the horrific killing that was committed on one of their own. Her murder was a tragedy. Abby Williams left behind a father and a mother, a husband, friends and most of all her baby son, Olav."

He nearly whispered the words "baby son Olav" to the jury and stayed silent for a few seconds to let the thought of a small motherless child sink in.

Morgan recounted the scene of the crime and the events leading up to it in detail, placing emphasis on the long relationship between Mose and Abby. He referred the jury to the testimony of various witnesses including the pathologist and that of Eleanor Rowe and Trish Paul.

"Ladies and gentlemen, two things to consider in a murder such as this, although not proof itself, but combined with other elements of evidence that you have heard, is whether the accused Mr. Strickland had motive and did he have opportunity? The Crown suggests the opportunity is clear. Mr. Strickland admits to being on the scene within the time period of the murder. As to motive, the Crown submits that he was still in love with Abby and acted in a state of extreme jealousy and took her life."

Morgan went on to talk about Mose's upbringing and how his Native American father had abandoned him and his mother and that, as often happens in fractured family relationships, Mose was not always on the straight and narrow. Without directly saying that Mose was a half-breed and likely a drug dealer, he managed to make those hints clear.

"Now today, ladies and gentlemen, we are here to determine the truth. To try and bring some measure of justice to the family of the deceased.

"So what is the truth about why Abby is no longer with us? It has been my job as prosecutor to present you with the evidence that will lead to the conviction of the accused, Mr. Mose Strickland. It has been my job to show that Mr. Strickland acted out of jealousy because Abby had denied Mose his child in 1988 and that she had later chosen another man over him.

"You heard evidence describing Mr. Strickland as having an explosive temper, and by Mr. Strickland's own admission he was in Abby's house at the site of the killing during the time period which Dr. Nolstrom, an expert witness, said that her death occurred."

The jurors were clearly engaged and seemed to be hanging on every word Morgan was saying.

"Now much has been made by defence counsel, that there was no eyewitness to the murder. And that is true. Except for Abby's small baby, and we can only hope that there are no long lasting, traumatic effects left on baby Olav from having been present during his mom's violent death. Defence counsel will have you believe that by some outrageous coincidence some other person showed up at Abby's house just after Mose left the scene and did the killing. While that may be possible, it is not probable.

"Think about it this way. The body of a fire victim is so badly damaged that it can only be identified by dental records. What are the chances that the victim is not who everyone thought it was because there was another person in that fire who had the very same dental work? The possibility is too minute to even imagine. I suggest that the kind of coincidence that the defence will attempt to make you accept is just too absurd to be considered.

"The Crown submits to you, ladies and gentlemen, that when you piece together all the facts, they can only lead you to one outcome. And that outcome has to be that Mose Strickland intended to kill Abby. That's why he drove her to her home and in a jealous rage he executed his deadly plan even while baby Olav was looking on."

Morgan, shaking his head as though in disbelief, looked toward Mose who was sitting bent over with his face in his hands.

"Ladies and gentlemen of the jury, you have to find Mose Strickland guilty of first degree murder in the death of Abby Williams. Thank you for your service."

Morgan nodded at the judge. "And thank you, my Lord."

He went back to his table and sat down rustling a few papers.

"Thank you counsellor. The court will recess for fifteen minutes and come back with opposing counsel's final argument."

* * *

Susan was no stranger to a courtroom. She had spent most of her twelve-year career practicing criminal defence with legal aid. She was quite comfortable on her feet and had become accustomed to the legal nuances and curve balls that people like prosecutor Morgan tended to throw around. This was her fifth murder trial, though her first time acting as lead counsel.

Susan paced in front of the jury for a moment appearing to compose her thoughts.

She began by talking about Mose and how he was such a hard worker in the community. He had a steady job, recently entered a new relationship, and was just finishing up building a house. She said that, yes, he may have a temper and may have gotten into the odd scrimmage, but that does not make him a killer. Mose Strickland, she said, had too much respect for Abby to commit such an act against her.

"Ladies and gentlemen, what we have seen here is an unusual case. Unusual because you have nothing to consider that clearly and without doubt points to the person who took Abby's life. The Crown has not presented evidence such that you the jury can decide beyond a reasonable doubt that our client Mose Strickland did the killing.

"The Crown has tried to gather as much evidence, albeit circumstantial, to build its case against Mose. Statements about his Native American ancestry and his explosive temper are statements that, we submit, are intended to inflame you and unfortunately stereotype my client through a particularly racist lens. These statements unfortunately border on hate propaganda."

"Counsellor, I caution you against such speculation and accusation," Estridge said, glaring down at Susan.

If only the judge would have cautioned Dr. Nolstrom on all his speculation!

"My Lord, I will ask the court reporter to strike my last two statements from the record."

"Thank you counsellor."

"Ladies and gentlemen," Susan said, "the facts are that no one saw Mose Strickland inflict any harm on Abigail Williams. In fact, the Crown and the police are responsible for conducting ineffective and incomplete investigations. The murder weapon was not located, yet the police coached Dr. Nolstrom to speculate on a potential murder weapon—that being a length of electrical wire—while advancing the notion that because Mose was building a house he would have somehow had easy access to a weapon. The defence submits to you ladies and gentlemen that this is pure conjecture and was meant to stack the deck against my client, Mr. Strickland."

Susan continued pacing in front of the jury.

"Where is the DNA evidence?" Susan continued. "People, especially Mayor Rowe, wanted Mose targeted and that set off a witch hunt against our client, which has brought him to this point, where he is now fighting for his very freedom.

"Now let us consider Eleanor Rowe's testimony. What was her motive or interest in contacting the police? Why did the Crown add her as a witness? Was it because she is mayor and the Crown felt that her position could help influence the outcome of this case? What other questions are underlying here that remain unanswered? Was Eleanor Rowe being truthful on the stand? She was not forthcoming about her relationship with Travis Williams, Abby's husband, and what does their affair represent? I leave that for you to think about.

"The reality is, ladies and gentlemen, no person other than baby Olav saw what happened that evening in February, 1996. And at just over two years old it is obvious that he cannot testify.

"Members of the jury, without such direct evidence before you—that is, evidence from an eyewitness or evidence of an admission of guilt, neither of which you have—you have to find Mr. Strickland not guilty in the murder of Abigail Williams.

"Thank you ladies and gentlemen and thank you my Lord."

Susan bowed to the bench and sat down.

Although she had to censor some of her comments, Susan still managed to get statements in that would sit deep within the consciousness of the jurors.

* * *

Judge Estridge, in his charge to the jury, reminded them that he was the judge of the law and they were the judge of the facts from the evidence that they had heard during the trial.

He talked about the right of the accused to be presumed innocent until proven guilty and that the duty to prove guilt rested with the Crown. He explained the standard of proof to be met for a guilty verdict—that the jurors must be satisfied beyond a reasonable doubt if they are to find the accused guilty. The accused has nothing to prove, the judge said.

The judge explained that there are two things to consider in order to return a guilty verdict in the case of first degree murder. First that the accused had to have intended to kill the victim—that is he planned her murder—and secondly, that he carried out that plan. To find a verdict of guilty of second-degree murder, intent and planning is less of a factor, but the perpetrator still commits the act perhaps as in a rage situation. To find manslaughter, intent is not a factor at all. Manslaughter can even be accidental, the judge explained. "If you are not satisfied that the conditions have been met to bring in a finding of either first degree murder, second degree murder or manslaughter, then your verdict must be acquittal," Judge Estridge explained.

The judge also reminded the jury to disregard certain statements that came forward, as in the case of witness Trish Paul.

After his statements to the jury he asked them to retire to consider the evidence and return with their verdict once they had decided.

CHAPTER 26:

Verdict

FRIDAY, OCTOBER 17, 1997, GOOSE BAY, LABRADOR

The leaves had fallen now, and people were getting ready for another avalanche of a Labrador winter. It was that time of year when health authorities note a distinct uptick in cases of depression and pharmacies would routinely see increased sales of anti-anxiety medications.

Mose was in a state of depression, but not because it was fall.

Dawn broke overcast and cold on the day the verdict came down. Mose hadn't eaten over the past twenty-four hours. It was impossible for him to rid himself of that feeling of helplessness.

The call came to Susan at twelve-thirty p.m. The jury had reached a verdict and the court was being called back together at one-thirty.

Mose sat with sweaty palms and seemed to be having some difficulty breathing as he watched the jurors file in. He looked toward his mother who was sitting staring straight ahead. Jackie had given up hope that this trial was going to produce a result in her son's favour.

Crown prosecutor Morgan wanted a conviction. The more criminals he could put away, the quicker he could be considered for the bench. He sat there whispering to his law clerk who was nodding and whispering back.

"All rise."

The judge resumed his position on the bench and the jurors began filing back in.

"Have you reached a verdict?" Estridge asked the foreman once they were all seated.

"Yes, we have."

"Please read the verdict on the charge of first-degree murder."

"We find the accused guilty."

For a few moments, Mose felt like he was inside of a big bubble, disoriented, with all the sounds in the courtroom being muffled and running together. He became nauseous but managed to avoid throwing up. The thundercloud had now stuck with all the ferociousness of a bolt of lightening. Mose and his mother could do nothing now but let the shock of those words penetrate their bodies and souls. Even though they expected that verdict, they were not prepared for it when it was spoken aloud. It felt as though the earth had opened up beneath them and they were falling headfirst into hell's fire. The crack of the gavel adjourning the court sounded like the final nail in the coffin.

He looked toward his mother. She was in her seat and sobbing.

Mose was going to a federal pen for a very long time.

PART 2

––––

"The truth will set you free, but first
it will make you miserable."

- James A. Garfield

CHAPTER 27:

Memorial University Campus

St. John's, Newfoundland, Fall 2013

Dr. Lau's office was on the second floor of the student union building. I had to walk down a long hallway before I came to a door that said Dr. L. Lau and Dr. J. Bailey, Counsellors.

I went into the reception area where the person at the desk, whose name was Vicki, gave me a sheet of various health questions and vital statistic type stuff. I returned the paper to her and went and sat down to wait my turn to see the shrink. I had never been to one so I didn't know what to expect.

The reception area had three chairs and a love seat. I always wondered why they were called love seats. They were a little short for lovemaking but I suppose one could be creative!

I sat in a chair and observed the paintings on the walls. Most were of nautical themes—tall ships, schooners, fishermen in trap boats hauling aboard a net full of cod—that sort of thing. Somehow the paintings gave me a sense of peace as I scanned each of them thinking about the lifestyles in Newfoundland fishing communities, ages past.

I wondered how the conversation would open with the doctor.

I was fresh off another round of nightmares that once again left me in a state of terror and wishing for daylight.

The nightmare happened just a couple of nights earlier. The dead man was sitting up on the roof of a house. Same somber look on his face. Dressed again in similar clothes to what he was wearing the last time I saw him. The next thing I know he is standing close to me. He reaches out his hand as his mouth starts to come open. His eyes are very dead. Empty of light. I have chills running down the back of my neck and I want to cry out for my mother. A moment later I am standing inside the house where I am looking into an open, empty coffin. Several people are sitting there and do not seem to find it strange that a dead man is up walking in their midst. The dead man takes a seat with the people and a voice somewhere in my head is saying to him "give up—be dead—you cannot be half dead!"

He remains sitting and staring at me. Then a baby cries. Far away at first, but the sound gets louder. Closer. I turn around and a baby wearing only a diaper is sitting on a chair next to the coffin. Somehow I know the baby is a girl but she is speaking to me in an adult male voice. I hear the words clearly but cannot understand what she is saying.

"Mr. Williams?"

The voice made me jump, bringing me back to reality.

It was Doctor Lau. "Please come in."

"Yes, thank you," I said.

Dr. Lau pointed me to a chesterfield.

She was straight-faced and did not appear to be all that friendly. She was short and studious looking. Very fit. She had the wall behind her desk plastered with diplomas and there were bookshelves and different ornaments scattered around the office. I noted some native art that included a dreamcatcher and some Inuit soapstone carvings.

She sat in a chair across from me with a coffee table of sorts between us. She offered me a small bottle of water.

"So Olav—may I call you Olav?"

"Yes, of course."

"What brings you to me?"

"Not sure why I am here myself, actually," I said.

"Well, tell me how the thought first occurred to you that perhaps you should see someone like me."

"My girlfriend. Sophie. I was telling her some of my history. She made the suggestion that I should see you, Dr. Lau."

"Why don't you tell me about the conversation that led to her making that suggestion to you?"

"First, I want to understand some ground rules. Is stuff I say here held in confidence?" I asked.

"Yes, our conversations are confidential," Dr. Lau explained. "The only exception is if you tell me something and I conclude from what you tell me that you may be at risk to harm yourself or you may be a threat to another person, then I am bound by law to notify the police. Anything else is strictly confidential and I cannot disclose anything without your specific written permission. I want you to understand that this is a safe place for you."

"Okay, thank you. I understand all that."

"Great, now let's go back to that conversation between you and your girlfriend."

CHAPTER 28:
Meeting Mandy

ST. JOHN'S, JULY, 2014

I flew into a foggy St. John's from Twin Rivers on a connecting flight through Deer Lake, feeling anxious, excited, and a little nervous. I was about to meet my half sister and spend the weekend getting to know her.

I called Sophie on her cell shortly after I landed. She was working a summer job at a pharmacy and said she would meet me after work. I decided to stay in a not-so-expensive hotel on Elizabeth Avenue. I didn't have a lot of money, but my minimum wage job in Twin Rivers, moving about merchandise in a warehouse, allowed me to save up some cash that I could use for the trip.

Mandy was scheduled to arrive in St. John's the following day, which was a Saturday. I didn't have a car, so I planned to borrow Sophie's Kia to go to the airport to meet her. Sophie felt I should meet Mandy alone at first, so as not to overwhelm her. One step at a time, she suggested. I thought that was smart of her.

Mandy and I had emailed each other several times since we met by phone. We exchanged photographs during that time so there would be no trouble recognizing each other when she came into the terminal with all the other passengers.

I must say though I was not prepared for what I saw when we did meet in person. Mandy's likeness to our mom was uncanny.

I cannot describe how I felt when the thought struck home that this person who looked so much like my mother was now in my life. It was as though a terrible weight had been lifted and now it was almost like my mother was standing here in front of me in another form. Providence really does work in some mysterious ways that us mere mortals cannot even begin to explain.

I could not hide my joy as I walked up to Mandy holding out my arms. She was gracious and beautiful. She put down her carry-on and we embraced in a full-on bear hug. We said very few words in the first few moments and as we released each other from our intro-hug, I noticed a few tears had trickled down her cheeks. She said she was anxious to talk and to find out as much as she could about the biological side of her family. Her Atlantic Canadian heritage.

* * *

We had to tell Mandy about Abby's death. She was aware of some of the details of how she died and how Mose, her biological father, was now in jail in New Brunswick serving a life sentence for her murder.

We also had to tell her about Abby's parents, the bishop and Rhoda, Mandy's grandparents, and mine, who were living in St. John's. There would be time for that, but first I wanted her to meet Sophie so the three of us could start getting to know each other.

I called Sophie and told her I was on my way to pick her up and we would find a deck downtown to have lunch. The fog had cleared away and the summer sun was out with a strong breeze blowing from the south. The wind churned up the waters outside the entrance to the harbour with whitecaps looking like scattered clouds in a deep blue sky. It was spectacular. I couldn't ask for a better day.

All three of us talked about where our academic careers were taking us. She said she was the only child in the Reynolds family. I told her about life in Twin Rivers and she was very interested in Newfoundland culture. The next time she visited she said she would like to go to Twin Rivers and Dark Harbour to see where her mother grew up and to visit her grave.

Mandy got quite upset at different points as she listened to us tell the story of how Abby died and the guilty verdict that had come down on Mose. She wanted to know every detail even though she had read the court transcripts of the trial and newspaper reports.

"Have you accepted that Mose committed the murder?" she asked. The question took me aback some because up to then, while I had not out and out questioned the legitimacy of the verdict, deep down I did have concerns about it.

"I am not sure what to believe. My understanding is that the prosecution had no direct evidence from anyone who had witnessed the murder."

"My guess is that it should have been relatively easy to establish reasonable doubt," she speculated. "Perhaps there was a miscarriage of justice and an innocent person is paying for the crime."

"Raising doubt was what his legal team was trying to establish, but obviously the jury didn't buy it."

Sophie explained to Mandy, that even though the Crown said there was no eyewitness to the murder, "in fact Olav was at the scene when his mother was killed but being just a baby he could not give evidence."

I was a little embarrassed to bring up stuff like my photographic memory and recurring nightmares so Sophie did. "Is it possible that the events could still be with Olav, filed away in his sub-conscious?" Sophie asked in a rhetorical kind of way.

"I don't know, but it is a question that a specialist in that area should explore," Mandy suggested. "It is not unusual for verdicts to get overturned in cases where evidence comes forward that was not available at the time of trial. This may be such a case."

She offered to get in touch with the Society for the Rights of the Wrongfully Convicted in Toronto to give them a heads up that we may be seeking their support.

Where Mandy was doing her articles in Toronto she was well placed to make some contacts there. It could not hurt to have such an organization take up the case.

I was not a hundred per cent certain about whether we should go that route. I knew there would be a lot of hills to climb, including legal stuff, science, DNA, and submissions to a judge. But mostly what concerned me was how it might affect my relations with family and others in Twin Rivers. I would have to weigh these issues. I asked Mandy and Sophie for a bit more time to think it through.

In the meantime, Mandy expressed interest in meeting her grandparents, Absolom and Rhoda. I told Mandy about the bishop's disposition and that meeting them might be quite a challenge. I offered to call them to see what we could arrange.

We spent the weekend debating the question and the possibility of getting Mose's case re-opened. I became convinced that we should proceed with our efforts. It was going to take a lot of work and some risk on our part, but I was all in.

CHAPTER 29:

Breaking the Mold

I thought I would wait until Monday to call the bishop's residence. In his line of work, I figured they would be pretty busy on Sunday.

"Hello." A female voice came on the line.

"Hello, this is Olav Williams calling. May I speak with Rhoda please?"

"This is Rhoda, and you are my grandson."

Good start!

I tried to make some introductory talk telling her about my being a student at Memorial University and my plan to go to law school. That seemed to impress her. She sounded like she became a bit withdrawn though when I mentioned that I had tracked down Abby's daughter, my sister Mandy, in Thunder Bay.

"In fact Mandy is here visiting in St. John's right now for a few more days and she would like to meet you," I told Rhoda.

"I would love to meet her and you as well," Rhoda said. "Absalom is at the cathedral right now, so I will talk to him when he gets back for lunch. May I call you back?"

I gave her my phone number and waited for her to call me back.

* * *

Even though Rhoda was on cloud nine and excited to tell Absolom the news, she could feel some dark strains of disappointment below it all as she anticipated the reaction she was likely to get from him.

"I have some news," she said when they both got settled at the table.

"Oh? I'm listening."

"Our grandchildren," Rhoda said. "They are both here in St. John's."

"Both?"

"Yes, Olav tracked down his sister," Rhoda explained.

"How is that possible? Abby's baby was put up for adoption and the files were supposed to have been closed. Someone up there on the mainland has broken the law," the bishop snarled.

"No, there was no law broken," Rhoda said. "Olav started a legal action to get the file opened."

The bishop was becoming more distraught by the minute.

"I will get to the bottom of this!" He slapped his hand on the table, startling Rhoda.

"We are at the bottom of it for heaven's sake! Can't you see? Rock bottom, and we have been there ever since you forced Abby to let her baby go for adoption! She did that against her will, and you ought to be so ashamed of yourself! She might even be alive today had she been allowed to keep the baby."

The bishop's eyes widened into an uncomfortable stare.

"Rhoda, you know why the baby was put up for adoption and you did not oppose the idea at the time."

"How could anyone argue with you? It was your way or no way! In any case they want to meet us. Their grandparents," Rhoda said, her eyes filling with tears.

"I am not meeting them and neither are you!" Absolom roared.

"I am meeting them whether you like it or not!" Rhoda screamed at the bishop. "As of this moment, I am no longer letting

162

you deny me my right to see my two grandchildren. I am getting old and I am not leaving this earth without spending time with them and getting to know these children who are our flesh and blood. So get out of my way!"

Absolom's mouth was hanging open as he struggled for words.

"Think about the church, Rhoda. The church that has been so good to you all your life."

Rhoda had promised herself years earlier that there would come a time when she would give him a piece of her mind. That time had come.

"I don't give a damn about the church! It's your church! What are you worried about? That because Abby had a baby out of wedlock is somehow a scandal? Get with the times for God's sake! I am sorry Absalom, but I cannot sit here and take this any longer. I cannot live under this oppression and be subservient to you— not when Abby's two children are here and wanting to meet us. I have to tell you Absalom, I have made up my mind. I am leaving you and I want a divorce. The sooner the better!"

The bishop sat there, not believing what he just witnessed. He crossed himself, mumbled something, kissed the metal cross he had strung around his neck, and crossed himself again.

Rhoda just glared at the man sitting there in the purple robe and a white collar. If looks could kill, the bishop would be dead and buried. She jumped to her feet, pushing her chair back so hard from the table that it toppled over backwards. She left the dining room and went upstairs.

Rhoda looked at herself in her dresser mirror and smiled even though she felt a little disoriented from the severity of the confrontation. Never before had she had such a feeling of freedom, and it was sweet! Abby would be proud of her. Of that she was certain. If only Abby were here to share it. Even so, she could feel her daughter's presence.

She would let herself be guided by Abby's spirit. She could hear her darling daughter whisper, "You are Rhoda, you are a strong and free woman. You are in charge of your life."

Damn the bishop! That would be her mantra from here on in.

Rhoda put on her coat and stormed out of the house. The only person she knew to call on at that moment was her younger sister, Francine, who was living in St. John's west end. She would cool down there for a couple of hours and then give Olav a call.

She was dead serious about the divorce and loved the idea of it.

CHAPTER 30:

Pieces of a puzzle

I was now into my third session with Dr. Lau. It seemed to me that so far we were just exploring the territory. Getting to know each other sort of thing. She started out having me talk about my growing up in Twin Rivers, the loss of my mother, and my experiences of abuse that I suffered from my father.

I told her about those recurring nightmares and how long I had been having them. If they meant something, I needed to understand what that was. It was torture having to live through them, to the point where many nights I would be afraid to fall asleep.

"Do you recall when they started?"

"I was really young, about four, maybe five."

"Were they the same dream back then as now?"

"Similar, always a dead person who keeps moving around and a small child or sometimes children are most often there."

"And they have never ceased?"

"No, I would say I have one every couple of months."

"Describe one to me."

I told her the details of my most recent nightmare—the one with the baby girl talking in an adult male voice. I kept getting chills as I recounted the story for Dr. Lau.

"It seems to me they have to mean something. Like someone or some thing is trying to tell me something," I said.

"Who do you think the people are in your dream?"

"I think the dead man is a relative. Maybe an uncle who was lost at sea. In some dreams he is soaking wet. But I never knew him so I am not sure."

"Have you ever seen a dead person?" Dr. Lau asked.

"Yes."

"Were you afraid to see dead people when you were younger?"

"Yes."

"Do you recall if anyone ever read scary stories to you when you were small?"

"No one read me stories after my mother died. My father didn't pay enough attention to me for that sort of thing."

"What about television or movies. Do you remember any particular thing you might have seen back then that really scared you?"

"No. That stuff never really scared me because I knew it was all fake."

"In your dreams, have you ever speculated as to who the baby might be?"

"Yes, I have tried to figure out who the baby is but I am never certain."

"And who have you been thinking it might be?"

"Sometimes I think the baby might also be a relative. Specifically who? Don't know."

Dr. Lau shifted in her chair and put down her pen.

"To have a recurring dream is not unusual Olav. Many people have them. I've had them. What is puzzling, though, is that you have had the same or similar dream over such a long period of time."

"Do I need some kind of exorcist?" I asked, almost rhetorically.

"No, you are not possessed and you do not need an exorcist or a shaman or anything like that. We just need to keep talking and exploring. Like putting together the pieces of a puzzle."

Just as we were concluding the session I thought I would tell her about my memory.

"Let's get into that a bit more on your next visit," Dr. Lau suggested.

* * *

Two weeks later I was back in her office again. After some small talk and questions about my sleeping, she got to the point of the session.

"Now you mentioned your memory at our last session and you wanted to talk about that."

"Yes, I believe it is photographic. I retain everything I see or hear. Do you have expertise in that area?"

"I have done some studies into the functions of the brain and recall ability."

I glanced up at the certificates on her wall, squinting my eyes to see if anything there was relevant.

"Let us take a quick test. It is not that I am doubting what you are telling me, it's just that I want to position ourselves to see what we are working with."

She went outside and picked up several books.

Coming back, she pointed to two or three asking if I had read them. I hadn't.

Then she came to a biography called, *Jack: A Life Like No Other*.

"Have you read this one?"

"Yes, I have," I said. "I think I told you early on that I always had a fascination with the history of the Kennedys in the United States and their impact on the world. So I have read as much about them as I could. Everything I could get my hands on. That is a biography of President John F. Kennedy by Geoffrey Perret."

"Impressive," Dr. Lau said. "Recite for me the last line in the biography."

I closed my eyes for a couple of seconds and called up the page.

"Okay. It is on page four hundred and it reads '*Oswald fires again. He is doing this for Cuba. The bullet flies*'."

"Olav, that is amazing. Tell me the author of *Uncle Tom's Cabin*."

"Harriet Beecher Stowe," I said. *Easy.*

"*The Catcher in the Rye.*"

"J.D. Salinger."

"*To Kill a Mockingbird.*"

"Harper Lee. All easy"

"Okay let's try something a little more obscure. Have you read *Cold War: Warnings for a Unipolar World* by Fidel Castro?"

"No, I haven't."

She gave me the book, told me to read it, and when I returned for the next session she would give me another short quiz.

* * *

Two weeks later I found myself climbing the stairs to the second floor at the Student Union Building once again.

"So did you read the Fidel Castro book?" Dr. Lau asked.

"Yes, I did," I said, handing the book back to her. "The book is in conversational format. A CNN journalist is interviewing Fidel Castro."

"Ok then. Recite the first full paragraph on page twenty-nine."

I took a moment.

"It reads, quote—*I was afraid that the [Soviets] would make a mistake. As I am telling you, I could see the situation was difficult, there was no way out for Kennedy in that predicament, and so it seemed that war would break out at any time. It looked imminent, or at least an attack looked imminent.* Unquote."

"The subject here is the Cuban Missile Crisis of October, 1962," I added.

I was watching for reaction from Dr. Lau, but there was none. She just sat there. Stoic. I could see the wheels turning in her head.

"Wow," Dr. Lau said. "It seems clear to me that you are quite gifted Olav. Remember I said our work here is like the pieces of a puzzle? Let's see what we can connect between that memory of yours and those night terrors. We have work to do."

I left her office wondering what would come next.

Dr. Lau decided to consult with Dr. Benjamin Schumer, a psychologist at the university who had collaborated with her to co-author a study titled *Eidetic Memory: A Deep Dive into the Science of the Mind.* The report was published in 2010 and had been widely reviewed and quoted in Canada and the United States, including citations in the *New England Journal of Medicine.*

CHAPTER 31:

Rhoda's Surprises

Rhoda called me the morning after her conversation with Absolom. She said she wanted to meet Mandy and I. She asked if we would be available the following day for lunch downtown. We both assured her that we were available, and she suggested we meet at the Hotel Newfoundland. She said she would be waiting to meet us in the rock garden there.

The next day at noon Mandy and I drove up to the parking lot at the hotel and made our way through the lobby and down a flight of stairs to the rock garden.

We gave each other a wondering glance as we walked toward the table where Rhoda was sitting—alone.

Rhoda appeared to be of average height and weight and dressed in a pale blue pantsuit something like those that Hilary Clinton wears. She had wire-rimmed glasses and her grey hair was held back with combs on either side of her head. She struck me as being very Anglo-Saxon and I would have expected a British accent had I not spoken to her earlier on the phone. Her appearance came across as distinguished, grandmotherly.

I felt good about meeting her, but we were puzzled that the bishop was not with her. Neither of us wanted to ask where he was. Perhaps he was in the bathroom or maybe he planned on joining us a little later.

Rhoda seemed a bit shy to be meeting us, especially when it came to Mandy. We took turns hugging in a kind of tentative way, but she had a glorious smile on her face.

I could see that she was struck by Mandy's resemblance to Abby.

She started by telling us of her origins and her ancestry. She was a descendant of one of the Water Street merchant families, the Kavanaghs, who had made their fortunes from the cod fishery along the Labrador coast. The salt cod industry, built around trade with the West Indies, had made a lot of St. John's business elite very rich.

Historically, the merchants' relationships with fishermen and their families, were a lot like having a person attached to your company in an indentured sort of way. So while fishermen were technically independent, they were more often than not beholden to the merchant year after year. The merchant enabled that dependent scheme by allowing the fishermen to receive credit for their supplies, thereby giving the fisherman little choice but to sell his product to that merchant.

Those days are long gone now.

But it was one of those families from which Rhoda, Abby, and now Mandy and I were all descendants.

Guessing that we were wondering where Absolom was, she told us about her confrontation with him following my call. She said it was a terrible argument and unfortunately she had to tell us that she'd left him and would be filing for divorce.

Our jaws dropped!

"Don't be surprised," she said. "That man has been controlling my life for fifty years and I decided that I'd had enough. The realization that Mandy was now in our lives is what drove me over the top."

"He forced Abby to do what she did with you, Mandy," she continued, "and I have had to live with that consequence and guilt all these years, craving a relationship with both of you. It broke Abby's heart to have to part with you. I should have been stronger back then. I should have prevented it from happening. You have no idea of the elation I felt when you called me, Olav."

I could see the pain on her face as she was telling us this. All three of us fought back tears.

We told her that she must have incredible strength to do what she was doing. A divorce at that level of the church is almost unheard of, and for her to go against that kind of tide was a remarkable testament to her resolve.

She told us how proud she was of both of us, and how we would have loved our mother had she lived.

Before our meeting was over she told us some other distressing news. Not long before, she had been diagnosed with cancer and would be starting treatments in a couple of weeks. She was hopeful these would work, but it was very hard to predict how her body might respond.

"But I have faith," she said and smiled.

As we got up to leave, she kissed and hugged us both and told us how much she loved the two of us and that she wanted a chance to make things right.

CHAPTER 32:

Papa

I awoke in Hebron, not certain how I got there. Hebron is an abandoned Inuit community in northern Labrador. I am among the ghosts of Moravian Missionaries. The spirits of Inuit, who lost their lives in the Spanish Flu still roam these hills.

Hebron was one of several Inuit communities that were coerced by the Newfoundland government in the 1950s into relocation to communities farther south. The places left behind became ghost towns.

Today's Inuit come back here every year to honour their ancestors.

What am I doing here?

The only way to get to Hebron other than by snowmobile in winter is by seagoing vessel. I look out toward the harbour. There are no seagoing vessels in sight.

I am alone with the ghosts.

There is a huge building in Hebron that the missionaries built in the eighteenth century to support their work in Christianizing their flock. The building still stands.

I find myself peering into the building through what once was a window.

An Inuk man is staring back at me.

Funny, in this place of ghosts, that doesn't startle me.

He has long hair and a goatee kind of beard. The man's face is gaunt and he appears to be very old. It looks like he has been starved of food and water. Within seconds he collapses in front of me gasping and groaning. Then all is still.

I walk around to the other side of the building and go inside to where I saw the man. His body is no longer where it fell. I look up and he is now hanging from the rafters. The grin on his face sends chills down my back. His dead eyes are open and fixated in a stare in my direction.

Down a long hallway I hear children. It sounds like they are playing games. I walk toward the sound but it seems to elude me for a moment. Turning a corner I see children playing with dolls. Their faces are pale and not smiling. One is crying.

I move past them and come to a place where an old man is dancing around a fire. Chanting.

Strange, the fire is not burning the building down.

I move closer and I see several more people who appear to be Inuit sitting around the fire and respecting the man doing the dancing and chanting. They seem to worship the spear that he has in his hands. It is burning on one end and he touches each person on the forehead with it, but it leaves no mark.

Then all eyes are suddenly on me. Unfriendly eyes. As I try to run to get out of the building, I am stopped in my tracks by a caribou. The animal looks like it is starved and dehydrated. Its ribs are showing through. Next to the caribou is a walrus with one tusk. Both animals are frothing at the mouth and shaking. Then they kind of melt into the ground.

I glance behind where I came from and the chanter is following me. I can smell a strange unearthly smell. He looks at me and says something I cannot understand. He is clutching the spear. His eyes blood red. Then he opens his mouth which just keeps getting bigger and bigger. Blood is spurting from his pores and his mouth. I fall back against a wall and slide to the ground. He approaches me with his spear aimed directly at my throat. He pulls it back and raises it to the strike position. A voice, one that almost hisses, comes at me from somewhere "Uppisâgiven?"

Like a miracle it translates in my head—"are you telling your truth?"

Screaming something unintelligible and breathing heavily, I awaken in the darkness once again bathed in sweat.

Why the hell does this happen to me?

It was my phone that buzzed at four-twenty a.m. waking me up. Sophie is on the other end of the line, crying. My skin crawls as she tells me, between sobs, that Papa Bear is dead. Someone found him a half-hour earlier in the living room. He was unresponsive.

CHAPTER 34:
Shaking an Establishment

Rhoda's lawyer told her that she would need to live apart from the bishop for a year before she could file for divorce. She asked whether the divorce could come earlier if she could claim that she was subject to mental abuse. The lawyer suggested that her case might be weakened on that ground due to the length of time they were together and her not acting on it sooner. Her grandchild being adopted out went back over twenty years without her taking any action.

Neither did Rhoda have any grounds with respect to infidelity on Absolom's part, at least none that she knew about, so that ground was not available to her either.

"What about my inheritances?" Rhoda asked.

"They are protected in your favour," the lawyer explained. "But that does not mean Absolom won't try and countersue."

As to the timing of the divorce, Rhoda's only option was to wait it out.

She did that—the months dragging by.

Over that time she had begun her treatments in chemotherapy and radiation and so far she was responding well to those. The tumor appeared to be shrinking. That improved her spirits and it made her feel she had bright things in her future.

When Rhoda did file for divorce, the court, God bless the judge, upheld the law that she could keep all her inheritances, despite the bishop's attempt to counter sue for half of her assets.

The court threw out Absolom's claim, but not before he aired some dirty laundry. He got on the stand disputing Rhoda's claim that she had suffered mental abuse. He said her statement of claim was all lies and that both he and the church had always respected her.

Once on the stand however, he opened himself up for cross-examination.

Rhoda's lawyer dissected him about his controlling nature and his efforts to keep Rhoda subservient to him. The lawyer accused him of forcing Abby to give her child away, which had a demoralizing, long-term effect on Rhoda's mental health.

The bishop, facing death by a thousand cuts, could not do much more than sputter incoherently on the stand. I read all the media coverage of the divorce and it sounded like he was delivered a serious ass-kicking that day.

Rhoda was happy with the outcome and after the expiration of the thirty-day appeal period, the court issued her divorce decree. It was final.

She never felt better. The world around her would be of her own making now, and she loved every minute of it. She was finally able to tell the bishop, in Archie Bunker's words, to kiss her "where the sun don't shine."

The media in St. John's was all over the story. "Bishop Dragged into Divorce Scandal" one of the headlines read. In an editorial one writer, perhaps an anti-Christian, commented, "This is just desserts. The bishop's attempt to claim half his wife's assets failed spectacularly. It puzzles me as to why he would even make that claim. Does he have no faith in the very gospel he preaches? I wonder what Matthew's Gospel means to this man? In 6:24, Matthew writes '*No man can serve two masters—Ye cannot serve*

God and mammon.' Or did he ask himself what Jesus would do in this case? The bishop struck back hard and didn't exactly turn the other cheek as Jesus did. We should all be happy today for the very brave Mrs. Peters."

.

CHAPTER 35:
A Cat in a Hat

When I arrived at Dr. Lau's office for my next session, she introduced me to a Dr. Schumer. He was probably in his mid-forties and wearing a tweed sports jacket, open collar, and blue jeans. His hair was quite long and unkempt. John Lennon glasses. Dr. Schumer would have made a really good advertisement for the typical image of a shrink, if there be such a thing.

Dr. Schumer and I shook hands. I sat in my usual place and he sat near Dr. Lau.

She said the two of them had collaborated on a joint study related to memory, which was recently published. Dr. Lau said she was wondering if it would be okay if he sat in on our session today.

"Perhaps I should have called you first about that," she said. "I'm sorry."

I gave her a puzzled look.

"Do the same rules of confidentiality apply?" I asked.

"Yes, they do," she said.

Dr. Schumer spoke up. "Let me assure you, Olav, that the same rules do apply, I promise you that. I want you to feel safe. However, if you do not feel comfortable by my presence, please say so and I will respect that and leave."

I took a few seconds to think before I responded. I was beginning to feel a little like someone was taking advantage of me, or that I was some sort of lab rat.

"Let's see how this session goes with the three of us," I said finally. "If I feel uncomfortable or intimidated in any way, I will ask that we end the session and re-schedule."

"Agreed," Dr. Lau continued.

"We're all good?" she said, glancing around. Everyone nodded.

"Now Olav, please tell us what you think is your very earliest memory," Dr. Lau suggested.

She gave me some time to re-wind the reels. But it did not take me long to get there.

I could see that some of this was going to be painful.

"I can remember my mother looking after me. Standing over my crib. My crib was handmade. My aunt Grace bought it at a flea market and she gave it to my mom just before I was born."

"How old do you think you were around that time?"

"Less than a year."

"What other kinds of things do you remember about that time?"

"I remember her rocking me, feeding me, looking in my face and smiling at me. I remember her singing to me, reading little stories, giving me soft toys to play with."

"What books do you remember?"

"I remember two Dr. Seuss books, *The Cat in the Hat* and *Green Eggs and Ham*. There was a book called *Curious George*, a book called *Hand, Hand, Fingers, Thumb*, and one called *But No Elephants*. Right after my mother died, my father renovated the house. While he was doing that he put all my books in a trunk with a lock on it, and put the trunk in the attic. I guess he didn't want reminders or something. I haven't seen the books since."

"How old were you when your mom died?"

"I was a year and a half."

"Do you recall anything that might indicate what your parents' relationship was like?"

"My dad was very often angry with her. Shouting at her a lot. He often mentioned my name during those times."

"Why do you think he would mention your name?"

"I don't know. I think most likely he was blaming me for something."

"Why do you say that?"

"Years after Mom died he often said I used to slow him down—that I was a burden on him. Just a big useless cost to him, he would say. He would say that I should be not seen and not heard. Things like that."

"Did you ever have confrontations with your father?" Dr. Lau asked.

"No, I was afraid of him. He scared me most of the time. I told you earlier that he had seen action in the Gulf War, and his trauma from that came out at times and it always created scary situations."

"Do you remember how you felt around other people as you grew up? People other than your father."

"I felt invisible. I would think that my presence was so insignificant that I meant nothing to anyone and therefore I was invisible. Really I felt that way all through high school and still do to some extent."

"Can you tell us any specific incidents that caused you to feel invisible?"

I thought for a moment.

"I remember meeting a priest several times in Twin Rivers when I was fifteen. He would call me by name in the community when he'd see me around. He would say, 'Hello Olav. I hope you are having a good day' and stuff like that. I thought that was nice. For the first time it seemed like someone was able to see me as a person. But then I saw him in the mall here in St. John's not long ago. I went up to him to say hello and he could not remember me. I felt like shit. It only reinforced that feeling of invisibility."

"Did you re-introduce yourself?"

"No. If the bastard couldn't remember me, too damn bad. I said the hell with him. I didn't want to talk to him at that point so I just walked away."

* * *

"Olav, you haven't talked much about losing your mother," Dr. Lau said. "Can you tell us what you know about that?"

I looked at the clock. We were getting close to the end of the session.

"I think I would rather take some time to prepare myself, mentally, for that. I am not ready to talk about it today," I said.

"Fair enough, let's schedule that for the next session. If you are okay, I would like Dr. Schumer to sit in again."

"Yes, that will be okay," I said after a few moments.

"Also, Olav I am going to give you a copy of the study Dr. Schumer and I did on the mind and memory. I suggest you read it and jot down anything that jumps out at you that you that you might want to raise with us—any words or expressions that you read in the study that might have a familiarity with you. That sort of thing."

I spoke to Vicki on the way out and scheduled another session for the following week.

CHAPTER 36:
Fake?

I shuddered thinking about what the doctors had in store for me at my next appointment. I was feeling as though Dr. Lau and I had developed a good rapport but testing my memory and talking about my mother's death was bringing this to a new level. I was starting to feel uncomfortable.

Even as I write this, five years later, I sweat and tremble.

I was torn about whether I wanted to go through with any exercises they might want to do and I began to seriously consider cutting off my sessions completely with Dr. Lau.

I read the study that she and Dr. Schumer had done. It didn't take me long, but pieces of it were of interest to me. I did note that what they are calling eidetic imagery, another word for photographic memory, mostly occurs in small children and less so in adults.

I was no longer a small child, but I was still seeing certain images that I saw as a small child, so I must have been the exception rather than the rule.

I needed to understand this further, so I decided I had to continue the sessions.

I also noted that the studies indicated the presence of a lot of expertise out there that suggests eidetic imagery does not exist.

How one can fake it, though, is beyond me.

* * *

Sophie and I got together downtown for lunch a couple of days after I read the study. I told here that in the next session the doctors were going to ask me questions about my mother's murder.

"I have flashes of memory where I see the crime taking place," I said. "My guess is that they will try and hypnotize me or something and ask me to recount what I see. It all sounds a bit weird to me."

"What comes back in your flashes of memory?" Sophie asked.

"Mostly sounds. Something breaking. Someone screaming. And then it is gone from me."

"This is going to be traumatic for you I imagine. Are you sure you want to do it?"

"I've thought it through and yes, I should do it," I said. "Would you consider coming to that session with me? I will need the support if I agree to do this."

"I don't want to be a distraction, but yes, of course," Sophie said. "I am here for you."

"I will call Dr. Lau and tell her that you will be with me as support, because I anticipate it will shake me up quite a bit."

"Yes, okay. These are your sessions so I am sure that is quite acceptable," Sophie said.

I called Dr. Lau right there from the table. She was not certain as to whether it was a good idea to have Sophie there.

"Her presence may cause you to stray from your trains of thought. That is what would concern me. I don't think it would be helpful for her to be present," Dr. Lau suggested. "But please understand that I do appreciate your need for emotional supports as we go through this and I don't mean to be dismissive of that."

"Well, they are my sessions. Not being arrogant or anything, but I pay for them. And I think it is not unreasonable to try and view things through my lens," I argued.

"Yes, and I agree with all that, but from a professional standpoint, I have to put your best interests ahead of anything else."

"You don't think helping to find a way to address my need for emotional support is in my best interests?"

"No, I didn't say that," Dr. Lau said. "What I am saying is that we need to create the best possible space for you as we try and get to the root of what has been troubling you for so long, so we can figure out a strategy to help you move forward. And I think at this point the less distraction the better."

"Okay, but if I go crazy in there and start beating out your windows, don't say I didn't warn you!"

"I don't think that will happen. Thanks for calling and see you in a few days."

We hung up and I explained to Sophie what I understood to be the doctor's take on the idea.

Sophie rolled her eyes slightly. "That seems a little reckless to me. But she's the expert." She leaned forward and touched my hand. That always comforted me when she did that.

"We will see how it goes," I said.

CHAPTER 37:

The Journey

I continued my pilgrimage to the second floor of the student union building and to Dr. Lau's office.

I was on tenterhooks. Butterflies galore.

Why was I pursuing this? Do I really feel it is going to result in anything positive?

I got to the waiting room about eight minutes before my appointment. I sat down and just kind of stared at the wall. I thought about calling Sophie and I even considered bolting out the door and back out into the street. But something was telling me not to do that. I could sense a voice in my head.

"Keep your appointment Olav! Tell your story. Dig deeper. You owe it to your people and the world."

It was probably Sophie's voice encouraging me to go on.

Like storms that rage around you, things often have to get worse before they get better. You will get through this and come out in peace on the other side.

Okay, that was poetic. But I am not sure if it was putting me at ease or whether it was causing me more anguish. Rubbing the sweating palms of my hands against my pant legs, I went over to the water cooler and filled a plastic cup.

I just sipped water and waited.

"Olav? Come on in." Dr. Lau was standing in her open door way.

I went in to her office.

Again Dr. Schumer was there and he also greeted me. I noted one additional item in the office—an easel on a tripod, with blank flip chart paper.

I sat in my usual place and raised both my hands in the palms up position.

"Well, what's next," I said.

"Okay, the document we gave you," Dr. Lau began. "Did you get a chance to read that?"

"Every word is right here," I said tapping the side of my head with my right forefinger.

"Do you have any questions, or did you read anything there that you wanted to raise with us?"

"I noted that it is usually in small children where eidetic imagery is most prevalent. Am I an exception?" I asked.

"We will get to that, Olav. We are going to have to do some work before we can say with more certainty that you have that imagery."

I nodded and looked at the flip chart.

"We are going to do a test with you today," she said. "It will involve my blindfolding you."

"Why am I feeling like a guinea pig?"

"Please don't feel that way. If we have any chance of helping you, we need to have a good picture as to how your brain functions."

Dr. Schumer walked over to the flip chart while Dr. Lau blind-folded me.

I could hear Schumer flipping over pages.

"Now we are going to ask that you look at an image," Dr. Schumer said. "Dr. Lau will take off the blindfold. Keep your eyes closed until she tells you to open them. Look at the image for ten seconds only. After ten seconds, close your eyes while we remove the image. Then we are going to ask you to recreate the image on a blank sheet of flip chart paper. You okay with that?"

"Yes."

Dr. Lau removed the blindfold. Okay, now look at the image," she said.

It was a barcode. The kind you see on walls or in magazines that you scan into your phone for information. It was about a foot square. They had me standing about four feet back from the flipchart.

Ten seconds.

"Now close your eyes until I tell you to open them."

I could hear papers rustling.

"Okay. Open your eyes. Now take this marker and re-create what you just looked at," Dr. Schumer instructed.

I took the marker, stood in front of the flipchart, closed my eyes and gave myself a moment.

I first sketched three corners of the square to its exact measurements. Then I began building the maze, setting out every right angle in north, south, east and west directions. I colored the blocks and shapes in black as I went along.

The doctors sat looking at my work, then at each other. The sheet with the original barcode was on a transparent sheet of plastic so that they could place it over my drawing to compare its likeness. After I completed the drawing, they brought back the transparent sheet with the original barcode on it. Dr. Lau placed it over my work positioning it for levelness and precision. She and Dr. Schumer stood next to the flipchart, staring, I think in awe, at what I had done.

It was a match! In every nook and corner, it was precise. They could not tell it from the original. Then she took the original barcode and put it out of my sight and shredded the one that I drew.

Dr. Lau turned to me unfazed. "That is part one of the test," she said. "Part two will happen at our next appointment."

"We will take a short break about five minutes, just to relax your brain a bit. Dr. Schumer and I will leave you alone here for that time."

They left the room and I just sat there. My brain didn't need relaxing! That was an easy exercise. I smiled and began feeling a bit better.

* * *

When they returned, Dr. Lau asked me if I was ready to go through my images and sounds of what I remembered from my mother's killing.

"Yes, I'm ready."

She invited me to sit in a recliner style chair and she asked me to push it into the stretched out position.

Dr. Lau turned all the lights down low and pulled down shades to reflect light from the outside so as to make room was quite dim. Then she lit a candle that burned of some sort of essential oils.

She sat close to the recliner on one side of me and Dr. Schumer on the other. They had notebooks in hand and on the table in front of us, with my permission, Dr. Lau placed a tape recorder.

Everything seemed completely still, quiet.

"This is not full blown hypnosis, Olav, but we are going to guide you into something of a trance."

"Interesting," I said.

"Why do you say that?"

"That was my father's nickname when he came back from the war. Trance. His comrades called him that for his ability to spot objects that could present danger and to focus directly in on them. Maybe I inherited whatever ability that is, if that's possible," I said trying to lighten the mood.

"Well, maybe you have. The trance that you will go in here is very similar to hypnosis but you will be semi-conscious and aware of the things that you are saying to us. In hypnosis, it is deeper—you become unconscious and you are not aware of what you are saying," Dr. Lau explained.

The mood in the room was calming and chilling at the same time.

"Now I am going to give you a few minutes to clear your mind of all clutter, and relax. When you feel you are ready, move your fingers on your right hand. "

After about thirty seconds I moved a couple of my fingers.

"Olav, I am going to count backwards from ten. All you will hear is my voice. By the time I get to one, you will be ready to focus on your vision."

"Ten, nine, eight—"

A few seconds of silence.

"Now, Olav, let your mind travel back to February 26, 1996. What kind of day is it?"

After a few more seconds of silence, I say, "It is very cold."

"Did you go anywhere that day?"

"To the Co-Op store with my mother."

"Do you see your mother?"

"Yes."

"Who else do you see in the store?"

"A man she is calling Mose."

"What else is happening?"

"Checking out groceries. Then we are leaving the store. Mose is with us."

"Keep going."

"We are getting aboard a bus. Mose is driving us home."

"What is the next thing you are seeing or hearing?"

I start to fidget. Sweat starts to run down my brow and my mouth goes dry. I manage to find some saliva and wet my lips. I can feel tears running down my face. I nearly holler out to my mom.

"Stay with us here, Olav. You are doing great." Dr. Lau's voice was gentle. "What are you looking at?"

"Something violent is going on in front of me. A piece of furniture is crashing close to where I am."

"Do you know the person in the house?"

"The person's back is to me. I see the person holding one of those bungee cords."

"What kind of a bungee cord?" Dr. Lau asks.

"The kind with hooks on either end."

"What colour is it?"

"It is red with specks of yellow in it."

By now I am shaking all over and feel like I might throw up. Dr. Lau asks me to tell her more.

"What do you see or hear now?"

"Someone screaming 'fuck'."

"Is it your mother's voice?"

"Can't tell for sure."

"What about now?"

"The person is kind of wrestling with my mother and she is gagging."

I start to moan and sob at this point. I feel I cannot go on.

"Please continue, Olav," Dr. Lau was saying despite my obvious distress.

"My mother cannot get any words out and she is falling—"

I am shivering from head to toe.

"She is falling to the floor. Now she is still. Oh no! Oh God!" I am whimpering, tears streaming. "Someone is laughing like a sinister, crazy laugh."

"Can you tell who the person is who did this to your mother with the bungee cord?"

"Yes—it is not Mose Strickland. Oh my God, he is innocent!!"

"Mose is the person who is in jail for this?"

"Yes. In jail for life."

"How can you tell it is not him?" Dr. Lau asks.

"Because the person is shorter than Mose. I saw Mose at the store just a bit earlier and he brought us home. I know what he was wearing. He left the house after he brought in our groceries only about five minutes earlier. It is not Mose Strickland. Mose did not kill my mother!"

"The person who attacked your mother, can you tell who that is? Was it a man? A woman?"

I continue to sweat and fidget. I bring my hands to my face to cover my eyes, breathing heavily.

"A man. He is looking at me now. Staring."

"Do you recognize the face, Olav?"

I whimper, "Yes."

"Whose face is it?"

"Oh God! God help me!" I am uttering words that seem to just come out automatically.

"Who is it Olav?"

"It's my father," I almost whisper.

"Okay, Olav, we are going to bring you out of your trance now. By the time I count to ten you will be back to the present with us. One, two, three—"

I kept my tear-filled eyes closed for a few moments and just sat there resting back in the recliner, my hands pushing in on my abdomen. Then I pulled the recliner upright and looked around.

"Jesus," I said after doing my best to compose myself. All three of us look at each other. "What now?"

"Well Olav, I am really sorry we had to put you through this," Dr. Lau was saying. "It must have been very hard for you to have to re-live that."

"Yes, it was. I feel sick."

"Do you need the washroom?"

I got up and almost ran to the washroom, just getting there in time before I threw up. Someone in the stall next to me asked if I was okay.

"Yes, thank you."

I returned to the doctor's office, apologizing for the interruption.

"That's quite alright. It is understandable," Dr. Lau said. "Do you feel better now?"

I nodded.

"Now, obviously you would have been too small to be in the courtroom at the time of trial," Dr. Lau continued. "May I ask if anyone ever described the scene to you? Or have you ever read any of the court transcripts, or police records, newspaper reports perhaps?"

"I think I know where you are going with that, but no. I haven't. Up to now I have tried to blot it from my mind as much as I could. So no, I have had no outside source that would give me the information I described to you. I know what I saw. And I know people will say it's impossible. But it is real."

"I think Dr. Schumer and I will take some time to discuss what we just learned from you, " Dr. Lau said. "But I should tell you, and Dr. Schumer can give us his opinion, that I believe this is a circumstance where we may have to give information to the police."

I just looked at the two of them. I knew it would come to this.

"I say that because an innocent third party may have already been seriously affected here. Mr. Strickland," Dr. Lau continued. "Dr. Schumer?"

"I agree with you Dr. Lau. I think it would be helpful if Olav gave us his permission for disclosure. If you are willing to give us that, Olav," Dr. Schumer said.

"Yes, I understand," I said.

Clearly this was going to have to be approached with very delicate hands. Should the Mose Strickland case be re-opened based on my evidence and its reliability as proof, the police would have to find more evidence, likely DNA that would work to corroborate my story.

"Let's talk more at our next session. Are you okay to go home? Perhaps Sophie will meet you?" Dr. Lau asked.

"No, she is in class."

"Okay. You okay to go home on your own?"

"Yes."

"Olav, I think we should not wait until next week to meet again. If you are okay, we should meet in a couple of days."

I nodded.

"I will come out with you to reception and set up a time. I may have to move around some of my other appointments."

We set up a time and I left the office feeling like I was staring into a deep, dark chasm.

CHAPTER 38:

Consent

I walked to the residence feeling the world pressing down on me. I had a decision to make—to consent or not to consent to the doctors' request for my permission to disclose.

I needed to have a conference with Sophie and Mandy. We would have to flesh out the pros and cons of disclosure, although I was pretty sure I knew which side they would come down on.

I called Sophie and told her what happened. We decided to brief Mandy by email first and suggest a call when she could be available.

Mandy's reply indicated she was pretty eager to talk and to move forward so Sophie and I decided to get together that evening at my quad and to link with her in Toronto by phone.

Even though I knew where we were headed, having the support of Sophie and Mandy was comforting to me. Our conversations put me at some level of peace with myself.

Mandy was awestruck as I described in detail the experience I had that day at Dr. Lau's office.

"There will be a process, obviously. But your doctors will give professional opinions and offer proof that your level of recall really does exist, and you have that from two doctors, not just one," Mandy said.

"But there will also be professionals to cast doubt on it, won't there?" Sophie suggested.

"Yes," Mandy said, "but they have done tests that prove your recall ability is real. What the Crown will question is that, while it is real, is it reasonable that a very small child will keep that imprinted on the brain all these years? We may need to find some precedent for that."

"I would imagine that the doctors would have knowledge of preceding cases, but there is no reason why we cannot do some of our own research," Sophie suggested.

We all agreed to that.

"In the meantime, I am going to give them my authorization to disclose the matter to the police. They can probably disclose it anyway, but my permission to disclose will show a level of cooperation. Yes?"

"Yes," Mandy said.

"At what point do we make contact with Mose?" I asked Mandy.

"I have spoken to a person at the organization here who works on behalf of the wrongfully convicted. I will get in touch with her again and give her this update. We may have to make a formal request that they engage. They are going to have to be convinced that there is a reasonable chance of success," Mandy explained. "I will ask them for guidance on how and at what point we contact Mose. All good?"

"Okay. Talk soon." Sophie and I hung up and looked at each other. I wondered what we were about to put in motion.

* * *

I went back to Dr. Lau's office at the appointed time two days later.

Dr. Schumer was there again.

They ran the same barcode experiment, except they didn't show me the original on the transparent paper this time. I was just expected to call it up from memory. I aced it without any hesitation. They said they would do it one more time, increasing the time between tests. Dr. Lau suggested two weeks down the road.

"How have you been sleeping?" Dr. Lau asked.

"Sleeping well actually. Nothing disturbing. But it's been only two nights."

I told the doctors that I was starting to feel a financial pinch from all these sessions.

"Look, we have no choice but to continue this with you Olav," Dr. Lau said. "We would be professionally negligent otherwise. We would rather get paid of course, but if you cannot come up with the money we will figure out a way to continue the sessions anyway. We have to be satisfied, and you need to be satisfied that our work results in a plan that will improve your quality of life, and ensure your safety."

"Thank you," I said.

"Now, have you thought about giving us your written consent to disclose information from our last session to the police?"

"Yes, I have and I am prepared to do that."

"You are doing the right thing Olav." Looking at each other, the doctors said this almost in unison.

Dr. Lau opened a khaki file folder and brought me a sheet that was headed "Authorization for Disclosure." I read it to make sure that I was consenting only to the disclosure of information from that one session and signed the form. Vicki came in and witnessed my signature.

"We will schedule our next session for two weeks from now," Dr. Lau said. "In the meantime we will immediately begin the process of working our report through to the police. We have done this before, so we know the procedures. We will keep you informed every step of the way, Olav."

I thanked them and left the office.

To some extent I felt like a dark cloud was gathering. It wasn't so much a feeling of confusion as to what I'd started here, but feelings of self-doubt and second-guessing my actions. But Mandy and Sophie had the ability to reason.

CHAPTER 39:

Quidi Vidi

Three weeks later, Sophie and I were at a Finbar Furey concert in the Arts and Culture Centre in St. John's. I considered Finbar to be one of the godfathers of Celtic music—a king with a banjo.

A half hour in, my cell phone vibrated in my pocket. It was a text from Dr. Lau. She said she had something to report and could she see me first thing in the morning.

I discreetly gave her the thumbs up and asked what time.

"Nine?"

"Will be there," I replied.

A week earlier, I had done my third experiment with the doctors and their barcode. Again I re-created it from memory without any difficulties. The doctors were coming to the conclusion that my memory was indeed a rarity and very real.

What they needed to do at this point was to somehow show conclusively that my memory of the terrible incident I witnessed in 1996 was real. How were they going to do this?

Sophie and I chatted as we were leaving the concert. We were both a little anxious and wondering what I would hear the following day.

"You okay being alone tonight?" she asked.

"Yes, I will be fine. I will call you after my appointment with Dr. Lau." I knew Sophie would have stayed but she was up to her ears in a term paper and had to get home.

We said good night and went our separate ways.

My roommates who shared my quad had all gone home on a break so I was alone in the apartment that night.

I went to bed about ten-thirty.

* * *

Early the next morning, I decided to get up and walk down to Quidi Vidi Lake. It was about a half hour to the lake, and then about another half hour to walk the trail that encircled it. I thought this would be a great way to get some fresh air, relax and clear my mind.

There were few people around at that hour, little traffic. The odd taxi cab here and there.

The streets were blurred with early morning mist. I expected to meet Sherlock Holmes at any moment but alas, no such luck!

I joined the walking trail not far from where Her Majesty's Penitentiary sits bordering the lake. I began walking north.

The low mist hovering around the lake sent a dull pain to my bowels as I trudged forward.

I finally come to my favourite spot on the south side. A small bridge, something like a moat. It was situated just past a little patch of trees. On either side of the moat were park benches.

I thought I'd sit for a few minutes.

Suddenly I hear a dog bark, bringing me out of some drowsiness.

How is it even possible to nod off in this cool and damp place?

Looking up the trail I see a big northern husky. He is frothing, growling, and showing his teeth.

Holy shit! That might be a wolf. He looks to be rabid. I'd better get the hell out of here!

Jumping up from the bench, I start running in retreat. Back over the moat and through the small patch of tall trees.

Stopping to look back, there is now no dog, and in his place is an Inuk man carrying a flaming spear. It's the chanter from Hebron and he is coming in my direction!

I continue through the trees. Looking up, I see dolls hanging by their necks from tree branches. Eight, ten of them!

On the ground small children with pale, serious faces and blank eyes are poking at the dolls with long sticks.

They have bare feet and are staring at me, expressionless.

Then they start chasing me!

I have goose flesh all over my body.

What the hell is going on?

"OLAV!" the chanter roars, "Uppisâgiven?"

Once again the word translates to an expression in my head. "Are you telling your truth?"

I can hear my heart pounding on my chest and there is throbbing in my ears as I continue running. Sweat is pouring down my face and I wipe my hands across my forehead.

Jesus Christ! It's blood! Where is it coming from?

I stop and fall to my knees, muttering in tongues as I bury my face into the ground. I look up and the chanter is glaring down at me. Spear raised. I pull back and sit on the ground with my knees up to my chest. My hands and arms cover my face as I try to shield myself.

Bathed in sweat and blood, I close my eyes, waiting for the strike.

When I open them, my mother is standing in front of me. She is aglow in a brilliant light, and so beautiful.

Arms outstretched, she says my name.

She looks at me smiling. I hear a voice inside my head saying, "Don't be afraid, Olav. Peace is coming. I am with you and will love you always."

As I am waking up I try to say, "I love you," but my words are jumbled like I am trying to talk with a mouth full of food.

The bed is soaked and I get up and I open the window blinds. Sitting by the open window, the fresh breeze that comes in helps wake me and bring me to me senses.

Thank you mom for saving me.

CHAPTER 40:

Where are the Books?

When I arrived at Dr. Lau's office, Vicki told me that the doctors were on a conference call and should be free any moment.

They kept me waiting ten minutes. I was getting agitated. *I have a class at eleven. But I guess this takes priority.*

Finally Dr. Lau's office door opened and she came out to greet me.

"I am sorry for the wait," she said.

"It's okay," I smiled. "I've learned the virtue of patience."

Smiling a rare smile back, she agreed. "Yes, patience is indeed a virtue."

We entered her office and I sat where I normally sit.

Dr. Schumer, in his usual rumpled outfit, rubbed his eyes, and looked at me as though he still not had his morning coffee.

"Olav," Dr. Lau said, "we hand-delivered our report to Sgt. Will Brocklehurst at Police Major Crimes unit. Here is a copy of the report. Unless you feel you need a copy for some reason I would suggest your leaving it here at the office once you've read it, because it is in strict confidence. You would have it all filed away in that computer brain of yours anyway, yes?" She smiled again.

Wow, she must have had happy flakes for her breakfast this morning! Two smiles.

"Shortly after we filed it with him, we had a call from the senior Crown prosecutor for the province, a Mr. Charles Morrison. They wanted to inform us that the matter had been brought to his attention and further that Mose has never admitted guilt. Even after serving time now for nearly twenty years, he has maintained his innocence. That is something that should work in his favour."

Dr. Schumer weighed in, talking like a lawyer, "In our system, the law is not about winning cases, so much as it is about seeing that justice is done. That is how it has been explained to us, at least. So it seems there is a level of interest, I might even say there is a high degree of interest, in looking into the matter further and putting it to a judge."

"Go on, I am following," I said.

"There are a few things that will need to happen," Dr. Lau explained. "One is that someone is going to have to make application to the court to re-consider the verdict in the Mose Strickland case. Now, the Chief Justice of the Trial Division is I. P. Morgan, the man who prosecuted Mose. That is a concern but it is something that the lawyers will explain."

She took a sip of water.

"The other thing is that we will have to present some evidence to the court that your memory is what it is. We can do that. But the court will also want to be satisfied that you had the ability to retain what you saw at the time your mother died," Dr. Lau went on. "One of the pieces that you told us about was the children's books that you named that you have not seen since your mother's death."

I nodded.

"Are you willing to swear an affidavit that your mother read you these books and that you haven't seen them since her death?"

"Yes, I would do that."

Clearly the doctors were preparing for a meeting with lawyers.

"Do you recall anything else about the books that would be unique?" Dr. Lau asked.

I thought for a moment.

"Yes, each book had my name and address printed on the inside cover. I am sure mom would have done that since the old man was not interested in that sort of thing or in anything to do with me."

"Do you think that the books would be still in the attic in your house in Twin Rivers?"

"Yes, I am pretty sure that they would be."

"Good, the other thing the prosecutor will do in order that the court can consider all angles, is to present a professional opinion challenging the legitimacy of eidetic memory. We need to prepare for that but again Dr. Schumer and I will handle that."

"My sister, and Sophie and I are doing some research to come up with a preceding case or two that will support my claim. Is that a good idea?"

"Yes, continue with that," Dr. Lau said.

"Now the last point we want to cover today," Dr. Lau continued, "is that it would bolster the case to have the intervention of a group that works for justice for the wrongfully convicted. In fact they are probably the people who should make the application to the court."

I told her that Mandy was already working on that in Toronto where the organization is located.

"What are the next steps?" I asked.

"The lawyers are going to want to depose us and maybe you. So that will have to be set up," Dr. Lau said. "They will be in touch with us about that and we will keep you informed."

"Okay," I said and got up to leave.

"Olav, one other thing, the police may decide they want to do a lie detector test. Will you be okay if they want to do that?"

I nodded and left the office.

CHAPTER 41:

A Precedent

Sophie was spending hours researching in the science section of the library. She was focusing her research on cases that had not been cited in the Lau and Schumer study.

I had a feeling she was about to discover something directly relevant, and I was right.

It was a case from 1951 in Gdańsk, Poland involving a child, a girl, who demonstrated signs of eidetic memory at an early age in elementary school.

One day a teacher asked her pupil, Maria Lewandowski, to read a story out loud to the class from one of their readers. Maria left her reader on her desk, walked up to the front of the class and recited the entire story from memory.

Her teacher was astounded and immediately reported to the school administration, recommending that they seek permission from her parents to subject Maria to a professional assessment.

The school received her parents' permission and set about recruiting a team of psychologists. The work and tests revealed that as soon Maria began learning to communicate, she could recall pictures in every detail that she had seen only one time. She would say to her mother and father that she could still see them in her mind.

When she started school, her parents had told the school officials that they thought she was gifted, but the teachers thought that they were just being overly proud parents so they did not pay much attention to it at the time.

At age seven Maria was able to recreate precise images from memory of things she had seen days and weeks earlier.

To get an idea of how far back Maria began recording in her brain, the psychologists needed to consult with her parents.

Maria had told the doctors about a small rubber toy puppy that her mom and dad had given her on her first birthday. The puppy would bark when squeezed. Maria liked the toy, but a day or two after she got it, the family's real pet dog chewed it to pieces and it had to be thrown in the garbage.

In the meantime, the doctors shopped around various toy stores to see if that exact toy was still in circulation. The toy had gone out of circulation several years earlier, they discovered, but a store clerk gave them a suggestion where to try, and they managed to locate one in a small store in Sanok in the south reaches of Poland.

When they went to visit Maria and her parents, they asked the child to describe the toy puppy that she had when she was one year old. The one their dog chewed up.

Maria gave every detail, the dog's colour and its spots, the dog in sitting position with its mouth open, its ears perked, and the sound it made when squeezed,

They kept the toy they tracked down, hidden from her until after she gave her description. Then they took the toy out of the box and showed it to Maria and her parents. It was the same model and exactly as Maria had described.

The doctors explained that Maria's recall ability seemed to prove that she began saving images and sounds in her memory even at the age of one, such that they can be recalled years later.

Maria, they told the parents, was truly a gift to the world.

The doctors continued to follow Maria all through school, concluding that eidetic memory, though very rare, was a real thing, and that it could manifest even while a child is still a baby.

The doctors' work was written up in an extensive report in 1970 and published in numerous medical journals around the world.

Maria's recall ability became a major asset to her in later years. Career-wise she rose swiftly through both military and government ranks leading significant files in intelligence services, though she did not accumulate a lot of money.

She died from lung cancer at the age of forty-eight. Upon her death, her brain was donated to the University of Gdańsk.

* * *

Sophie emailed a copy of the abstract with the citation to Mandy.

"This is excellent," Mandy said. "It is highly authoritative and reputable. Olav, perhaps you should take a copy of this in to your next meeting with Dr. Lau."

"Yes, I will do that," I said.

"Should we try and find one more case?" Sophie asked.

"It cannot not hurt to get another," Mandy said. "At least one more."

"The other thing," Mandy went on, "we have to be very careful that none of this gets out in the open. If word gets back to Twin Rivers that a process is going on which may result in the verdict being overturned, it could lead to the destruction of evidence that police may need to corroborate your information, Olav. That includes leaving Jackie out of it. She cannot know anything until after the search warrants are executed. We cannot be too careful in holding this very close."

We all agreed that confidentiality was of the utmost importance at this stage.

The last thing we covered with Mandy was the suggestion that the organization for the wrongfully convicted should be the agency that makes the application to the court. Mandy thought about this for a moment and agreed that made sense.

"The organization is national in scope—even international, I guess," she said, "so it is likely they have lawyers in each province that work on their behalf. It would be simpler if that is the case rather than flying a lawyer down from here. Be prepared to get a call from a lawyer in St. John's on this. I will speak to my contact tomorrow at the SRWC and report back."

* * *

I had an appointment with the doctors again the following day.

I showed them the study that Sophie had researched. They were pleased with that and told me it would support the theories that they would be advancing. They expected to use the case in their evidence.

They didn't do any further tests with me this time, but they were concerned about my well-being.

I told them about my most recent night terror—the Quidi Vidi Lake scene.

"You may very well continue having those for a while," Dr. Lau said. "Our thinking at this point is that you have been suppressing a lot of feelings of guilt—the fact that you were an eyewitness to your mother's murder and not able to tell your story. This is in your subconscious and it comes to the surface in those nightmares."

"Perhaps," I said. "But God, I need to move past them!"

"We are hesitant to prescribe any medication to help you sleep at this stage, Olav. You would not want to risk your having any confusion or distraction given what lies ahead for you," Dr. Lau explained.

"That sounds ominous."

"Sorry, I didn't mean it that way. Look at it this way, if you were taking medication, whatever it might be, it could give the lawyers who are going to oppose us some ammunition with respect to your brain and memory. You are not taking any meds now, correct?"

216

"Correct."

"We are pretty certain that you are suffering from a form of post traumatic stress disorder at witnessing the death of your mother," Dr. Lau said. "In addition to that, your father's treatment of you has added to that PTSD."

"The cause of your night terrors is that suppression Dr. Lau just spoke about," Dr. Schumer said. "We think what you need is a chance to make things right. Make things right with Mose, who you see as innocent in all this. You want the chance to tell the court and the police that they need to release Mose and they need to find the real killer. If those things can play out, we believe you will find relief from those nightmares. You need to hang in there through this process, Olav. You can be a lifesaver here to an innocent person. We are here to support you."

"Thank you. I appreciate your opinions."

"A question," Dr. Lau said. "Before the session where you went into the trance, you were having only flashes of memory of the incident, like something crashing and someone screaming and so on, yes?"

"Yes, that's correct."

"Since the session that day, can you now recall all the detail you told us about?" Dr. Lau asked.

"Yes," I said. "Every detail."

Dr. Lau was making notes.

"Now one last thing. Sgt. Brocklehurst called me and said that Major Crimes does want to do the lie detector test I mentioned. I think this is an indication of how seriously they are taking the matter."

"When do they want to do this?"

"Early next week."

"Will either of you be with me?"

"Unfortunately, no. They won't allow that. It can only be the interviewer and you in the room."

"Can I refuse it?"

"You shouldn't," Dr. Lau said.

"Okay. I'm not really worried about it, but I am going to run it by Mandy and see what she has to say about it."

I left the office and walked back to my quad. Thinking it through on the way home, I decided I had nothing to worry about with the lie detector. I suspected it was the prosecutor who would have demanded that it be done. But why should I worry? After all I reasoned, I am not the one being accused of anything here.

While I was getting something to eat, my cell phone buzzed. An officer from Brocklehurst's office was calling to schedule an appointment for the polygraph.

* * *

I thought I'd better get Mandy on the line. She said she was happy I called because she was just about to call me. She had spoken to her contact at SRWC and briefed her on events. The organization was fully on board and their lawyer contact in St. John's would be in touch. The lawyer was a fellow named James Joseph. He would act on our behalf on a pro bono basis.

"That's great news," I said.

"Mandy," I continued, "I wanted to mention to you that the police want to do a polygraph on me. They called me a few minutes ago to schedule a time."

"Really? How do you feel about that?"

"A little like being re-victimized to some extent. As though I am a suspect or something. I don't feel good about being subjected to that, but I feel confident that I can handle the test."

"Let me think about that and call you back a little later," Mandy said.

I hung up and got into my books.

About an hour later, James Joseph called to introduce himself. He told me about some cases he had worked on in other parts of the country. He was also a member of the bars of Ontario and New Brunswick. His origins were native Mi'kmaq he told me, from one of the communities in western Newfoundland. Somehow that put me at ease.

We planned to meet the next day.

I waited for Mandy to call back, which she did. I told her that James had called and that we had set up a meeting.

"At any point when you want to link me by conference call, please do," she said.

"For sure," I said.

"About the polygraph," she went on, "if you are comfortable doing it, I think it is best that you do. If you were to refuse it that may send messages that you don't want communicated."

"I can understand that."

"It is probably better that you take it and fail the test than to refuse altogether. These things fail all the time. People are nervous, heart pumping beyond normal and stuff like that, which can affect the outcome."

"Um-hmm."

"Besides, the results of a polygraph are never admitted as evidence in court, in any case. So, I think do it. It will show your level of cooperation and commitment."

"Okay. We're on the same page. I will call you after it is done."

"Thanks. I love you, Olav," Mandy said.

Oh my God. She said she loved me! My sister. My family.

"I love you too."

CHAPTER 42:

James Joseph

James and I met at an independently owned coffee shop called *Grounded*. It was located in downtown St. John's, not far from George Street. I don't know where they sourced their coffee, but it sure was a winner. The place was uniquely themed in Newfoundland culture and had so much more character than the carbon copy versions of Tim's and Starbucks.

James was about six feet. Great build, mid-forties. He was dressed smart casual with a charcoal coloured shirt under a navy jacket. His black hair was medium length, not too long, and he wore a fedora. Sharp looking character. Friendly smile. I noticed a thin rawhide strand around his neck, relatively inconspicuous. It was joined at the ends by four beads, black, white, red and yellow.

Honouring his native heritage.

"Are we okay meeting here in this public place?"

He looked around. It was not overly crowded.

"Yeah, we're okay."

He had lots of experience so I trusted his judgment.

In between his questions, I briefed James on everything right up to last night's call with Mandy. He made notes here and there. We spent about an hour together.

I told him how much I appreciated the pro bono nature of our relationship.

"I enjoy this kind of work, Olav. When I went to law school my goal was to follow the ideal of working for justice for those who have been mistreated. That may sound cheesy, but it is what motivated and still motivates me."

"Wow, that *is* honourable," I said.

"Now, here is what I think should be our immediate next steps."

"I'm listening."

"First we need to speak to Sgt. Brocklehurst about getting search warrants. They need to be executed like yesterday. Second, we need to get a message to Mose and bring him up to speed as to what is happening. Third, I will need to meet with him as soon as possible, and fourth I will need your permission to meet with your doctors."

"You have it. I will email it to you."

"Thank you. After I meet with the doctors I will begin drafting the application."

It was evident that James had been down this road before.

I asked his advice on whether Mandy and I should accompany him in the meeting with Mose.

"For the first meeting, I should meet with him alone to keep things as focused as possible," James said. "At that time I will get an idea where he stands about meeting with you and Mandy. Hopefully he will be open to that, but one never knows what twenty years of time spent in a maximum security prison can do to a person."

I looked at him and nodded.

"At some point," he continued, "this is all going to become public. Very public. The news media will be all over it. Television, national networks, newspapers. Social media. But right now we need to keep it in confidence. Like Mandy says, until after any search warrants have been executed. That is essential."

"Yes, I agree. I will report to Mandy after this meeting. We will need to keep her in the loop at every turn."

James nodded. "Anything else we haven't covered?"

"I understand that the Crown lawyer who prosecuted Mose is now the Chief Justice. What role might he have?" I asked.

"None," James assured me. "I.P. Morgan is Chief Justice of the Trial Division. Our application will be in the Newfoundland Court of Appeal."

"Okay. That is a relief."

"Anything thing else you're wondering about?"

"What will the police need as evidence?"

"The murder weapon, if possible. They will need it for DNA. If they find it, any DNA assessment may require exhuming the body."

I looked down at my coffee.

"I am sorry to have to say that, Olav," James said. "Also, to substantiate the truth of your story and state of mind, they will want to take custody of that trunk in the attic of your home in Twin Rivers. This is why we need swift action, so evidence is not destroyed."

"Yes, that's true," I said.

"Olav," James said, "you described my work and commitment as being honourable. Well, I am here to tell you that what you are doing is honourable, more so than what I do. I am a means to an end. But your decision to go forward with this is truly a brave act. After all, your own father is in the equation here. I do look forward to working with you."

I left the coffee shop and began walking back to campus.

Now that is a role model that I want to follow! Yes sir. Maybe I will even get a fedora. I smiled.

I was feeling centred. I had clear goals to work toward. A mission perhaps. It felt good and purposeful.

CHAPTER 43:

The Lie Detector

I spent the weekend thinking a lot about the polygraph test that was coming up in a couple of days. I tried doing a little research but realized that it is probably something that is next to impossible for which to try and prepare.

At times I would feel a bit angry having to go through something like this, then I would dismiss that anger. I'd call Sophie when I would feel that way. She always had a way of reassuring me that the feeling was natural and that I would do well.

On Sunday afternoon, I'll be damned if my father didn't call. I immediately got my guard up. It was the first time he had called in all my time at university.

I began to wonder if he had gotten a tip as to what was going on. I listened as close as possible trying to interpret every word he said in the small talk.

He said he was sick of living in Twin Rivers. He said people here still gossip about that day in February, 1996. He asked me if I ever heard any rumours.

I started to fidget and felt a sweat coming on.

"No, I've heard nothing really."

"Okay" he said. "I don't want you getting tangled up in any of that shit."

It turned out that he was calling to say he would not be home at the time I came back after the semester. He and Ellie were going on a trip to the Caribbean for two weeks, so the house key would be at Aunt Grace's.

"Okay. Thanks for letting me know."

As usual everything was about him. Or him and Ellie. He didn't even ask me how my studies were going.

Prick.

* * *

I had to do the polygraph at police headquarters downtown. I arrived there about twenty minutes before it was due to start.

I spoke to the person on the front desk through a two and a half inch diameter hole in some heavy Plexiglas. The door beside the glassed-in desk was locked and people had to punch in a code to open it.

Very secure place and so barren.

After a while, someone came out to shepherd me through the building to my destination. At the end of a really long hallway I had to go through a screening process something like at airports. I had to leave my shoes behind as well as my cell phone and any loose objects I had in my pockets.

Holy shit, those guys mean business.

An officer met me on the other side. The man was friendly enough. A Sgt. Ryan. He was the interviewer and the guy who would hook me up to the polygraph equipment.

He smiled and we chatted about the foggy weather. I think he sensed my uneasiness. He looked at me and told me to relax and just be myself.

I found his friendly disposition a little out of place in a cold office like this. I expected beady eyes staring out from a stone-carved face.

I better be on my guard. This could be good cop, bad cop shit!

Sgt. Ryan started with what I think were called control questions. He asked those before he hooked me up to the polygraph machine.

"Have you ever been caught speeding, Mr. Williams?"

"No."

"Have you ever had a parking ticket?"

"No." *Hell, I don't even have a car to get a parking ticket!*

"Have you ever been arrested?"

"No."

"Have you had sex outside of marriage?"

"Yes."

"Have you ever stolen anything?"

"No."

After a few more questions he placed a couple of censors on my chest. I took it that those were to monitor my heart rate. Then he put a blood pressure cuff on my left bicep.

He went back to his computer screen. I couldn't see the screen, but I imagined it was producing a readout something like lab technologists get when they do an EKG on a patient.

Then he looked up at me. He was unsmiling now.

Bad cop!

"How old are you Mr. Williams?"

"Twenty-one."

"Have you ever colluded with anyone to make up a false story?"

"No."

"Were you abused as a younger person?"

"Yes."

"Physically?"

"Yes."

"Sexually?"

"No."

"Mentally?"

"Yes."

The sergeant maintained firm eye contact when asking the question. Then glued his eyes to the screen for about thirty seconds after each answer.

"Mr. Williams, is the report you gave to your doctors about witnessing your mother's death true?"

"Yes."

"Did you see who killed your mother?"

"Yes."

"Are you recalling the murder scene right now?"

"Yes."

"You told the doctors that it was not Mose Strickland who did the killing. Did Mose Strickland kill your mother?"

"No, he did not."

"Do you know who did?"

"Yes."

"Who killed your mother, Mr. Williams?"

"My father, Travis Williams."

"Mr. Williams, do you have something referred to as a form of eidetic memory?"

"Yes."

"Would you swear an affidavit that what you told the doctors is true?"

"Yes."

After several more questions that were more like control questions, Sgt. Ryan shut down the machine and removed the censors and the cuff from me.

"We are done," he announced.

"Okay. How long before I hear some results of this test."

"There is a little bit of a process before we can submit the report. I have to meet with a couple of people who will review it, kind of like peer review. Once that's done we can then move it up to the Chief at Major Crimes, so I would give it a week to ten days before you hear the result."

"Okay. Thanks. Am I free to go now?"

"Yes, I will walk you back to where you left your stuff and someone else will show you out."

I left the building about an hour after I arrived.

CHAPTER 44:

Searching

James Joseph was a man of action. He wasted no time in arrang-
ing to meet with Drs. Lau and Schumer.

He called me to tell me that he'd spent an hour interviewing
them and they gave him a copy of the report that they submitted
to Sgt. Brocklehurst.

Dr. Lau also gave him a copy of the study that she and Dr.
Schumer had published and the Poland case that Sophie had
researched, as well as one other that we came up with.

The second case was one from the late 1950s. It was a set of
Mayan identical twins born in the Yucatan region of Mexico.
The circumstances were similar to the Polish case as to how it
came to be discovered. The twins were in primary school when
teachers began noticing their unique ability to recall sights and
sounds with great accuracy. Their school also engaged a team of
specialists to follow the children over a period of years. The difference was that in this case both children had displayed exceptional
evidence of sustained eidetic memory. In addition, it brought new
perspectives to the study of the often incredible ability of twins to
communicate with each other.

Both cases added weight to the claims by Lau and Schumer
that my memory was active in 1996 when I saw the murder and
that I had retained those images and sounds.

James told the doctors that he would be with them and act as their representative at the under oath, fact-finding process known as discovery, that the Crown prosecutor had planned.

"Also, I have drafted an affidavit for you to sign, effectively swearing to your information that you gave to the doctors about your witnessing the crime. We will need to meet for you to sign that."

* * *

The court issued search warrants to the police, following Sgt. Brocklehurst's application.

He explained to the judge in chambers that new evidence had come to light in the murder conviction involving Mose Strickland. Brocklehurst referred to the report he had received from Drs. Lau and Schumer. The report indicated that this evidence could not have been available at the time of trial and that the police have reasonable grounds to search the properties of two other suspects in Twin Rivers. Brocklehurst told the judge that they would need to do an exhaustive search to locate the murder weapon and subject it to DNA analysis, although there was no guarantee they would find it.

With search warrants in hand, Brocklehurst got on the phone to his contacts in Goose Bay. He sent the warrants by secure fax at the same time. He told them to arrange, without delay, for two teams to fly to Twin Rivers—one to search the Travis Williams property and one to search the property belonging to Eleanor Rowe.

Brocklehurst explained that in the Williams property they would be looking for a red bungee cord with yellow specks, "but whatever bungee cords you find, retrieve them all. Same in the Rowe property," he said. The court also extended the search warrants to outbuildings associated with the two properties, as well as vehicles.

In the Williams property, officers were also told to search the attic to locate a locked trunk and if there were more than one trunk to retrieve them all.

* * *

Caleb Moores, now in his last year of service before retirement, met the teams at the airport as the police Twin Otter arrived. Six officers headed by two inspectors got off the plane and aboard the police van.

Caleb first dropped the officers and the inspector at the Williams property and the other team at the Rowe property five minutes later.

It was eight o'clock in the morning.

Travis, now a supervisor at the town works department, was just finishing coffee when a firm, impatient knock came on the door.

"Mr. Travis Williams, we have a warrant to search your property."

Travis stood speechless, motionless.

The inspector ordered one officer to search the back yard shed and the other two to go through the house. Travis was instructed to remain in sight of the inspector at all times. He sat at the table not saying a word.

Similar orders were given at the Rowe property, where Ellie still had not left to go to her office.

CHAPTER 45:

"What the Hell is Going On?"

Travis and Ellie did not openly become a couple until about three years or so after Abby's death.

For some reason, they chose not to marry and maintained separate homes. I was okay with this because I did not want that woman as a live-in at my home, though if Travis had wanted that I would not have had a lot of choice.

In the early 2000s Ellie was elected to the provincial legislature. In due course she became the minister responsible for municipalities. This brought many opportunities for travel and for both to spend a lot of time in the capital city and elsewhere. She was now into her third term.

Ellie was very proud to go to public events sporting a decorated war veteran on her arm. She would play that up at every opportunity, especially during campaign time. She maintained a very high profile and with her ambition, being what it was, she could ill afford any kind of negative publicity.

So when police showed up at her door and her boyfriend's door that day to execute warrants, the rumours began circulating all over the coast and the media went into overdrive.

On the noontime news broadcast that day, one radio station reported that:

"Police officers from the Major Crimes Unit are in Twin Rivers this morning conducting searches of properties owned by residents Travis Williams and the local member of the legislature Eleanor Rowe. Rowe is also a member of the provincial cabinet. Nothing further is available at this time, but we will keep you up to date as more information comes in."

This was bad news. Eleanor was in her last year before the next general election and she needed to find a way to do some damage control.

Calls were coming in to her office and her staff had to scramble to make excuses for her unavailability.

Once the searches were complete, she called Travis and summoned him to her house.

"What the hell is going on?" she demanded.

"I don't know any more than you do!"

"Well, this is not going to end well if we don't do something right away."

"What do you think we should do?"

"We should go to St. John's right now. I need to meet with the attorney general."

"Is that a good idea?"

"Do you have a better one?" Ellie snapped at Travis.

"No. Not yet anyway."

"I am not waiting for any scheduled flights," Ellie said. "I am calling for the government aircraft to get in here today. We both need to get out of the local spotlight here for a few days, although it's going to be just as bad in St. John's. But we can hole up in my apartment for a while."

"What will people think of your using government aircraft for this?" Travis asked.

"It was all a pre-planned trip. Cabinet meeting and so on. Don't worry about it. It is the least of our worries right now. Now go on home and pack some things."

* * *

On arrival at her apartment on Elizabeth Avenue, Ellie got on the phone to the attorney general. She and Hal Cowie had had a longstanding working relationship. She arranged to meet with him first thing the following morning.

The two met at the AG's office at eight o'clock. It was just the two of them with no other staff in attendance. Ellie asked if he knew what was going on.

Hal told her he had been briefed just days before.

"Why didn't you call me?" Ellie said.

"I couldn't do that."

"I want whatever the hell is going on in this cluster-fuck to stop. Shut it down now!"

"I cannot interfere, Ellie, and you should know that," the attorney general said. "In fact I am a little uneasy about your coming in to meet me here this morning. The premier and the government won't put up with any evidence of impropriety or even any perception of impropriety."

Ellie gave Hal a look of surprise.

"I have a fucking election to win in less than a year," Ellie said.

The attorney general just sat shaking his head.

"I thought we were a team," Ellie was pleading now.

"We are a team Ellie, but on matters like this we have to keep our distance. It's the way things work," the attorney general stated.

"Then maybe you can advise me as to what to do about my cabinet position. Should I take a leave of absence until this is all over?"

"That will be up to the premier, Ellie. You should take the matter to his office."

The attorney general walked toward the door to show her out. "Have a good day," he said.

CHAPTER 46:

Hitting the Media

A fter the news story aired, I had a call from Jackie in Dark Harbour.

She asked me if I had heard the news about the searches and if I knew anything about what was going on.

I had to tell her what was happening, but I needed to warn her not to get her expectations raised at this time. We still had a lot of bases to cover and any number of things could go sideways. Court processes can be very unpredictable I told her. James had already spoken to Mose, and I suggested to Jackie that if she is talking to him to not communicate in any way that this is a done deal.

She agreed to follow my advice to stay realistic and focused.

I offered that Sophie, Mandy and I could call her in a couple of days if she would like. She was happy to do that and we arranged a time.

Jackie became engulfed in all kinds of emotions and was sobbing as we hung up the phone.

* * *

James called me the next day. He had gotten a report from Brocklehurst on the results of the searches. He said rather than talk on the phone he felt we should meet in his downtown office.

He said he was in court most of the day, but the following morning would be good.

I hung up and called Sophie. She was down the shore at her parents' place. Her grandmother had been quite sick and she wanted to spend some time with her, so she'd been there for a few days. She said she would be in town later and we could meet for coffee.

Even though we had been in touch on text, I still needed to meet and bring her up to date as to where we were. I also wanted her to know how much Mandy and I appreciated everything she'd being doing. She was a real team player.

I was afraid I was not acknowledging her support as much as I should have been and I wanted to correct that. Things really would not be where they were had it not been for Sophie. I had a lot to be thankful for.

* * *

The day that James and I were to meet, the main newspaper in the province ran a story on the case. The story was picked up by national networks. It reported that the Society for the Rights of the Wrongfully Convicted was now actively building a case related to the Mose Strickland conviction and had hired St. John's lawyer, James Joseph, to work on his behalf.

The front page headline that morning screamed.

Possible Wrongful Conviction in 1996 Murder case.

"Mose Strickland was convicted in 1997 of killing his ex-girlfriend Abigail Peters Williams in Twin Rivers, Labrador in February, 1996.

"Court records show that at trial the Crown produced no eye witnesses and based its case entirely on circumstantial evidence.

"According to sources, new evidence has recently come to light that casts doubt on the legitimacy of the first-degree murder verdict.

"Police have carried out searches on two properties in Twin Rivers and at this point are awaiting forensic results.

"Lawyer James Joseph will be making application to the Court of Appeal but did not specify when that might be, indicating they needed to be in possession of the reports from the searches.

"Strickland has served nearly twenty years of a life sentence. He has never admitted guilt."

The paper carried side-by-side photos of Mose and of James Joseph under the headline.

* * *

Sophie and I met for breakfast and read through the news article. We emailed a copy of the story to Mandy.

"You know what's next, right?" Sophie said.

"What?"

"The media will be after you. On a couple of levels. First your evidence that will go to the court, and secondly, your memory itself. It being so rare. It will definitely make for a good human interest story as journalists like to call it," she suggested.

"I dare say you are probably right," I said, "but at this point I need to keep things low-key."

"For sure."

We finished breakfast and walked to James's office. I had alerted James that Sophie would be with me as she was fully a part of the team.

He had reserved the boardroom at his office for our meeting. This time he had an assistant, a paralegal, with him.

He said the searches resulted in the recovery of a number of bungee cords at both sites and that it included one that matched the description I gave to the doctors.

They had also recovered the trunk from the attic. They had asked the doctors to come to the station when they opened the trunk. I was invited to the police station to be there when they opened the trunks, but I chose not to go. The doctors knew what to expect and told me I didn't need to come down. They didn't want to risk any unnecessary trauma to me. I agreed with them. James was now telling us that the trunk contained some magazines, a couple of cushions, knitting yarn, some old CDs, and the very books that I had identified in my interviews with the doctors. The books also had my name and address written on the inside cover, just as I had described.

Sophie and I looked at each other and smiled.

James went on to tell us that the Crown had destroyed the tissue samples that had been taken at the time of the autopsy. They preserved samples for a number of years as a matter of course in case it would ever be required for DNA analysis. They destroyed it after a ten-year period.

We were left without my mother's DNA.

"This will set us back some because it means that a forensics team will have to go into Twin and exhume the body to harvest some samples. I regret having to tell you that," James said. "Anyone who knows Labrador would know that, as morbid as this might sound, interned human bodies are preserved for a very long time due to the extreme cold. The terrain is not permafrost, but close to it. Forensics tells us they will have no trouble getting samples for DNA testing."

"When will that happen?" I asked.

"I will talk to Brocklehurst and find out," James said.

I sat quiet, thinking, for a long moment.

"I want to go in with them," I said.

Both Sophie and James looked at me wide-eyed.

"Are you sure that is something you should do?" Sophie asked.

"Yes. I want to be there," I said firmly.

"I will talk to the police and get back to you. I don't think they can refuse you," James said.

After another long moment with James making notes, Sophie spoke up.

"Olav, were you at your mother's wake?"

"Yes, Aunt Grace took me there to kind of say good-bye I guess."

"Did you see your mother in the casket?"

"Yes, I did."

"Can you recall what clothes she was wearing when she was ready for burial?"

"Yes, I can."

"Did anyone ever tell you what she was wearing?"

"No. Aunt Grace and the family tried to keep all that stuff from me."

"You know, if you went there it could further corroborate the claim your doctors are making about your ability to call up images from when you were a baby," Sophie said.

"Wow!" James exclaimed. "That's brilliant Sophie! But Olav, you need to tell us now what you remember seeing. How was she dressed? Can you do that?"

I thought for a moment and nodded my head.

Finally I said, "She was dressed in a pale blue outfit, a dress, with a brooch on the left side just above her heart. She had ribbons in her hair and a couple of combs. She also had rings on two fingers. Two rings on the wedding band finger and one on the forefinger of her right hand. They had a type of white satin kerchief around her neck, I think to hide the marks from the attack. She was also holding a small book. I couldn't see it properly but I think it might have been a testament. The Gospels. She was a sleeping beauty."

James was writing down every word.

I looked at Sophie. Her eyes were filling with tears.

"Okay, I am on to this," James said. "I will also speak to Brocklehurst about obtaining photos of those things you just identified, Olav."

"Now, one last thing," James said. "I know that Travis's girlfriend, Eleanor, is a powerful person with access to a lot of resources. I want to caution you about texting and telephones. That goes for all three of you, including Mandy. When you talk to her, call from a landline. We cannot be too careful, and some people may become desperate enough to bug your lines. I'm not saying that will happen, but be on the lookout for that. Behave as though you are walking on thin ice."

We thanked James and headed down the street for lunch. Both Sophie and I felt a little drained by the meeting and at the thought of what lay ahead, but at the same time, we both felt as though we were walking on air.

We had lunch and made a plan to call Mandy that night to brief her.

CHAPTER 47:

No Nightmares

It was a pleasant ride into Twin Rivers aboard the police aircraft. James told me that he had to argue a little with Brocklehurst to allow me to come along. But Brocklehurst seemed sympathetic, he said, when James told him that it could help bring some closure to me.

The officers in Twin Rivers received instructions from Major Crimes to get a start on the retrieval of the body once they received the message that the plane was in the air. The officers hired three local guys to help them unearth the casket. They decided to get close to the target and stop. They were told to stay at the site at all times. They would finish what was left of the shoveling once the officers and I arrived at the gravesite from the police plane.

With a good tail wind, we landed in Twin just about four hours after we left the Torbay airport. We stopped at St. Anthony for fuel and one of the officers went to the terminal and picked up some sandwiches and pop. We all ate on the last leg of the journey to Twin Rivers.

I was surprised that I didn't feel any uneasiness as Caleb drove us to the cemetery.

The forensics team with the local officers set up a large tent—the kind you see at weddings—over the site.

Then the fellows continued digging.

The lead forensics officer equipped everyone including me with plastic yellow cloaks, masks, and plastic gloves.

Once the diggers had reached the casket, they worked with ropes in order to bring the casket up to ground level.

The first job they were instructed to do was take close up photos of each of the things that I had told James about, including the colour of the dress, the brooch, the kerchief, the rings and the book.

Then they would harvest tissue samples and the work would be done.

The officers were very gracious in leading me to the casket to view my mother.

Except for the withering of her face, everything else was just what I remembered seeing when I looked down at my sleeping mom from Aunt Grace's arms.

I stood for a moment with an officer alongside me and said some silent prayers. I imagined her from that dream about Quidi Vidi Lake telling me she would be with me always and that she loved me. I cried as I returned to the police van to sit and wait while the people under the tent carried out their work.

Our flight back to St. John's was smooth and quiet. Solemn even.

I caught a ride back to campus in a cop car with two of the officers. I told them how much I appreciated the trip and thanked them.

It was dusk. I showered and went straight to my room and to bed.

I was out as soon as my head hit the pillow and slept soundly for a full ten hours. No dreams. No nightmares.

CHAPTER 48:

No Regrets

In September of 2015, I received a call from Rhoda's sister in St. John's.

Although I had been visiting Rhoda on a regular basis after our first meeting at Hotel Newfoundland, I had not noticed any apparent change in her health. But that's just me. I can be slow on the uptake when it comes to stuff like that.

I hadn't seen Rhoda in a couple of weeks.

Rhoda's sister, Francine Kavanagh, whom I had never met, told me that Rhoda's cancer had spread to other parts of her body, including her lymph nodes, and that she had taken a turn for the worse. The treatments had been stopped and she was now going into palliative care.

I was shocked to hear that news. That seemed so fast.

"Have the doctors given you any estimates of time?"

"They don't expect much more than three to six months—the most likely scenario being closer to the three-month end of the spectrum. I am so sorry to have to tell you that, Olav."

"Thank you," I said.

"Rhoda asked me to make sure that you and Mandy got the message."

Francine explained to me where the palliative care unit was located at the Health Sciences and told me the specific room number.

"Maybe at some time, Olav, we could meet for lunch. Would you like that? I am your great aunt, after all." I couldn't see her smile, but I could hear it in her voice.

"Yes, that would be great. I will get on to Mandy now and give her that news. Thank you for calling, Francine."

* * *

Mandy was as shocked as I was to hear the news. She had come back to St. John's for a very brief weekend trip that spring to see me and to visit Rhoda. That was the only other time she saw Rhoda after Hotel Newfoundland.

That was a great visit. Rhoda was feeling well at the time and was just a joy to be around. She told us lots of Newfoundland jokes and stories. We also toured around the bay, visited Signal Hill and Cape Spear, and ate Newfoundland style fish and chips. It was a real fun weekend.

* * *

"Oh my God," Mandy said when I called her with the latest news about Rhoda's health. "I am so sorry to hear that about her."

"Yes, seems that stuff can move fast once it really takes hold," I said.

"I will take some time off from work and come over," she said. "It will probably be a couple of days before I get there. I will call my mother and let her know too."

"We'll see you soon."

I put away my books for the day and got ready to go and visit Rhoda. I called Sophie, and she came and picked me up to drive us to the palliative care unit at the Health Sciences.

I am never very good at knowing what to say in those circumstances.

Rhoda was cheerful and welcoming. I told her that Francine had called me and that I was so sorry to hear the news. She gave us warm hugs and asked us to sit. Someone brought glasses of water to us.

"I didn't want to call earlier," Rhoda said, "until I had a better idea what was happening. Have you talked to Mandy?"

"Yes, and she will be here day after tomorrow."

"This is a beautiful room," Sophie said, trying to make conversation.

"Yes, very nice and great people."

"You may be wondering what to say in times like this," Rhoda said, reading our minds. "Well, treat things like any other visit. Just be yourselves. I am okay."

"Maybe I could ask you one thing," I said. "Do you mind if I ask you if you regret divorcing the bishop? You don't have to answer if you don't want to."

Sophie shot a wondering glance toward me.

"You know, kids," Rhoda said. "I have had plenty of regrets in my life, but let me assure you, that is not one of them. We were married in the sight of God, lived in the sight of God, and I guess divorced in the sight of God. God wanted me to have more respect for myself, in the way He created me, and Absalom went against God's will and did everything he could to stifle that. So no regrets here. I will leave earth, whenever that might be, a contented person. And I have my two grandchildren who have made me so proud."

"Wow," Sophie said. "That is such amazing strength."

Rhoda was very fond of Sophie. She cried during an earlier visit when Sophie told her about Papa Bear. She had a big heart. She told Sophie to pass her condolences along to the family.

Mandy arrived two days later and we visited with Rhoda where, this time, I did notice some change in her.

During Mandy's visit, we also made it a point to meet and have lunch with James—more of a courtesy visit since we were all being kept in the know.

When Mandy left to go back to Toronto, we both wondered if this was the last time she'd seen Rhoda alive.

CHAPTER 49:

The Lie Detector Result

About a week after I had the polygraph test, I got a call from Sgt. Ryan at the downtown police headquarters. He wanted to see me.

I arrived downtown and went through the various security protocols to sit and wait while he finished a phone call. It was a stark waiting room, four walls with neither pictures nor windows. The floor was tiled and cold, sending off echoes at every step.

Finally someone motioned me to go in to Ryan's office.

I sat across from him.

The sergeant reached for a file, opened it, and handed me a sheet of paper.

"I am happy to tell you that you passed the polygraph test in a very decisive way. Not a mark of any indecision or hesitation on any of the questions. You should be very happy with the results," Ryan said.

"Thank you. That is a relief. Could you not have told me that over the phone?" I asked.

"No," he said. "Our policy is to meet in person when it's possible to do so, and not discuss results over the phone."

"Yes, I see," I said.

I kept my eyes on the results sheet.

"I understand," I said, "that these results are not admitted in court."

"That is correct, but the Crown prosecutor will be aware of the results."

I left Sgt. Ryan's office and headed over to get the report to James at his office. Besides, I needed to get there to sign the affidavit that he had drafted, and get updated on a couple of things. He also wanted to brief me on his visit with Mose at the federal pen in New Brunswick.

James told me that Mose was quite reserved in their meeting. James reassured him that he was representing people who are working to get the verdict overturned and have him released.

A greying, bearded Mose with a scar under his left eye was skeptical about what James was telling him. James said he expected that attitude. In most cases after a long period of incarceration even the most optimistic person can be turned into a raving cynic.

But when Mose realized that James had come all the way from Newfoundland to visit him, he began to show some signs of warming up.

James had to caution Mose to be patient and not get his hopes too high. There were some hoops to go through, he told Mose, but the team has lots to work with.

"What did he say about a visit from Mandy?" I asked.

"His mother had already told him that Mandy had been tracked down, so it was not a surprise when I mentioned her name. He said he would like to meet her," James said. "When I told him that you were a key player here, he said he would like to meet you as well."

"Okay. I will get those messages to Mandy. Thanks for that update."

"I don't know if you've heard or not," James said "but Eleanor Rowe has been asked by the premier to take a leave of absence from cabinet after all this became public. It was just reported in the news an hour ago."

"No, I hadn't heard that."

"She will continue to represent the district as its member in the legislature but she will step aside from her cabinet duties."

"Well, we'll have to see how that goes," I said. "Depending on what comes out in the court application, she may end up having to resign altogether."

"It could come to that. There could be a lot of bad press in her immediate future, and this is her election year," James said.

James also informed me that the results of the DNA analysis on the bungee cords should be available in a few days.

"I will call you as soon as I get them."

In the meantime, the discovery hearing with Drs. Lau and Schumer was also happening in the coming days. He said he would be there to represent them and that I was welcome to come and observe.

"Yes, I should hope so!"

James smiled. "I'll call you."

CHAPTER 50:
Ellie's Connections

Travis and Ellie had not had a good day since their houses were searched.

The news reports about a possible wrongful conviction kept coming out in local and national media, and that was doing little to cement her support coming up to the next election, to say the least.

Though Ellie craved attention and being in the spotlight, she sure as hell didn't need this hanging over her head.

Travis spent about a week in St. John's after Ellie's meeting with the attorney general and then flew back commercially to Twin Rivers. Ellie, now a cabinet casualty, had no more access to government aircraft. She came back a few days later, also on a commercial flight.

Travis went back to work as soon as he returned but did so only for the money. He could not focus on his duties anymore and became less and les committed to the job.

Ellie returned with instructions to let go two of her staff whose jobs were funded by her budget as a cabinet minister. She was able to keep one staff in Twin Rivers as part of the money that came with being a member of the legislature.

Ellie was very unhappy downsizing her office. She was more used to empire building.

She had expected more from the attorney general. She cursed him and the premier for being wimps. *The sonzabitches.* If circumstances had been different she would have switched political parties.

But this was not over yet. She felt she had one last angle that she could work to pull a few strings.

She had never told Travis about the covert relationship she had with Denis Lundringham about twenty years back. Lundringham had been a high profile lawyer at the time, and now he was the Chief Justice of the Newfoundland Court of Appeal. The top legal dog in the province.

The relationship happened when he was the deputy attorney general and she had met him at a cities and municipalities convention in Corner Brook. After that convention, she would arrange trips to St. John's so she could carry on her affair with Lundringham, who made plenty out of the fact that he was also a Queen's Counsel. Quite often Ellie arranged trips to other parts of the country, coordinated with Lundringham, under the guise of municipal business so their rendezvouses carried much less risk of public exposure.

Ellie carefully calculated how and when to contact him now and what she would say. She knew it was risky, but she felt her future depended on it. If she could not wangle some influence here, she thought, then things would be looking pretty damn gruesome. She had never before been in such a conundrum and she hated the thought of having to call in favours. She still had Lundringham's private email address and cell number and planned to use them.

She decided she would not tell Travis about this contact.

In the meantime, Travis was drinking heavily. He was drunk every night and began missing time from work. He was not crazy about the job he was in now anyway, even though he was making a bit more money. He didn't like the idea of moving from the outdoor job operating equipment to a desk job with some super-visory responsibilities.

More than once he got himself into trouble at the local bar and had to be put in a taxi and sent home. He eventually got himself barred from the club altogether for an indefinite period.

In drunken stupors followed by depressing hangovers, day in day out, he began to wonder what the hell was going to happen to him if he were to get charged with Abby's murder. Dark clouds were gathering fast and the drink just made him more confused. It all left him in a daze and clueless about how to move forward.

He cursed the community and his job and began looking for blame. He even began to curse Ellie for coming into his life. Although she had given him a good job with many benefits, he came to the realization that she was also going to be his downfall.

In his conversations with Ellie, she tried to encourage him to live his life and do his job as normal as possible. She said they could not let the police get the impression that there was some-thing to hide. "Don't let them see you sweat," she used to repeat, quoting something from the Internet.

A week later, Ellie arranged to fly to St. John's on business, a totally justifiable trip as the legislature was due to open in a few days.

She planned to get in touch with Lundringham as soon as pos-sible, but it was taking some time for her to build her courage. She was a nervous wreck and she worried about how Denis would react to her call. But she worked hard at not letting her nervous-ness show. She went about her business at her office in St. John's as though everything was normal.

CHAPTER 51:
Meeting Mose

The court procedure began with James filing an application to be heard before three judges of the Newfoundland Court of Appeal.

I was told that normally hearings at the Court of Appeal are restricted to submissions by lawyers on questions of law. But because of new evidence, James, with the concurrence of the Crown prosecutor, put a motion before the court asking that expert witnesses be heard in this case.

Since the application identified new evidence, the judges did not push back in any big way and granted the motion, clearing the way for Dr. Lau to testify. This also meant that the Crown could call witnesses to challenge the claims that Lau would make. They left the door open for Olav himself to testify as well, if he and his legal counsel felt that was necessary.

In granting the motion the court scheduled the application hearing and set the date four weeks away.

I called Mandy and told her the date for the hearing. She said she would come to St. John's for that. We also took the time to make a plan to go and visit Mose at the pen in New Brunswick. We thought it would be best to do the visit almost immediately.

James felt that it would be helpful if he also came on the trip to visit Mose. We agreed to that.

* * *

We met Mandy at the Fredericton airport and had dinner that evening at a hotel downtown. The drive the next morning would be about an hour and a half. We were set to meet Mose at ten o'clock.

At dinner we talked about what lay ahead and James advised that I should be prepared to testify, although we would not make that decision right there and then.

James told us not to breathe a word, but that Major Crimes was looking very closely at the role that Eleanor might have played in the murder.

"So much so that they have tapped the telephone landline at her apartment in St. John's," James said.

"Holy shit!" I was taken aback. "Can they do that?"

"The court has already allowed it for a period of thirty days. The legislature is scheduled to re-open next week, so she will be in town for that."

"She may have been an accomplice," Mandy said.

"I am told, and I say this in the strictest confidence," James said, "that Eleanor carried on an affair with Chief Justice Denis Lundringham some years back, before he was appointed to the bench. It went on for a few years. I remember even hearing rumours of it the year I was doing my articles. The talk was out there locally, knowing that Lundringham was a married man."

"Wow," I said. "That woman gets around."

"I presume they are expecting her to make some moves to have some people of significance run interference for her," Mandy suggested. "She could find herself on charges of obstruction of justice, no?"

"Yes, she could," James said.

"Is she stupid enough to take that kind of risk?" Mandy wondered.

260

"Desperate people have been known to do desperate things," James said. "She is, or at least was, a very powerful person in high circles, but I suspect that is waning to a large extent after the media stories that have been out there. But she will use her influence, whatever it might be, to try and achieve her own ends."

"I guess the universe will unfold as it should," I said, quoting *Desiderata*.

We finished up dessert and headed off to our rooms.

* * *

If I thought the police offices in downtown St. John's were cold and unfriendly, they were absolutely rosy compared to the metal environment, clanging doors and razor wire at the maximum security prison where Mose was spending his time.

Armed guards guided us through various security points where we had to surrender our cell phones and any metal objects. They led us to a room that had a table attached to the floor and some very heavy chairs.

The room was devoid of character. It had a large glass window that was one way only—in. Two security cameras, both near the rather high ceiling opposite each other kept watch in the room.

We took seats around the table with Mandy on one side and James and I at either end. They reserved a chair for Mose to sit across from Mandy.

We were given the protocol on the way in that there would be no touching of any kind and no hugs allowed.

We sat waiting for about five minutes. Finally the door opened and two guards escorted Mose in to the room. We all rose to our feet. Mose was a skinny guy with a gaunt face. He looked like he was starving to death.

All this time Mose kept looking at Mandy. It is difficult to describe the look as his eyes met those of his adult daughter for the very first time. It was heart-wrenching. I think Mandy's incredible resemblance to Abby was jarring to him. He was very moved by her presence and I believe he must have felt a painful, haunting love in those moments.

Mose could not hold back tears as he tried to say something. It was difficult to understand what he was trying to communicate at that moment.

"Take your time, Mose," James said. James poured some water from a non-glass pitcher and passed it to Mose in a plastic cup.

Mose did his best to compose himself.

"I hear your name is Amanda Reynolds," Mose said.

Mandy looked at him and smiled.

"Yes, that is my name," Mandy was speaking in a soft voice. "I grew up in Thunder Bay but I live in Toronto now. I am so glad that Olav contacted me and now, here we are."

"I am as well," Mose said looking in my direction.

He made a few comments about how sorry he was that we had to see him under these conditions. Clearly he had tried to clean up as best he could before he came in the room. He was also a little bashful about the couple of scars on his face.

We tried to reassure him that that was the least of our concerns.

"Thank you," he said.

Mose looked from Mandy to me.

"I do want to say to the both of you, though," Mose continued, "that I did not kill your mother. Even though she had gone to another man and allowed you to be adopted, I could never do something like that—certainly not to her, or to anyone for that matter. I always loved her. I am not a killer."

Both Mandy and I looked at each other, then at Mose. The sincerity in his shaking voice was profound.

There was silence for a few moments. We all let the moment sink in.

"So what do you have new to report?" Mose asked looking toward James.

"The Court of Appeal has agreed to hear our application in about two weeks," James said.

"So my future is in the hands of another judge? The record on that has not been too good to date. Denied appeal. Denied bail again and again."

"This time is different. We are going to be in court. We will be presenting new evidence and that makes us optimistic," James said. "But I don't want to lead you down the garden path. Prepare for the worst. You never know how a court might rule."

"Well that is hopeful and depressing at the same time! What are my chances?"

"As I've said, Mose, we are optimistic. At the discovery hearing, the doctors who assessed Olav were excellent in their presentations," James said. "The Crown presented one witness to rebut their evidence, but it was not a strong rebuttal, so that might be a good sign."

"Do I come over to be in the court?"

"No, there is no need, so we won't go through that expense." James said. "We hope the judges will make a quick decision. You have been in here for a big part of your life. The judges understand that justice needs to be swift."

"They have taken away a lot of my life. You got that right," Mose said.

"Two minutes," the guard at the door barked.

"Mose, I will be in touch as necessary, but I will definitely call you the night before we go to court, ok?" James stood as Mose got to his feet to be escorted back to his cell. We all stood once again.

"Okay. Thank you for coming," Mose said, "and thank you for all that you are doing."

I'll never forget the look Mose gave Mandy as he was being led out. It was just so desperate, like a drowning person pleading for a lifeline.

After the door closed, Mandy took a moment. She turned her back to us to dry a tear and compose herself.

Neither of us spoke as we were shown out of that God-awful place.

* * *

The news broke four days before the court hearing into the Mose Strickland wrongful conviction case.

The front-page headline in the city's main newspaper was huge and loud.

Legislature Member Eleanor Rowe Arrested

An old photo of a smiling Ellie, shaking hands at some social gathering, appeared just under the headline.

The story was short on details, merely mentioning that the member of the legislature was arrested on charges of obstruction of justice. There were no specifics on the infraction or how it came about. The story did include, though, that Ellie was released on bail, but considering her a flight risk, the court ordered that she be required to wear an ankle bracelet while she awaited trial.

CHAPTER 52:

A Visit with Rhoda

Sophie and I drove out to the St. John's airport to meet Mandy in the early afternoon before the court hearing.

I had visited Rhoda just two days before and though her health was continuing to fail, she was still managing to cling to life. "Some days better, some days much worse than others," she'd say. She was bedridden for the most part, but was able to get out and move about in a wheelchair now and then.

Rhoda was very interested in what was happening and told me she wanted to hold on as long as she could, partly to see what the outcome would be from the court. That pained me some because her weakening health was clearly evident and I didn't hold out a lot of hope that she would be alive when the judges handed down their decision.

After picking up Mandy, we went straight from the airport to visit Rhoda at the Health Sciences.

She was asleep when we arrived. A nurse gently woke Rhoda and told her she had some company.

She became wide-awake and apologized for being asleep when we arrived.

We all took turns hugging her.

"Oh Mandy, I cannot get over how much you look like your mother," she said. "It's like having her right here."

"Yes, I've seen the pictures and there is a resemblance," Mandy smiled and said.

"A strong resemblance. Abby was very beautiful and so are you."

We had a fun couple of hours with Rhoda. She even told us some more funny Newfoundland stories. Some that included four letter words, which made us all burst into side-slitting laughter.

She loved the arrangement of flowers we brought her, and she opened the box of chocolates and shared those around. Someone brought in four cups of tea and biscuits for each of us.

Rhoda was clearly considering not only Mandy and me as her family, but Sophie too. She talked with Sophie again about Papa Bear and wondered if the family planned to get another dog. Sophie told her that they are waiting to hear from a breeder now, so hopefully they would have another one in the next few months.

Rhoda sure had those two ladies on a pedestal—and that was okay. As far as she was concerned, they were two princesses. I think our visit cheered her so much it made her stronger, because she got out into her wheelchair on her own power so she could sit up at a table with us.

All afternoon, Rhoda sat there with a smile on her face that just glowed. It was such a joy to see.

We were careful not to mention anything about the bishop because we did not know what, if any, contact he was having with her during her illness and we did not want anything to spoil her mood at that moment.

Rhoda wept as the time came for us to leave. She hugged us all and said she loved us. It was a painful moment, but we told her we would come to see here again before Mandy went back to Toronto.

We left and went to our appointment with James to discuss some last minute stuff before the hearing. I did not expect James to make a decision as to whether I would testify until he got a feel for how things were going in the hearing.

CHAPTER 53:

The Hearing

ST. JOHN'S, MAY 10, 2016

St. John's was fog-covered in the morning on the day of the hearing. Fog is almost a tourist attraction for this tough, ancient north Atlantic city. The fog is one of the things we all love about the place. It always brought with it that sense of mystery. And you appreciated the sun more when the fog cleared away.

I was sleeping well and had not had a nightmare since my work with the doctors. That was a promising sign, and maybe I was actually coming out of that PTSD that they suspected was causing them. I was optimistic, but there was still more work I needed to do with them.

I called Mandy and Sophie at seven a.m. We planned to meet at Mandy's downtown hotel for breakfast. It was not far from the building that housed the court.

They were both up and raring to go. Sophie came to pick me up and we headed downtown.

I had made a reservation for the three of us. We invited James, but he chose not to come he said because on days like this he liked to meditate for a time to clear his mind and focus. He also did his workouts in the early morning.

We all met in the hotel restaurant called the Tip of the Iceberg. Its walls had beautiful photos of a multitude of shapes and sizes of icebergs, some that stood in a majestic way near outport communities. There was also fascinating photography of humpback whales breaching and rolling with their fins high in the air.

Mandy remarked on the neat names of the businesses in the city, especially the restaurants and bars.

"There is so much history and culture here," she said. "I've read a lot about the history of this place since our coming in contact, Olav, and it really is what those tourist ads on television say it is."

"Well, your roots are here too," I said. "We know your family is in Thunder Bay, but you also have family here."

Sophie took time to tell Mandy all about her family down the shore and we made a plan to do a quick visit there so Mandy could meet them, once the court hearing was done.

We ate breakfast and laughed some more at Rhoda's jokes. Knowing what her life was like with the bishop, we felt the freedom she was experiencing, but at the same time there came that nagging dread of the toll that cancer was taking on her. Life could be so unfair, but we thanked our gods for having brought us together.

* * *

The courtroom was located in an ancient brownstone building in downtown St. John's. It looked like it was probably constructed in the early nineteenth century. James told me that the grounds just outside the building was where the gallows used to be, back in the hanging days. Each time I would pass the building I would imagine such a structure with crowds of witnesses in bowler hats leaning on walking canes and looking up in horror as some poor soul swung from a rope.

Now that would give a fellow nightmares!

Inside, the room itself had very high ceilings with cathedral like arches. There were wooden panels behind the judges' bench with Latin expressions about justice and fairness carved into them. The bench, which sat well up from floor level, also held the Canadian flag, the provincial flag and even a Union Jack that had probably been there since Newfoundland was a colony of Great Britain. Of course, at the centre of this backdrop was Her Majesty in her 1960's portrait projecting the very picture of law and order.

The fixtures, desks and benches where the public sat, were all made of oak and finished with a dark stain. It had the character of old courtrooms or law offices you might see in movies. The place had to be designed to intimidate, it seemed.

James was completely at home in the building. He seemed to know everything about the law and legal procedure and I expected that he would litigate like the star that I was beginning to consider him to be. I pictured myself some years in the future doing this kind of work.

* * *

The door behind the bench opened and some crier hollered out, "All rise!" as the three judges paraded out to take their seats.

The Honourable Mr. Justice Martin Barnes, the Honourable Madame Justice Connie Beale, and the Honourable Madame Justice Cora Augustine of the Newfoundland Court of Appeal made up the bench that would hear the application submitted by James Joseph in the matter of the first-degree murder conviction of Mose Strickland.

None of them looked very happy to be there. Stern, scowling faces looking down at the lawyers. These did not look like people that you might invite over to your house for a barbecue. Based on what I was seeing, James was going to have to make a pretty compelling case. But that was just my first impression. I could be proven wrong!

Down at the level of the public, James was appearing on behalf of the Society for the Rights of the Wrongfully Convicted, representing Mose. He had an associate with him. It was James's application that the judges would have read before coming into the courtroom.

Mr. Charles Morrison appeared for the Crown. He was the senior counsel in the department reporting to the deputy attorney general. He had a pleasant way about him, and not all stuffy like so many in the business. He didn't seem to think that his robe could heal the sick or cause the lame to walk. He was in his early forties, tall, clean-shaven with dark hair.

Since this was the Court of Appeal, both lawyers were fully gowned with formal dress and tabs. James knew Morrison quite well and they made small talk with each other before the court was called to order.

I looked at James in his lawyer's outfit and could not help but admire how sharp he looked.

I asked Mandy if she had appeared yet in Supreme Court and had she worn this kind of outfit. She said yes she had, and noted with a smile, "There's power in the robe." I wasn't sure what that meant.

"You will know what that means some day in the future," she said.

I noted there were several people present from the media. The newspapers, radio and television had reporters were there, although the cameras were outside the courtroom. This story was about to get a lot of attention, but I wanted to keep as low a profile as possible.

CHAPTER 54:

A Descent into Hell

After her release on bail, Ellie remained at her apartment in St. John's to lie low and wallow in her troubles. She did not want to be back among her constituents having to deal with questions and all the embarrassment that would come with that. She had hired a lawyer in St. John's, though she held out little hope that she could avoid a jail sentence. She simply could not look for the nomination for her seat in the next election and had to accept the fact that her political days were at an end.

She had plenty of money to continue to maintain her apartment in St. John's, so it made sense to stay there out of sight.

Ellie tried to disguise herself as much as she could, even colouring her hair and wearing hats and sunglasses each time she left the apartment, which wasn't often.

She also disconnected her old telephone number from her apartment and installed a new unlisted number. The only two people who knew the number were Travis and her lawyer in St. John's.

Ellie was sealing herself off from the world.

Although relations were strained between Ellie and Travis, she called him and suggested he come into St. John's. She was in need of some company because her spending too much time alone was proving to be damaging to her mental health.

Who else could she talk to but Travis?

She also wanted to hear what people were saying back home and on the ground.

Ellie was only charged with a crime at this point and not convicted, so she was free to hold on to her seat in the legislature. Speculation was rampant in the media though that the premier was about to kick her out of caucus. These stories were depressing her to no end.

Travis said he would advise work the following day that he was taking a leave of absence for a period of time. He said he would fly into St. John's in a few days.

* * *

Unbeknownst to most, Travis had two contacts in the city that he had used on many occasions to supply him with methamphetamines and opioids—fentanyl often being the opioid of choice. Ellie knew this as she had often shared their use, and even paid at times for Travis.

It was not long after he hit the tarmac at the airport in St. John's that Travis paid a visit to his friends, his suppliers. He dropped a thousand dollars that evening.

Their first evening back together in St. John's was just a blur.

CHAPTER 55:

Dr. Lau, Star Witness

May 10, 2016

The Court of Appeal was now sitting with Judges Barnes, Augustine and Beale presiding. The public benches were packed to overflowing.

"Are you ready for an opening statement Mr. Joseph?" It was Judge Barnes speaking for the court.

"Yes, we are my Lord. May it please the court," James began. "This application, my Lord and Ladies, is about justice, or more appropriately we submit, the miscarriage of justice in the matter of the 1997 conviction of Mose Strickland, currently serving a life sentence at a maximum security facility in New Brunswick.

"Our application sets out clear, new evidence that was not available and could not be available at the time of trial in 1997.

"The applicant will show that while the Crown's case went to the jury based only on circumstantial evidence, that in fact there was an eye witness to the murder and it has taken medical and psychiatric expertise to bring that to the attention of the police and the Crown.

"The applicant will show my Lord and my Ladies that after this evidence came to light, searches of properties in Twin Rivers resulted in the retrieval of the murder weapon with proof through DNA analysis.

Olav's Story

"My Lord and Ladies of the bench, Mr. Mose Strickland has spent over nineteen years in a federal maximum security institution. He has had a huge part of his life and freedom taken from him. He has suffered wrongs while in custody that we can never imagine, and yet the real killer has been walking free.

"The applicant also informs the court that Mr. Strickland, while in custody since 1996, has never once admitted to being guilty of the crime for which he is incarcerated—even when such admission may have been helpful in his parole applications. He's never admitted guilt.

"My Lord and Ladies, we appreciate and thank the court for opening this hearing to the testimony of witnesses, and we will bring forward two witnesses that we believe will provide the court with the evidence you need to overturn the 1997 verdict. Thank you, my Lord and Ladies."

James bowed and sat down.

"Thank you, counsellor," Justice Barnes said. "Mr. Morrison, do you have an opening statement?"

"Thank you my Lord and Ladies, may it please the Court," Morrison began. He had a bit of a nasal-like voice. A bit irritating, which kind of canceled out his otherwise welcoming smile and the pleasant way he had about him.

"The Crown offers a brief statement at this time my Lord and Ladies. The Crown will bring forward one witness to challenge the expert evidence that will be presented by the applicant. This will give the court an alternate scientific viewpoint for consideration. Thank you."

Morrison sat and waited for James's next move.

"Mr. Joseph, please call your first witness," Judge Barnes said.

"The applicant calls Sgt. Devon Harris of the forensic unit of the Major Crimes section of the police department."

274

A bailiff opened the door and Sgt. Harris strode in. I hadn't seen him or heard his name before. Whenever James would update me, he would just refer to forensics.

Once seated, someone swore him to the truth and nothing but, and at James's prompting, he proceeded to describe his background and experience to the court. It was impressive. So much so that Justice Barnes asked that a commendation go back to Sgt. Harris's commanding officer on the excellent and forthright summary in the way that he articulated his expertise to the court. That was a gold standard, Judge Barnes said.

"Thank you my Lord," Sgt. Harris nodded his appreciation to the bench.

"Now Sgt.Harris," James said, "please tell the court what you were given following the searches of the properties in Twin Rivers four months ago."

"Yes sir, I was given five bungee cords of various lengths that were retrieved from the searches. These bungee cords are the type with hooks on either end and are strong with considerable elasticity. They are a common tool used for strapping things in place, for example when someone is transporting items in a truck, or a boat, or on a bicycle."

"Go on."

"I was also presented with tissue samples that had been harvested from the body of murder victim Abigail Williams. Samples that were retrieved by exhuming the body."

"Anything else?"

"Yes, I was also given tissue and blood samples harvested, with his permission, from Mr. Mose Strickland."

"What was your assignment, Sergeant?" James asked.

"I was to examine the cords using the DNA process to determine whether either of the cords held any material such as tissue or blood that may have come from the body of the victim, Abigail Williams, and further, to determine if there was any DNA evidence in the cords that matched the profile associated with Mose Strickland."

"What was the result of your examination?"

"We found samples of blood and tissue that were ingrained and preserved in the cord. When I say 'in the cord,' I mean that the samples would have become present at a time when the cord was extended, or stretched. When the cord was returned to its normal length, the closing up of the material on the outside captured and preserved the blood and tissue fibre. It was preserved quite well," Sgt. Harris explained.

"What was the length of the bungee cord from which you harvested the samples?"

"Thirty inches, sir."

"What was the colour of that cord?" James asked.

"It was mainly red with yellow speckles throughout."

James paused for a few moments to let that sink in.

Morrison sat staring straight ahead.

"What did you do next?" James continued.

"We then analyzed the samples retrieved from the cord and compared them to the analysis of the tissue samples from the body that was being carried out by my partner in another lab."

"Please tell the court the result of that analysis," James said.

"Our analysis, which was independently peer reviewed, was that there was one chance in two and a half billion that the samples were not a match."

The judges were all making notes and seemed to be very much engaged in the sergeant's testimony.

"And the matter of whether there was anything in your analysis that matched the Mose Strickland DNA?"

"We did not find anything, sir, on either of the cords."

"Sgt. Harris, did your instructions include information as to where this particular cord was found?"

"Yes sir. It was located in the attic of the Travis Williams residence in Twin Rivers, Labrador."

"Thank you Sgt. Harris. One final question, what did your conclusion say in plain language?"

"That we are certain that the blood and tissue preserved on the bungee cord came from the victim, Abigail Williams," Sgt. Harris told the court.

"Nothing further, my Lord."

"Any cross?" Judge Barnes motioned his head toward Morrison.

"Yes, my Lord," Morrison stood, looking down at his notes. "Sgt. Harris, your work has determined that the particular bungee cord you put under DNA analysis is the murder weapon that was used on the victim, yes?"

"Yes, sir, that is correct."

"But it does not conclude who the person was that would have used this weapon on the victim Abigail Williams, is that correct?"

"Yes sir, that is correct."

"Nothing further, my Lord."

Morrison took his seat.

* * *

"Mr. Joseph, please call your next witness," Judge Barnes instructed.

"The applicant calls Dr. Lynda Lau," James said.

At James's prompting, Dr. Lau took a few minutes after her swearing the oath to inform the court of her academic and professional background, including studies she had researched, authored and published.

"Dr. Lau, you work out of the Student Union building at Memorial University, in Student Health Services, is that correct?"

"Yes sir. That's correct."

"Thank you, Dr. Lau," James said. "Dr. Lau, can you confirm that Olav Williams has been or is a client of yours?"

"Yes, I can confirm that."

"Is Mr. Williams in the courtroom here today?"

"Yes, he is," she said, pointing me out. I stood for a moment.

"What was the nature of your relationship with Mr. Williams? I will call him Olav," James said flashing a smile toward me.

"Olav came to see me about a year ago concerning a number of issues that were troubling him."

"What kind of issues?"

"He told me about recurring night terrors that he had been having since a very early age. He told me about the loss of his mother, Abby Williams, when he was a baby, and of abuse he suffered as a child, from his father, Travis Williams. We also talked about what he considered was his tendency to be somewhat socially dysfunctional," Dr. Lau said.

"Anything else?" James asked.

"After several sessions into our work, he told me that he had a photographic memory. I was very interested in discussing this with him since I, along with Dr. Schumer, had conducted an extensive study into the science of the mind, with memory being a large part of that work."

"How did you follow up with Olav?"

"We tested him for what is called eidetic imagery, or photographic memory."

"Would you describe the test to the court please?"

Dr. Lau went through the test involving the barcode and explained that the test was carried out multiple times. She told the court how they increased the length of time between each of the tests.

"What did you conclude from the tests?"

"Dr. Schumer and I concluded that Olav was exceptionally gifted with a very pronounced form of eidetic memory."

"Dr. Lau can you explain to the court what eidetic memory actually is?"

Looking toward the bench, Dr. Lau said, "Actually we all have eidetic memory in varying degrees. I should qualify that and say all who are not blind, have eidetic memory. For example, we have all experienced looking at something for a few moments and then closing our eyes only to continue to seeing that image against a black background. It may be only for a second or two or a nano-second, but your ability to see that image once you have closed your eyes is very common. It can sometimes be like looking at a negative from a flash camera. That is a form of eidetic memory."

"If we all have it, then what was unique about Olav's memory?" James asked.

"Where it becomes a phenomenon is when someone, as in Olav's case, can register and maintain an image in their brain over long periods of time, like the barcode, and be able to recall it with precise, demonstrable imagery. As though he is calling up a computer file."

"Thank you, Dr. Lau," James said. "So how does all this relate to the death of Abby Williams?"

"The court would know," Dr. Lau said "that at the trial, the case against Mr. Mose Strickland was not based on any evidence from an eye witness present at the time of the murder. The only other person at the scene was a small baby, a year and a half old, that being Olav."

"Can you tell the court what you learned from Olav?"

"He told me that he had retained images of the murder scene— just flashes of memory that would keep coming back to him. He said he could remember the sounds and some of the scenes of what happened at his mother's death."

"What did you do about that?"

"The question then became, not so much that he had, or has an elevated form of eidetic memory, but how far back over his life time did it go? How early in his life did it begin?"

"What did you do next, Dr. Lau?"

"We questioned him some more on his memories of his mother and he described her doing things like singing to him, reading to him, seeing her above his crib. Then he named books that she read to him. Books that, right after her death, his father gathered together and put away in the attic of their house, storing them in a locked trunk. Olav told us that he hadn't seen them since. Even now after they have been recovered through the search warrants, Olav chose not to look in the trunk that was brought to the police headquarters. For emotional reasons."

"If it please the court, my Lord, when the search was executed on the Williams property in Twin Rivers, the police recovered the trunk to which Dr. Lau refers. It contained the books that Olav identified to the doctors and it is set out in a sworn affidavit that the Crown has also seen, and we hereby submit it into evidence."

A clerk walked over to James and he handed her the document.

"Thank you," James said. "Now continuing, Dr. Lau, what did you do next with Olav?"

"After telling us of his recall of his mother's death, Dr. Schumer and I subjected Olav to a semi-hypnotic state that for working purposes we called a trance. In other words, unlike full hypnosis, Olav remained conscious and was fully aware of what he was saying and describing to us."

"Go on."

"Once he was settled and had cleared his mind, we asked him to go to the date and time that his mother was killed. We asked him to describe what was he hearing and seeing."

Dr. Lau went into detail describing the test they carried out that day when I brought back the images and sounds of the murder, noting my description of the murder weapon.

There were emotions starting to come out in the courtroom as Dr. Lau talked. Jackie was among the spectators and she couldn't hold back tears.

"Dr. Lau, did Olav see the person strangling his mother?"

"Yes."

"Did Olav say who it was?"

"Yes, he did. It took us a little while to get it from him. He was in a very emotional state, as one would expect," Dr. Lau said.

"Who did Olav identify as the person who attacked and killed his mother?"

"He identified the person as his father, Travis Williams."

A not so quiet gasp came from Jackie's direction. The judges looked at her but said nothing. In fact, their look seemed to be more of compassion if anything.

"Thank you, Dr. Lau. I have nothing further for this witness my Lord," James said and sat down.

"Mr. Morrison, do you have any questions?"

"Yes, my Lord," Morrison said as he got to his feet. "Dr. Lau, that was indeed very powerful and compelling testimony, and I thank you for it."

"Thank you, sir."

Dr. Lau was a pro in the witness box.

"Dr. Lau, in the research that you have conducted have you ever come across cases where eidetic memory has existed in persons where it manifested at an early age as in the case of Mr. Williams?"

"Yes, we have," Dr. Lau said. "The application cites at least two cases of children, one born in Poland and a set of identical twins with eidetic memory born in Mexico. In both cases the children were born in the 1950s, and once it was diagnosed they were followed for years by teams of doctors."

"What did those cases determine?"

"That eidetic memory is measurable and scientifically provable, and that it can be life-long and sustaining." Dr. Lau said.

"By that you mean it is present at a very early age as in the case of Mr. Williams?"

"Yes, it has been shown to begin even at the age of one."

"But you would agree Dr. Lau, that cases are extremely rare, yes?"

"Yes, I agree with that."

"Perhaps one in a billion?"

James objected to this question. "My Lord," James said, "while the science of eidetic memory is, as Dr. Lau said, measurable and provable, it is not an exact science. So to expect the doctor to put a precise measurement on how frequent it appears in the global population, we submit, would be misleading the court."

"I agree," Judge Barnes said. "Please continue Mr. Morrison."

"Now, Dr. Lau," Morrison said, "while I am not accusing Mr. Williams of fabricating anything here, could his memory have been influenced in any way, by say, someone telling him about the things he recalled such that he could form images? Could he have developed the images and sounds based perhaps on newspaper stories, or court records and the like?"

"Mr. Williams took pains to try and blot out everything associated with the death of his mother. He has made that clear in sworn statements to the court being fully aware of the crime of perjury," Dr. Lau said. "For example, he was even able to describe in detail, items of dress and jewelry that his mother wore as she was being buried. His descriptions were matched perfectly when the body was exhumed.

"So while it seems almost too fantastic to be true, and I understand that there are skeptics out there, we must appreciate that the brain is a very complex organ.

"Eidetic memory has been proven to be a real thing, so why would it come into its own only in an adult brain, or an adolescent brain, or a seven-year-old brain and not in a baby's brain. Where do you draw the line?

"With respect, the cases we researched and our work with Olav proves that it can manifest itself such that recallable images and sounds are imprinted on the brain even at the age of one."

"Thank you, Dr. Lau. "I have nothing further, my Lord."

"Any re-direct Mr. Joseph?"

"No, my Lord."

"Mr. Joseph, will you be calling any further witnesses?" Judge Barnes asked.

"No, my Lord."

"The court will take a fifteen minute recess. I would like to see both counsel in chambers, please," Judge Barnes said and hit the desk with his gavel.

In his office, Judge Barnes asked James and Morrison if either of them had any objection to his calling me to the witness box just to do a brief test to show my recall ability. The judges were concerned about whether this might contribute to further traumatizing me. They did not want to do it if being in the witness box presented any risk like that to me.

James told the judges that the doctors had diagnosed me with PTSD and that this condition was what was contributing to my night terrors and my insecurities. But in recent months, James said, I had been showing improvement, especially after the recall session with them.

Both counsel answered in the negative. No objection.

The judge asked James if he knew whether I had read the Bible. James answered yes, that I had. He said he had even done a couple of tests with me himself, using the Bible, and I aced it each time.

"Well, we would like to see this thing close up ourselves," Judge Barnes declared.

Once James and Morrison left the Judges' chambers, Morrison requested a private meeting with James and the two went into a small office.

"What's up?" James asked.

"A couple of things," Morrison said. "In light of this new evidence, and the relevant circumstances of the case, the judges are going to consider everything on balance of probabilities. Given that, I think they will vacate the verdict, resulting in the release of your client."

"Okay. We will see," James said. "Dr. Lau did offer some very compelling testimony, and although the DNA still does not prove Travis Williams held the weapon, it does prove that Mose was not the perpetrator. So likely, yes, I'd be surprised if he doesn't walk."

"So from a constructive standpoint, everything is pointing to Travis as the killer," Morrison concluded.

"Agreed."

"Now that I have said all this, I have decided not to call my rebuttal witness, the one who you met in discovery. So here is what I suggest. That we make a joint submission accepting the evidence presented by the expert witnesses, including the DNA, and we submit that the court vacate the jury's verdict."

James shook hands with Morrison and thanked him for suggesting the approach. They left the small conference room and returned to the courtroom.

* * *

"Mr. Morrison, please call your witness," Judge Barnes ordered.

"My Lord, the Crown has since chosen not to call any witnesses," Morrison advised.

"Thank you Mr. Morrison." Judge Barnes looked a bit surprised and took a moment.

"Now before we get to closing statements," Judge Barnes continued, nodding to James and Morrison, "I would like to ask Mr. Williams to step forward."

I stood and moved to the desk where James and his associate were seated. James had prepared me for this.

"Mr. Williams, this has been a fascinating day of testimony," Judge Barnes said. "Now let me begin by saying how truly sorry we are for the trauma you suffered over the years after the loss of your mother and what must have been a painful childhood."

"Thank you, my Lord," I said.

I suspect I will be saying those words a lot in the future.

"I understand you are a student at the university here, at Memorial?"

"Yes, I am doing my undergrad here, my Lord."

"What are you going to do your graduate work in, if I might ask?" Judge Barnes asked.

"I have been accepted for law school at Dalhousie University in Halifax, my Lord," I said.

"Very good, young man. All three of us judges up here graduated from that school."

"Then I will be in good company," I said with a smile.

"Let me offer a different way of putting that Mr. Williams. I think we are the people who will be in great company with you among the alumni," Judge Barnes said with a smile. The other two judges nodded their agreement.

I think I might have been wrong in my first impressions of this bench!

"Would you mind, Mr. Williams, if you came up here to give us a demonstration of that memory of yours? This is optional, as the three of us are not eager to contribute in any way to further traumatizing you. So we'll not ask you to swear an oath."

"Of course my Lord, I don't mind that at all."

I walked up front and sat in the witness box. I looked back at the courtroom, toward James, then to Sophie and Mandy, and then at Jackie. From the perspective of the witness box, I got a better appreciation of just how many people were in attendance. Standing room only. A lot of media, it seemed.

"Now Mr. Williams, I am told that you have read the Holy Bible from cover to cover," Judge Barnes said.

"Yes, I have my Lord. The King James Version."

"And that's the one I am using," Judge Barnes said. "Now, can you recite for the court the first two verses of Psalm 139?"

"Yes my Lord," I said, looking toward the bench and taking a moment. "The first verse reads, quote—*O Lord, thou hast searched me, and known me,* and the second, *Thou knowth my down-sitting and mine uprising, thou understandth my thoughts from afar.* Unquote."

The judge shook his head in amazement.

I looked toward Mandy and Sophie. They were smiling contented smiles.

"Okay," Judge Barnes said, leafing through the Bible, the one that the court used to swear oaths. How about reciting verse twenty-five from chapter twenty-one of the Gospel of John."

"It reads, my Lord, quote—*And there are also many other things that Jesus did, that which, if it should be written every one, I suppose that even the world itself could not contain the books that should be written.* Unquote."

Silence in the courtroom. James sat there looking at me with a pleased look on his face.

"One more Mr. Williams. Verse eight of chapter one of the Book of Revelation, do you know how that reads?" Judge Barnes asked.

I looked toward the bench, then out over the crowded courtroom. Jackie, Sophie, Mandy, Drs. Lau and Schumer, and James were all looking up at me, supporting me and cheering me on in silence. Crown prosecutor Morrison sat there shaking his head slightly.

"My Lord, it reads quote—*I am Alpha and Omega, the beginning and the ending, saith the Lord, which is, which was, and which is to come, the Almighty.* Unquote."

Applause broke out in the court. The judges let it go on for a little while. It was the sweetest of moments that will live in my heart forever.

Finally Judge Barnes tapped his gavel and said, "Order, please."

"Mr. Williams, that is the most incredible display of recall ability that I have ever witnessed."

"Thank you, my Lord."

"It is phenomenal young man. You may return to your seat now. Take the best possible care of that brain of yours," Judge Barnes said. "I guarantee that it will serve you well in years to come. Thank you on behalf of the court."

I bowed to the bench and returned to my seat, the bow being another of James's protocol pointers.

* * *

When the court returned, James was asked to submit closing comments.

He rose to his feet.

"Before we do, should it please the court, I believe my friend opposite would like to address the bench," James said.

Judge Barnes nodded. "Go ahead Mr. Morrison."

Morrison got to his feet.

"My Lord and Ladies of the bench, in light of the evidence today, that is, new evidence which was not available at trial, the Crown sees no alternative but to join with the applicant in its submission that the jury verdict in the Mose Strickland conviction be vacated. Thank you my Lord."

A rustle among the spectators in gallery.

"Thank you, Mr. Morrison. Any further comment Mr. Joseph?"

"The applicant wishes to thank the court for its due diligence in bringing this hearing about in a timely way, my Lord. We also want to thank the Crown for joining in this final submission," James continued. "The evidence heard today stands alone. It speaks for itself, and the applicant submits that the court would be on solid evidentiary ground, my Lord, to move to set aside the

Mose Strickland verdict forthwith. Such days as these rarely come around my Lord and my Ladies, and I have had the honour of working with my client in this effort to right this serious miscarriage of justice. Thank you, my Lord and Ladies of the bench."

James bowed and resumed sitting.

Applause broke out again. This time not quite as long, but the judge had to use his gavel again to bring the court back to order.

"I want to thank both counsel for their work leading up to this hearing, as well as the witnesses who brought forth their testimony," Judge Barnes said. "We will adjourn now and the court will be in touch with both counsel once we have reached our decision."

The gavel swung once again.

CHAPTER 56:

Waiting

James accompanied us as we left the courtroom. Outside at the entrance to the court, several television cameras were set up, with reporters pointing microphones. James went and spoke briefly to the media saying only that we now await the decision, and that we felt we had a good day in front of the Court of Appeal.

The sun was setting and the breeze blowing off the harbour had his hair, tabs, and robe flickering this way and that. He was such a natural. I stood in awe of the guy who came from a culture whose people, only sixty odd years ago, were prevented by federal law from even hiring a lawyer, let alone practice as one!

"There is not much more we can say until we hear the judges' decision," James told the reporters. "I am sure we will have more to say at that time. Thank you, ladies and gentlemen."

James walked away from the gaggle of microphones and back to us to lead us away from the building.

I took some time to talk with Jackie as we walked in the same direction. She seemed to be a bundle of nerves.

"I am very proud of you, Olav," Jackie said. "What you have done is truly brave. Heroic even."

'Thank you," I said. "I hope that we were able to persuade the judges."

"I am hopeful," Jackie said.

"How long are you staying in town?" I asked her.

"Until I get to hear the decision from the court, however long that takes," she said. She gave me the number of a relative of hers where she was staying while in St. John's and I promised to call her as soon as I found out when the decision was coming down.

We hugged and went on our separate ways.

* * *

The following morning, Mandy, Sophie and I met again for breakfast at Mandy's hotel. Sophie and I both had a class at eleven.

"If we get a call early that the decision is ready to be released, it should be a good sign," Mandy said. "If it drags on and on over days perhaps, that won't look too promising."

"I agree," Sophie said. "What does the fact that the Crown joined with James on the final submission mean? Well, I know what it means I guess, but how much weight is that likely to carry in their decision?"

"It should carry a lot of weight," Mandy said. "The joint submission is pretty much an admission on the part of the Crown that there has been a miscarriage of justice, wouldn't you say Olav?"

"That would be my interpretation of the move," I said.

We finished up our breakfast and made a plan to connect after our classes and pay a visit to Rhoda.

* * *

Rhoda was wide-awake and pumped when we got to visit her in the early afternoon at the Health Sciences.

She said she had been following the news reports about the hearing. She noted that one of the media reported, *there were several stars that appeared before the Court of Appeal today, but the brightest among them had to be young Olav Williams, the son of the Abigail Williams, the victim.* My grandson, she said!

She looked at me with the biggest smile.

"You are such a star!" Rhoda gushed. "They reported that you even brought about a round of applause from the people in the courtroom. My heavens, I could never be made more proud."

We had another fun afternoon with Rhoda. We had tea and we played some cards. She had an old twenty-nine-shaped cribbage board in a drawer, so we were able to play partners—Rhoda and me against Mandy and Sophie. Everyone knew the game. We finished two games and were just starting to deal for the third when my phone rang. I picked it up. It was James on the other end.

"Get down here," he said, "the judges are about to release their decision."

That was quick. A good sign?

We had to hurry and move out. I sent a short text to Jackie and followed up with a call to her. She was on her way. Quick hugs all around with Rhoda and we were out the door.

As I was exiting the room, I looked back at my grandmother.

She was smiling and had two of her fingers held up in the "V" formation.

Sir Winston Churchill's "V" for victory sign!

I smiled, threw a kiss, and waved back to her.

CHAPTER 57:

Twin Rivers, Labrador

FEBRUARY 26, 1996, FIVE-THIRTY P.M.

Travis and Ellie left the town offices together on the evening of
February 26, 1996. Travis was driving her home from the meeting
in the boardroom. She was in the passenger seat of his vehicle. In
order to get to Ellie's he had to drive up Groswater Street and past
his house to drop Ellie off at her's.

"What the fuck is this?" Travis said. As the two got closer to
the Williams residence, they could see the school bus was parked
by Travis's house. Everyone knew that Mose was the driver of the
only bus in town.

Travis expected the worst. Something was still going on
between Abby and Mose. His blood pressure rose and he felt a
raging anger.

"Park around the corner," Ellie ordered.

Ellie and Travis had continued their covert relationship since
it had started the previous fall in St. John's at the municipalities
convention. But over the past couple of months their love affair
had taken on a whole new dimension that involved a sinister plan.

I often asked myself why did Travis not simply file for divorce.
There were probably a couple of reasons that he didn't. He knew
that Abby would demand alimony and child support and he would
most likely lose his house. He could afford none of those things.

The other thing was the power that Eleanor wielded. She convinced him that they could orchestrate Abby's demise when an opportunity arose, and blame it on someone else. And politically speaking, she was very well connected. That had to help!

Travis was easily led, being blinded by love and the perception of Eleanor's power.

They came to the conclusion that the only solution was that, quite simply, Abby had to die.

Once parked out of sight, but where they could keep an eye on the bus, Ellie took control of the situation. They had to act fast.

She looked at him straight in the eyes and spoke firmly and with authority.

"We are never going to get an opportunity like this again," she said. "The time has come and here is what you are going to do."

Ellie searched her bag and brought out a bungee cord. She said she used those things all the time for strapping things on her bike, keeping doors open and stuff.

"I am going to leave now and walk home from here," she said. "As soon as Mose pulls away in the bus, you are going to park in your driveway and go in the house, and you know what you have to do."

She instructed Travis that once the deed is done, "Get to the store and buy something." The cogs in Ellie's mind were turning at the speed of light. "That will be evidence on paper that you were at the store. Then get back to the house and call the police," she said. "Do you have all that straight?"

Travis nodded. He was not hesitant about what lay ahead. After all he was a war veteran.

Ellie left to walk home.

A minute later, at twenty five to six, Mose drove away in the bus.

Travis, parked around the corner only seconds away, pulled into his driveway and entered the house with the bungee cord.

CHAPTER 58:

False Crutches

ST. JOHN'S, NEWFOUNDLAND

Travis, with Ellie under disguise, managed to venture out in the city a couple of times for groceries, or the newspaper, but not much else.

Ellie had a treadmill at the apartment so she could continue her running. Travis didn't like to run.

He would leave the house after dark every three nights or so to meet his suppliers downtown in an alleyway, near the war memorial.

Ellie kept supplying him the money he needed for his transactions.

They would routinely get wasted every night, blotting out all their cares but becoming mainliners in the process. Sometimes it would be Adderall that they would crush and sniff. Sometimes it would be alcohol.

During the daytime they'd argue and scare each other about what was likely to happen to them. Travis at times threatened Ellie with violence, but he managed to restrain himself and not act on his impulses. He could not afford to have a battery charge laid against him with everything else going on.

They both cringed every time they heard a siren going down the street, expecting police to show up at their door in the next few moments. It was simply terror and their nerves were shattered into a million pieces.

Both were following reports in the media about the hearing at the Court of Appeal and each time new information broke they would listen or read, while sweating like hell.

Ellie's menopausal situation also complicated matters to no end. "Fuck these hot flashes!" she would scream and strip down, darting off to open several windows. The menopausal thing was enough to drive her completely off the deep end, let alone the charges she had against her and her loss of prestige. Now her drug addiction piled on top of everything else had her smothering.

Neither of them were eating or paying any attention to getting reasonable nutrition in their diet. It was all strong coffee, or Pepsi, day in and day out.

Ellie, overcome by this lack of nutrition and all her other pressures, fainted one day while on her treadmill. Travis heard the crash and found her curled up unconscious on the floor in the corner of her workout room with her nose bleeding and the treadmill still running.

He brought in tissues for her nose and a warm, wet facecloth that he put to her forehead. She came around wondering what happened.

"You fainted, I think. Maybe you are low on protein," Travis said. "I can make some eggs if you promise to eat them."

"Yes, I will do that."

Travis led her to the couch where she lay down with a cushion under her head. He opened the windows and put a thin comforter over her.

She dropped off to sleep right away and forgot about the eggs.

She woke about four o'clock in the afternoon, her head all fuzzy and aching from where she hit it in her fall.

Travis made a trip to the war memorial just after Ellie awakened, even though it still wasn't dark. He had to risk it.

About an hour later they both got to shooting up again, and the world began to seem more bearable to them.

CHAPTER 59:
The Decision

Sophie, Mandy and I met James in the hallway just outside the courtroom where a lot of media had already gathered. I noticed some reporters eyeing the three of us as we walked up and huddled with James.

The area was also flooded with security, and armed police officers walking about in bulletproof vests.

I guess it was to be expected since there was a high level of interest from the public in the case. A miscarriage of justice somehow always seems to get the attention of the person in the street, what with Donald Marshall Jr.'s and David Milgaard's wrongful conviction cases. They brought national and international attention. I was expecting that interest in the Mose Strickland case would extend far beyond Newfoundland's borders.

"They've scheduled the court to resume in twenty minutes from now," James told us.

Sophie and Mandy went on in and took their seats where they had sat during the hearing. I thought I'd go out on the steps and wait for Jackie to arrive.

While I waited outside, I noticed a fellow smoking and pacing back and forth and shooting glances at me. He was in his mid-fifties. Average height, very fit, skinhead. Finally he walked up to me and asked if I was Trance Williams's son. It was the first time I think I ever heard someone else call him Trance. That could mean only one thing. They had served together in Desert Storm.

"Yes, I am," I said.

"I am a veteran of the Gulf War and knew your father at that time. We were in the same regiment there together."

"I see."

"You seem to have no heart or soul trying to pin a murder on your father," he hissed. "You need to be taught some fucking lessons, kid. Trance served his country and saved lives, including mine! He doesn't deserve this nonsense that you people are making up against him!"

"I don't agree with you. Serving your country is one thing but a domestic murder is quite a different matter."

"And what are you basing that shit on? Something you saw as a baby?" he said. "Who the fuck do you think will believe that?"

His voice was raised now. Butterflies entered my stomach.

"I guess we will soon find out," I said.

"Yes, we will," he said, "and if the crooks in the court system can do one thing right they will fire this case in the garbage!"

He was talking very loud now, up close and in my face. A few people stood around watching what was happening.

I also noticed two police officers nearby who were keeping an eye on the man.

This guy got pretty bold and started screaming more and swearing at me. Suddenly, he raised his hand to either hit me or give me a push. I put my arms up to shield myself. Just as I did the two police officers, wasting no time, came up behind him. They each had one hand on their sidearm. The officers grabbed him and yanked him away from me. In seconds they had his hands cuffed behind his back and were walking him down the steps as he continued shouting obscenities.

Very much to my relief, they led him to a paddy wagon and drove away.

It was a close call but it only heightened my sense of how much people were impassioned by the case. My heartbeat that was pumping in my ears finally settled back to normal, and I realized how lucky I'd been that those two police officers were on the scene!

A couple of minutes later, Jackie arrived. I greeted her without mentioning the incident, and we headed in toward the courtroom.

* * *

"All rise." There was the court crier again.

The room was packed to overflowing.

Judge Barnes cracked his gavel and called the court to order. He looked down where the lawyers were sitting to make sure all were in attendance. "Now before we announce our decision," he began, "I want to note that tensions and emotions have been running more than a little high in the case before the court. In fact, a moment ago, I was told by the head of security, that Mr. Williams," the judge looked toward me, "you were verbally assaulted and nearly physically assaulted a few minutes ago outside the building. Are you okay Mr. Williams?"

I stood and addressed the bench. "Yes, my Lord. It was a sobering experience but I am fine and I do want the court to know that I am very thankful for the swift action of the two police officers, both of whom acted very quickly to take care of the matter. Thank you, my Lord."

James, Jackie, Mandy and Sophie all looked back at me with a puzzled looks on their face. I gave them the thumbs up and mouthed, "It's okay, fill you in later."

"Okay thank you Mr. Williams, and I will ensure your message gets back to the police officers and their superiors," the judge said. "Now let me continue." Judge Barnes elevated his voice. "I am going to say this just once and as firmly as I can. If any person, ANY PERSON, is found to intimidate ANY of the witnesses in this case, or their families or their legal counsel, now or in the future, they will be held responsible and dealt with in the strictest manner and to the fullest extent of the law. Newfoundland justice has zero tolerance for that type of thing. ZERO TOLERANCE." He lifted his left hand with his pointer finger extended. "I want to impress that upon everyone who is listening."

The judge's voice boomed out over the audience. I sat and inwardly applauded him.

The courtroom became pin drop silent.

"Now," Judge Barnes continued. "In the matter of the application from the Society for the Rights of the Wrongfully Convicted, in the case of the first degree murder conviction of Mose Strickland—represented here today by counsellor, James Joseph."

Both James and Charles Morrison stood at their tables looking up at the bench, awaiting the decision.

"This panel unanimously finds *for* the applicant," Judge Barnes stated.

The court broke out in shouts and applause. He had to use his gavel to bring it back to order.

I looked at Jackie. She had her hands and a handkerchief up to her face. Both Mandy and Sophie hugged and wept.

"Order please," Judge Barnes said. "This court finds that the applicant has made out its case and that verdict from the first degree murder trial in the death of Abigail Williams is hereby set aside. Mr. Mose Strickland is to be released from custody, forthwith."

Another round of applause. The judges did not seem to mind the cheering.

"Order please," Judge Barnes said again. "At this time, the court is also issuing a warrant for the arrest of Travis Williams of Twin Rivers, Labrador, to stand trial for the murder of Abigail Williams. This warrant takes effect as of this moment."

Applause.

Once the court settled down, Morrison addressed the bench on the question of whether there'd be any bail conditions associated with the release.

"No bail conditions," Judge Barnes proclaimed. "This innocent man has suffered long enough. He is free."

The judge brought down his gavel.

"This court is adjourned."

* * *

The media was all over the story. It was a frenzy outside the court.

They got a short comment out of Morrison to say that the new evidence could lead to only one conclusion and that had resulted in a good day for justice in Newfoundland.

Most questions were reserved for our lawyer, James Joseph—the man of the hour.

He explained that he could not be happier with the decision and complimented the judges for their level of diligence.

"This is a good day for justice in this province and indeed in the country. The decision is firm and it is clear, and I could not be happier for those around me who have suffered so much trauma over all these years," James said. "I believe they can now finally have some sense of peace and closure."

"Mr. Joseph," one of the reporters said, "some folks are calling you the star counsel on this achievement. What do you say to that?"

"With respect, I am not the star," James said. "While I appreciate the compliment, the real stars throughout this whole process have been Olav Williams and his doctor, Dr. Lau."

Man, I am seeing a side of James now that is clearly another unique skill of his. A communicator better than most politicians!

"Mr. Joseph, do you expect that a public inquiry will be held in this matter?"

"I would be very disappointed if there weren't a public inquiry," James commented. "I believe the attorney general has a duty to ensure that this wrongful conviction is given a full public airing and that there are reparations made to Mr. Strickland. There will be more to come on that. Thank you ladies and gentlemen."

James walked back toward me where I was standing with Jackie, Mandy and Sophie.

"I am pretty sure they want to hear from one or two of you," James said.

"Mandy and Jackie, would you want to speak to them?" I asked. "It would be most appropriate."

The two women looked at each other.

"Yes, I'd be okay with that," Jackie said. Mandy nodded and they headed toward the bank of microphones.

James went up first and introduced the reporters to Mose's mother, Jackie Strickland, and his daughter, Mandy Reynolds.

The media group was very respectful and quiet.

The first reporter addressed Jackie.

"Ms. Strickland, you must be very happy today with this decision concerning your son."

"Yes, I am. It has been a long and rough road for him, but thankfully he can now come home where he belongs."

There were tears in her eyes.

"I've held out hope all these years for a day like this," Jackie continued, "and I believe I am going to have bruises from pinching myself to see if it is real, or whether I am dreaming. It's a beautiful day."

"You are definitely not dreaming Ms. Strickland," another reporter said. "Mandy, what are you feeling today?"

"Relief," she said, "I am relieved that Mose is now free. His name is cleared and he will be forever absolved of this crime. I am so thankful to my brother, Olav, and his girlfriend, Sophie O'Brien, for their bravery, their commitment and strength.

Honestly, without them we would not be where we are today and Mose would still be incarcerated. And of course we have to thank our lawyer, James Joseph, and his team for their hard work and diligence."

"Mandy, the Court of Appeal took some liberties in hearing this case, such as allowing witnesses where normally that doesn't happen in Court of Appeal hearings. They also had an informal chat during the hearing with Olav. What do you think of that?"

"I am a lawyer in Toronto. Everything I have studied and seen tells me that it is very rare that a panel of judges will come down to earth in the way that this panel has. They are true jurists in every sense of the word, and I suggest that new and up and coming judges across the country would do well to take some lessons from this display of justice here in Newfoundland today."

"Ms. Strickland, when do you expect to see your son?"

"Very soon. Mr. Joseph, Mandy and I will be travelling to Fredericton on a flight tonight, and we will be driving straight from the airport to meet Mose and bring him home. Thank you."

"Congratulations everyone," a reporter said.

CHAPTER 60:

"Come to Me"

It was getting late in the day so Sophie and I decided we would go downtown for a celebratory dinner. James, Jackie and Mandy were already in the air, heading for Fredericton.

Sophie had a glass of wine—blueberry, from Newfoundland's famous Rodrigues Winery in Whitbourne. I stuck to Perrier water.

We were just into the main course when my phone rang. I didn't recognize the number but it was a local exchange.

I answered. It was someone calling from the Health Sciences, from palliative care.

"Is this Mr. Olav Williams?"

"Yes, it is."

"Mr. Williams I am very sorry to have to tell you this but your grandmother Rhoda Peters has passed away."

I must have gone pale by the look that Sophie gave me. I felt the blood leave my face and my whole body began quivering.

"We went to her room a few minutes ago and she appears to have died in her sleep. We found an envelope that she was holding in her hand, addressed to you, Mandy and Sophie. We will hold it here for you to pick up, Mr. Williams."

"Thank you," I said.

"Again I am very sorry to have to deliver this news."

"I appreciate your calling."

I looked at Sophie. She knew what the news was going to be.

"Rhoda is gone," I said. "She died in her sleep a short time ago."

Neither of us said anything. There was nothing to say.

I sent a text to Mandy but she was on the plane and probably would not get it for an hour or more. I told her to call me when she lands.

By this time Sophie and I had lost our appetites and we explained what had happened, to the servers.

"Oh I am so sorry to hear that," one of them said. "Please, do what you have to do and don't worry about this."

We got up and left the restaurant.

As we walked out to the parking lot, my thoughts went to a vision of my mother standing in a glow of light just as when I saw her at Quidi Vidi Lake. Her arms are outstretched and with that beautiful smile she says to her mom, Rhoda, "Come to me." It was a comforting thought. There was pain ahead that we would have to endure, but Rhoda was now free of pain and at peace. Her journey complete.

CHAPTER 61:

Mose and the Light of Day

Metal prison doors clanged and echoed through the prison. It was about midnight. Mose was pretty used to the sounds and had somehow managed to tune them out most of the time.

The heavy, steel-toed boots of the guards clicked and thumped up and down the hallways all day long.

Mose was still awake when one of the guards called his name.

"Strickland!"

"Yes," Mose said, sitting up.

"Get dressed Mose. You need to come to the front area to meet some people," the guard told him.

There were two guards. One of them keyed in a security code that allowed the cell door to slide open.

He pulled on his prison outfit and splashed a bit of water in his face.

"I'm ready, lead the way," Mose said.

Mose felt a spring in his step as they walked through long hallways leading to the main entrance of the prison.

The guards opened the last metal door that they needed to pass through before he could see who was waiting for him.

When he stepped into the lobby area of the front entrance, he was greeted with applause and cheers from his mother and from Mandy and James.

Mose got the message. He was being released! He didn't know whether to laugh or to cry.

Jackie and Mose embraced in a hug that seemed to go on forever. But he saved his biggest hug for his daughter Mandy.

"I'm sorry I'm not dressed for this moment," he said.

"Not a requirement," James said. "This is your moment. You can dress which ever way you want!"

"Is it real? Or am I living a dream?" Mose said. "I cannot believe this is happening."

"Pinch yourself," Mandy said with a smile. "It is very real."

Jackie was so overcome that she was stuck for words. She kept drying her eyes and smiling at her son.

"You're coming with us," Jackie finally managed to say. "Home with us!"

Mose, still in a bit of a daze, just nodded his head.

"We will have a bit of paperwork here at the office before you can collect your things and say goodbye to this place," James told him. "I will be there with you, as I will likely have to witness some documents."

A guard led James and Mose to the warden's office. The hour was late but the warden needed to be there for the clearance report.

Not long after, Mose, accompanied by James, Mandy and his mother, who held his arm, headed to the main gate and walked toward his freedom.

* * *

Epilogue

Sophie, Mandy and I went by the funeral home on the day of the wake. It was there that I had picked up the envelope that the nurse from palliative care told me about—the one that Rhoda was holding in her hands at the time of her death.

I read it aloud to Mandy and Sophie.

My Dearest Children.

I am writing this just after I heard the news about the decision from the court. I am proud beyond words. Without the three of you, justice would not have been done today. I know that Abby would be glowing with pride and she probably is, looking down on you from above.

You will never know the joy that the three of you brought me even though our time together was short. I would live a full life again if I could, just to have the chance to savour our moments together one more time.

Please do not be sad for me. Remember God is good. All things that happen are meant to happen. Like that song, 'Que sera sera, whatever will be, will be."

Mandy, Olav and Sophie, I love each of you and God loves you. Promise to be good to each other and be good to yourselves.

I am forever your loving grandmother and friend,

Rhoda
St. John's
Newfoundland

Her handwriting was a little shaky at times, but all her words were clear and legible.

From the language in the letter, it seemed she knew that her time had come.

We paid our last respects. I touched her on the cheek and said a silent prayer.

The three of us stayed around for the two-hour wake. We had coffee and Francine introduced us to several people, including the bishop. He himself looked to be in frail health but he did manage to have some polite words for Mandy and me.

He thanked us for coming. That was it.

Francine told us that the body would be cremated so if we had any requests we should let her know. I told her I wanted some of Rhoda's ashes. I planned to take them back to Twin Rivers to sprinkle them on Abby's grave.

Just before the wake concluded, we were approached by someone who introduced himself as Robert Westphal. He asked if we were Olav, Mandy and Sophie.

He offered his condolences.

"I am going to need you at my office downtown as soon as the funeral is over tomorrow."

"Okay," I said.

"I understand that the funeral is at eleven a.m. so can we meet in my office at two-thirty?" Robert suggested.

We all looked at each other and nodded. He gave each of us his business card.

"I will see you then," he said. "Again, I am very sorry about your grandmother."

Epilogue

*　*　*

The law offices of Westphal, Thomas was in another huge stone building not too far from the Court of Appeal. There were three floors, each with suites of law offices, different firms on different floors. Westphal, Thomas was on the top level.

The elevator door opened right in the reception area where we were greeted by a young man on the front desk.

It was about two-twenty p.m. The fellow showed us down a hallway to another receptionist who worked outside a door that had "Robert Westphal, Partner" written on it.

The receptionist offered us coffee and asked us to sit for a few moments.

"Mr. Westphal won't be long."

We each took a bottle of water, and made small talk about how these last few days were pretty eventful.

Finally the phone on the receptionist's desk buzzed. She answered and said okay, and hung up.

"Mr. Westphal is ready for you now," she said. "Right this way."

The door with Westphal's name on it opened to another room that had filing cabinets, some office equipment, a fridge, a counter with a sink and a coffee machine. Then there was yet another door with his name on it.

When we entered his office proper, he greeted us and asked us to sit at a mahogany boardroom table that could seat twelve people.

Robert sat at the head of the table and placed a legal size envelope with a red wax seal in front of him.

"Rhoda was a longtime client of ours," he began. "We are sure going to miss her. Again, my condolences."

"Thank you," I said.

"As per Rhoda's instructions," he said, "I am to meet with you immediately following her funeral to read you her will."

We all looked at each other. Sophie was looking a little uncomfortable. She was not a blood relative and was not sure why she should be there. She asked the lawyer about it.

"My instructions are to meet with the three of you. She was very specific about this," Robert explained.

"Okay," Sophie said.

We all looked at each other again with, I am sure, the same question. *Was the bishop going to be part of this?*

"Is it just the three of us only, to hear her will?' Mandy asked.

"Yes. Just you three," Robert said. "Anything else before I start?"

I looked at Mandy and Sophie who were shaking their heads.

"No," I said.

He buzzed for the receptionist to come in. A moment later, the door opened and his executive assistant came in with a notebook and sat at the table with us.

"Okay," Robert said, "let's get started. I am opening the envelope now. It contains the last will and testament of Rhoda Peters of St. John's, Newfoundland."

He was reading from the top of the legal size paper.

"I, Rhoda Peters, being of sound mind and body, do hereby bequeath all my assets consisting of both personal and real property, to Amanda Reynolds of Thunder Bay, Ontario, and Olav Williams of Twin Rivers, Labrador to be divided equally between the two said beneficiaries—"

Robert stopped there and noted a codicil that Rhoda had added about six months earlier, naming Sophie O'Brien of Renews-Cappahayden, Newfoundland as a beneficiary as well. The codicil, he said, forms part of the will. The assets Rhoda was leaving to Sophie would be taken off the top and the remainder divided equally between Mandy and me.

The bishop was not named in the will.

Robert continued to the end, reading each paragraph slowly and making sure we understood everything. The last page of the will listed all Rhoda's assets and the very last page was the codicil.

"Let's see what this has to say," Robert said with a smile.

The codicil naming Sophie as a beneficiary bequeathed five hundred thousand dollars to Sophie.

"What?" Sophie mouthed the word in our direction.

The list of total assets in the form of term deposits, investments, GICs, and shares in several technology companies, all amounted to eight point eight million dollars after tax and legal fees.

Deducting off Sophie's share left eight point three million to be divided between Mandy and me.

I nearly fell off my chair. It was like the dizziness effect you get when you spin yourself around and around. It was surreal.

All three of us were totally stuck for words.

Robert was enjoying the moment.

"Congratulations to all three of you," he said. "That is the complete will. We will now begin to work out the details with the banks and get the certification from the court, such that we can get assets moved into your names. It has been an honour to carry out Rhoda's final wishes. Do you have any questions?"

"No," I said. "Unless there is anything for us to sign, we can leave you to your business."

"There is one form there just to certify that I read the will to you today for each of you to sign and that will be it for the day."

We each signed the document, Robert and his assistant witnessed it, and we got up to leave, all of us shaking hands with Robert and his assistant.

The air outside the office was filled with fog, but for us, it had the smell of roses. The three of us stood on the steps of the building and looked at each other in wonder. Did this really happen? All we could do was embrace in one sustained group hug with Rhoda's memory at the centre.

* * *

Mose returned to Dark Harbour with his mother after his release from the pen.

About a year or so after Mose began his life sentence, Jackie discovered that Jennifer Morris, Mose's live-in girlfriend in Twin Rivers, had not been in contact with Mose at all and that she had in fact taken up with a new man who had moved into Mose's house with her.

That was a real slap in the face both to Mose and his mother.

Acting for Mose, Jackie was not going to allow him to be taken advantage of with this shit that Jennifer was pulling, so she devised a plan.

On a trip to visit Mose just after she learned about the new guy that Jennifer dragged home, Jackie had Mose transfer the deed to the property to her. It was a real smart move on Jackie's part. She was no fool when it came to business.

As soon as she had secured the deed in her name, Jackie went to Twin Rivers, knocked on Jennifer's door, showed her the deed and ordered the two of them out of the house and off the property within twenty-four hours. She had negotiated a deal with a buyer in Twin Rivers. The place was sold and the deal was closing in forty-eight hours.

Jackie showed no mercy whatsoever as she pulled the rug out from under Jennifer and her man.

When she told Mose about it later at a visit to the pen, they both got a great laugh. It was at least one little piece of poetic justice for Mose, if nothing else.

Now back in Dark Harbour, Mose felt like a fish out of water much of the time trying to adjust to his new life. He didn't like the stares he would get around the community and he imagined that a lot of people were still blaming him for the murder.

At times, especially at night, he would awaken from nightmares, sweating and hollering. It was clear to Jackie that he was suffering from PTSD and she began thinking about what they could do to make sure he got professional help.

She realized that his loss of sleep brought on by nightmares and his general social dysfunction was nowhere near improving, so she decided to run an idea by him.

Jackie offered that she would rent an apartment for him in St. John's so that he could have better access to mental health services and get counselling. She promised him that she would continue to rent the place and give him an allowance for as long as he needed it to get well. She also offered to lend him the money to buy a secondhand car, which he could pay back when he was in a position to do so.

Jackie also explained that a city like St. John's also offered a degree of anonymity for him, away from the prying eyes of Dark Harbour.

By moving to St. John's she suggested he would also be close to his lawyer, James Joseph, who had agreed to represent him in negotiating a compensation package with the government for his wrongful conviction.

A Commission of Inquiry into the Wrongful Conviction of Mose Strickland had been appointed and identified a number of things that came together to victimize Mose during the whole investigation and legal process. Day after day the media followed the work of the commission and reported on errors and the incompleteness of the investigations. It left the government no option but to assume responsibility for the miscarriage of justice and make reparations.

James advised Mose and his mother that it would be a matter of the attorney general receiving a claim from Mose and then opening negotiations with the government.

There were plenty of precedents for such settlements from various parts of the country, including Newfoundland.

So all things considered, Mose concluded that the idea of the apartment in St. John's made a lot of sense and he decided to take his mother up on it.

Jackie went to St. John's with Mose to help him set up the place. They found a small third floor, one-bedroom flat downtown off Military Road. The place was fully furnished, so there was not a lot of setting up to do. After they got the telephone and cable installed, they went searching for a secondhand car, eventually finding one in "Buy and Sell" for ninety-five hundred dollars, tax in. It was a 2010 Buick sedan.

Mose was starting to appreciate this royal treatment.

After speaking to Jackie, Dr. Lau recommended a counsellor for Mose and this gave Jackie a sense of relief.

Jackie stayed around for a few days cooking meals and shopping in the city.

Although she didn't mention alcohol and drugs to Mose, she was harbouring a concern that someone who's been through what he'd been through will often fall into addictions. She hoped and prayed this would not happen to Mose.

The day before she left to go home she called James Joseph while Mose was out of earshot and asked him to keep a close eye on Mose and to call her immediately if he began to suspect that he might be abusing alcohol or drugs. James promised her he would do that.

What Mose really needed, Jackie thought, was a good, honest girlfriend, but she was not going to play matchmaker. Mose had suffered enough and didn't need his mother interfering in that aspect of his life.

Before returning to Dark Harbour Jackie made sure Mose was equipped with a laptop and cell phone and that he was familiar with texting. But she told him that any sensitive information he might want to share with her, he could only do by a phone call from his secure landline.

Mose took a bit of time to settle himself and drove around the city to locate the addresses of his doctor, where James's office was, and where banks and other services were located.

About three weeks after Jackie went home, James, not wanting too much down time, called Mose and asked him to come to his office to begin drafting his statement of claim against the government. Mose was happy to do that and made an appointment for the following morning at ten o'clock in James's boardroom.

Mose looked forward to the conversation, but his years behind bars in the maximum-security facility meant he had developed a very cynical view of the world and he didn't hold out a lot of hope for much from the government.

Mose was right on schedule the following morning, showing up at James's office five minutes early. Everyone was gracious, offering him coffee and light refreshments.

James escorted Mose into the boardroom and both seated themselves at the boardroom table. There was also a fellow there, a Timothy Slater, who James introduced as an actuary.

"What is an actuary?" Mose asked. "I think I've read the word in magazines but never really knew what they did."

"Actuaries are something like accountants or insurance adjusters," Timothy said. "They work with numbers and look at monetary value over time and assess past, present and future value of money. In your case, we will need to estimate what kind of losses you would have had, for example in salary, over the twenty years that you haven't been able to work because of your wrongful conviction."

"Well, twenty years of back pay would not go astray," Mose said. "If we get that I would be very happy."

"Just a second Mose, that is not all we will be asking for, you understand?" James asked.

"No, please fill me in."

"The lost salary will certainly be a big part of the claim. But the bigger piece will be the pain and suffering stemming from your being a victim of mental and physical abuse due to twenty years of confinement. This is going to add up substantially. And it is why we need people like Timothy here to put as accurate a number as possible on the claim."

"I see," Mose said. "Do you have any estimates as to what those things might add up to?"

"Not yet," James said. "We are going to need some confirmation from you that will allow us to get employment records from your working at the school board in 1996. And this is where Timothy comes in. He will take that annual salary and project it over twenty years for increases due to inflation and cost of living and so forth. We have a paper here for you to sign on that."

"No problem," Mose said. "What about the pain and suffering as you call it?"

"We are researching previous cases for that and again Timothy will make upward adjustments for inflation," James explained. "You have been deprived of an awful lot over the years, Mose, and we want to make sure that the reparations government makes to you are adequate."

After signing the authorization to release information, Mose shook hands with James and Timothy and left the office.

He was feeling pretty good about things but wondered how long the whole process would take. He didn't have a chance to spend too much time trying to understand these things during his early life, but he did know that such processes could drag on.

* * *

After getting out of prison Mose began putting on a bit of weight, nothing too serious. He got his haircut and he trimmed down his beard to a reasonable length. For a man his age and despite what he'd been through, he still had much of his youthful good looks.

He spent a lot of time going to movies and working out at the YMCA. It didn't take long before his body was showing considerable definition muscle-wise. He would go to the gym about five or six times a week, lifting weights and doing cardio training.

Mose was friendly and struck up conversations with people at the gym, most of whom, when he told people his name, recognized it from the press coverage on his hearing at the Court of Appeal.

One day a lady came over to say hello. They had on a few occasions made eye contact. She was very fit, they were close in age, and she could stretch her body into various contortions from doing yoga. That impressed Mose.

Her name was Olivia Hale. She was a physiotherapist she told him, and had her own practice in St. John's. She recognized Mose's name when he told her.

Olivia was just a bit shorter than Mose and liked to hold her shoulder-length dark hair back with a headband, at the gym at least. Mose hadn't seen her anywhere else. She was very attractive and stood out. They would make small talk each day that they met at the gym.

Olivia had a great city accent and loved using Newfoundland expressions. She was fun to be around.

Finally one day, after getting on a first name basis with each other, Mose asked if she would like to go to a movie with him at the mall theatres. She accepted. After that they began meeting for coffee and lunch and started to get to know each other quite well.

Mose had already decided to take it slow so it was going to be some time before he invited her to his place. Or introduce Olivia to his mother.

But his personal life was turning a corner.

* * *

Three weeks after his meeting with James and Timothy, Mose got a call from James asking him to come meet with them again. They set it up for ten o'clock the next morning.

Mose got there at his usual time.

"Thanks for coming, Mose," James began. "We have run a lot of numbers over these past couple of weeks and we have to thank Timothy for his diligence on that."

Mose looked at Timothy and nodded.

"Using the precedents set for pain and suffering in similar cases of wrongful conviction we have come up with a number that we recommend would be a starting point for negotiations," James said.

"What does the loss of salary amount to?" Mose asked.

"We looked at your salary in 1996, adjusted for inflation and cost of living increases and came up with an average annual salary of forty thousand dollars over twenty years. That equates to eight hundred thousand dollars," Timothy said.

"Holy shit," Mose said. "I like that starting point!"

"As far as pain and suffering, and mental and physical abuse, as we said we used previous cases to come to a number on that," James explained.

Timothy weighed in. "The numbers, again after inflation and cost of living, round up to just under a million dollars a year for twenty years. Eight hundred and fifty thousand actually. In total for pain and suffering we are advising you to set your claim at seventeen million dollars. The claim then will total seventeen million, eight hundred thousand dollars with the loss of salary factored in."

Mose could only stare wide-eyed. He expected nothing like this.

"Is this real? I mean, are we serious here?" Mose's head was spinning.

"Well, Mose, you were a victim and the government has to make reparations for their mistakes and what they did to you," James said.

"I'm curious as to how you guys get paid," Mose said.

"We will not get paid until the settlement is made. Normally in these kind of cases lawyers charge thirty per cent, however this firm will charge twenty-five per cent of the final settlement and we will look after the fees charged by our friend Timothy here," James said. "You okay with all that?"

"Give me a paper and I will sign it," Mose said with a grin. "What happens next?"

"We will need to get you to sign the statement of claim as well as the agreement on the contingency fees, the twenty-five per cent, before you leave today," James explained. "Then we are going to deliver it to the deputy attorney general today so they can schedule the start of negotiations. They are already waiting for the claim. This whole thing has been an embarrassment to the government and they are anxious to get beyond it and move on."

Mose signed the papers and prepared to leave.

"The media has been following this every day, Mose," James told him, "so once the claim has been made I suspect they will report about the beginning of negotiations."

"I don't want anything to do with media," Mose said. "Will you speak for me?"

"I certainly can with your authority, so yes, I will make sure you are kept in the background."

"Okay then. Thank you," Mose said. "Oh, do I need to be at the negotiations with you?"

"No, it's not necessary. Timothy and I will be there. We will keep you informed every step of the way and we cannot make any decisions without you," James assured him.

Mose left the law office feeling as though he was in a dream. He knew enough about business to know that this was a starting point, but he also knew that he had two strong advocates in James and Timothy.

He got on his landline that night and called his mother.

* * *

James called Mose a month later on the landline to tell him that they were going into a meeting that might result in an agreement. "Stay close to your phone," he said.

Over the previous month, James and Timothy had had several meetings with senior people in the government and offers and counter offers had gone back and forth. Each time they would receive an offer they would get Mose on the line and recommend to Mose not to take the deal. Mose kept rejecting the offers and would come back with counter offers.

"But we are getting closer," James said. "I have a good feeling, so we need you standing by. If it looks like we can recommend you accept what they have on the table, I will call you and you should prepare to come down."

"Okay, I will be here and waiting," Mose said.

Within an hour, James was calling back. "You should come up here now and we can meet in one of the side rooms."

Mose got aboard the Buick and headed to Confederation Building, parked and made his way up to the third floor where James had directed him to go.

"Okay, here is what they are offering," James said. "They have agreed to accept the loss of salary without any deductions. On the pain and suffering, we have been going back and forth a fair bit. But what they are now proposing is four hundred and fifty thousand dollars per year over twenty years. Nine million. Add to that the eight hundred thousand dollars in lost salary, their total offer comes to nine million, eight hundred thousand dollars. Setting aside the contingency fees of twenty-five per cent, that leaves a return to you at seven million, three hundred and fifty thousand dollars. We are recommending that we settle for this. We are pretty sure it is the best we are going to do get out of them."

Mose looked at both James and Timothy. "I agree. Go in and tell them we have a deal."

* * *

Ellie's trial on charges of obstruction of justice inched closer and closer. The closer it got, the more of a basket case she was becoming.

After her dust up with the attorney general and the premier, her association with Travis Williams, as well as intelligence that pointed to Ellie's relationship with the Chief Justice, the police felt they had reasonable grounds to ask the court for an order allowing them to tap her phone line.

The police were convinced that Ellie not only knew who the killer was but that she was an accessory to Abby's murder. It is why she was making so many desperate moves.

The court order was granted.

James's intelligence in the matter, when he related the wiretap to Mandy and me in Fredericton, proved to be accurate.

Somehow the transcript of the call Ellie made to Chief Justice Denis Lundringham got leaked to the media and it became public knowledge that she had tried to influence the justice system by contacting the Chief Justice. Her call indicated that she was prepared to offer up the real killer in exchange for her immunity. This brought about the obstruction of justice charge. The media report of the transcript sure had people talking around the province.

The transcript never picked up a word from Judge Lundringham. When he got a sense of what Ellie was up to, he hung up the phone, but the transaction and what they caught her saying was enough for the police to arrest her.

Since her arrest Ellie sank further and further into the bowels of hell owing to her reckless use of methamphetamines, opioids and alcohol.

Travis was no better. He continued making his secret visits to the war memorial and coming home to Ellie with stash after stash of drugs.

The news that broke about Ellie's willingness to give up the real killer created some hardship for the two of them domestically. Every day they fought. But they seemed to accept that they had become the authors of their own destiny.

* * *

Fifteen minutes after the Court of Appeal issued the warrant for the arrest of Travis Williams, two police cruisers came to a stop in the parking lot outside Ellie's apartment building on Elizabeth Avenue.

Police had intelligence from the officers in Twin Rivers that Travis was holed up at Ellie's apartment in St. John's.

Four officers got out of the cars and went in the building through the main entrance.

One went and showed the arrest warrant to the building manager and retrieved a master key. Then all four armed officers went upstairs and knocked on Ellie's door.

"Police!"

No answer.

The next knock was a little more impatient. "Police! Open up."

The lead officer motioned his head to the one with the master key that he unlock the door. He did so and swung it wide open. The officers entered, guns ready.

No sound.

No one in the living room or kitchen. A naloxone product and several syringes lay on the coffee table. One of the officers picked them up and placed them in a plastic bag. They moved toward a closed bedroom door.

Epilogue

Swinging open the door, they found the dead bodies of Travis Williams and Eleanor Rowe.

Their deaths were ruled a double suicide.

Acknowledgements

There are several people I leaned on and need to thank, following this journey through the mind of Olav Williams. I am indebted to my editor, Valerie Compton, of Halifax who did extensive, meticulous work on my first draft (and then some!) Also to Morgan Flowers Winters of Happy Valley-Goose Bay, Labrador, for her creativity on the cover design. A few other folks I consulted on some finer points of the story were Gary Mitchell of Makkovik, Labrador, now living on Fogo Island in Newfoundland, legendary pilot Tony Powell of Charlottetown, Labrador and Ellen M. Torng of West Ste. Modeste, Labrador. Then there is also Charlie Flowers of Rigolet, Labrador. Believe me, I consider Charlie to be a world resource! Jim Bennett of Daniel's Harbour, Newfoundland, an old friend from our Memorial University days, encouraged me to write the story after I ran some early ideas by him, and a good friend in Halifax, who prefers to remain anonymous, gave me some valuable insights at the beginning of the project. I also thank the editors and staff at FriesenPress for their constant support and advice. Lastly, I need to thank my partner Joanne Trenholme for her never-ending support as I worked my way through *Olav's Story*.

I thank you all.

Bill Flowers
Amherst, Nova Scotia
June 9, 2022

About the Author

Bill Flowers was born in Rigolet, on the coast of Labrador. He holds a law degree from Dalhousie University. Bill lives in Amherst, Nova Scotia. *Olav's Story* is his first novel.

Lightning Source UK Ltd.
Milton Keynes UK
UKHW010630210922
409160UK00003B/79/J